TROUBLETWISTERS

— BOOK ONE —

TROUBLETWISTERS

GARTH NIX
— AND —
SEAN WILLIAMS

SCHOLASTIC INC.
New York Toronto London Auckland
Sydney Mexico City New Delhi Hong Kong

ISBN 978-0-545-39471-0

12 11 10 9 8 7 6 5 4 3 2 1   11 12 13 14 15 16/0

Printed in the U.S.A.   40

First Scholastic paperback printing, September 2011

The text type was set in Sabon.
Book design by Christopher Stengel

As always, for Anna, Thomas,
and Edward, and for all my
family and friends — Garth

For Amanda and the boys, and
my mother for getting me hooked
in the first place — Sean

TABLE
OF
CONTENTS

TROUBLETWISTERS

A BOLT FROM THE BLUE

The year the twins turned twelve, everything changed.

It started with a small black cloud scudding over a perfectly ordinary suburban landscape. Neither Jack nor Jaide noticed it, even though they were standing sentry outside their house, eyes peeled for the first sign of their father's arrival. Their attention was fixed on the street and its occupants, not the sky above.

A taxi appeared in the distance, and the twins craned their heads hopefully, but it turned off two blocks ahead of their house. They sagged in disappointment.

"I wish Dad wasn't late *all* the time," said Jaide.

"Here's hoping it's not genetic," Jack gloomily replied. This time, their father was a full day late . . . and counting.

Jaide sent a hard look her brother's way. "Speak for yourself, Jack. I'm not the one who takes after him."

This was true. Jaide had her mother's green eyes, red hair, and fair skin, though she never burned in the sun, whereas Jack had the brown eyes, black hair, and brown skin of his father's side of the family. Or at least they assumed their father's family looked like that; they had never actually met any of the other Shields. They all lived far away, the twins were told, and weren't very friendly. Even their mother had only met their father's relatives once. And clearly it hadn't gone very well.

Jack vowed to himself that if the Shields *were* late all the time, he wasn't going to be like them. Genes weren't everything, their mother liked to say. Jack wanted to believe this.

Several hundred yards behind their house, the cloud turned right at a church spire and spun twice counterclockwise, as though lost.

Instead of their hoped-for father, the next person the twins saw was the mailman. He smiled at them and put a letter in their mailbox.

"Hey, maybe it's a card from Dad!" said Jaide. Hector Shield was a treasure-seeker, hunting lost masterpieces for auction houses and galleries. Sometimes cards from him took even longer to arrive than he did.

"He's probably just making long-distance excuses," muttered Jack.

Jaide pushed past her brother, opened the mailbox, and took out the envelope.

"It's not from Dad," she said, examining the cream-colored envelope curiously. "But it *is* for us."

The envelope was made of a thick, flecked paper and addressed in ornate, formal handwriting that neither twin recognized. It also referred to them by their real names, the ones their mother only used when they were in big trouble:

"Who's it from, then?" asked Jack, peering over Jaide's shoulder.

Jaide turned the envelope over. There was no return address anywhere, and next to the stamp was a four-pointed star — like the compass symbol on a map — printed directly on the envelope.

Something about the star unsettled Jack. But he couldn't help asking his sister, "Are you going to open it?" Jack would rather know something disturbing than have to wait in suspense.

"Of course," Jaide told her brother, trying to sound as calm and cool as she usually did. It took a lot to bother Jaide. "What's the hurry?"

She didn't tell him that there was something about the card that made her hesitate, too. Something about it just felt . . . odd.

She ran her thumb along the flap and tore it with a satisfying rip. The smell of salt and sand hit her nostrils, as though a strong sea breeze had just rushed over her — even though they lived nowhere near the sea.

Jack wasn't hit by this strange sensation. As his sister hesitated, he pulled the envelope from her frozen fingers and tugged out the card from within. It was white, with the same four-pointed star embossed in gold on the front.

The day darkened momentarily. Then the single black cloud moved on, and the sky was immediately blue again.

"Maybe we should show it to Mom first," Jack said.

"It does have our names on it," Jaide pointed out. She flipped open the card.

Inside were five lines written in the same old-person handwriting.

My dear troubletwisters,

The cats have been very restless, so I expect I will see you soon.

With love,
Grandma X

"Grandma who?" asked Jack.

"That's not Mamma Jane's writing," said Jaide, thinking of their mother's mother, who lived with their aunt in an apartment on the other side of town.

"Let me see that."

Both Jack and Jaide jumped as their mother reached past them and snatched the card from Jaide's fingers. Neither twin had heard her coming.

After reading the message, Susan Shield's lips tightened and she shut her eyes for a moment. The twins watched her, puzzled by her reaction.

"This isn't really for you," she said finally. "I want you to forget you ever saw it."

"But it was addressed to us," Jaide said.

"I know, but it shouldn't have been," their mother replied firmly.

Jack couldn't help himself. "What's a troubletwister?" he asked.

"We're not going to talk about it now. I want you to forget it," Susan repeated in a warning voice. The twins knew that tone. They only ever heard it when they were caught doing something particularly bad, like climbing on the roof or blowing things up in the microwave.

"But we didn't do anything wrong," Jaide protested.

"I know," said Susan. She knelt down and pulled them both in for a quick hug, which typically Jaide resisted and Jack leaned into. "But let's move right along, okay? Why don't you go and have a jump on the trampoline?"

"We did that already," said Jack.

"Who jumped the highest?" Susan asked.

"I did," both twins declared. They glared at each other for a moment, then ran off through the house, since that was marginally faster than going around to the backyard.

Susan watched them run. As soon as they were out of sight, she read the card a second time, then realized that there was something else in the envelope. Susan pulled it out just far enough to see it was a map, with some instructions written on the side. Angrily, she stuffed it and the card back in the envelope, which she then shoved into her back pocket.

"Where are you, Hector?" she said savagely as she closed the mailbox flap with a loud rattle and went inside.

Half a mile away, the single black cloud stopped above a derelict building site and a single stroke of lightning flashed down. The muted clap of thunder that followed could have been a car backfiring.

The twins, busy on the backyard trampoline, didn't notice it. Jaide, the eldest by four minutes, was shorter by half an inch, but even so she could nearly always jump much higher than Jack, much to his annoyance.

"Do you really think I take after Dad?" Jack asked while gathering his breath for another challenge.

"I don't know. I guess we both do, a little bit."

"So you could be the late one, not me."

"Maybe, but I'll always jump the highest."

"Only because you hog the middle."

"That's not true!"

"You know," said a voice from the back fence, "I reckon you both hog the middle, given the opportunity."

The twins stopped jumping. For all their differences, the surprised looks on their faces were identical.

"Dad?!" they both asked.

The familiar floppy-haired figure of Hector Shield smiled at them over the fence.

"Better late than never!"

The twins practically bounced over the trampoline net in their haste to get to him.

"You made it!" Jack said.

"What took you so long?" Jaide asked.

"It's good to see you, too, kids."

The twins opened the gate and Hector stepped into the yard. He was dressed in his usual rumpled dark blue corduroy pants and jacket, and was wheeling a large and battered black suitcase behind him. His long arms easily enfolded them both in a great big hug.

Neither twin noticed that there were scorch marks on his jacket. But Jack, burying his head in his father's shirt, withdrew after a moment, sniffing. Hector smelled like burned toast.

"Why did you come this way?" Jack asked.

"My, uh, taxi dropped me off on the wrong street."

Jaide didn't care how their father had gotten there, just as long as he was home. "Did you bring us any presents?" she asked.

Hector smiled at Jaide. He always brought back a little bit of treasure for each of them from his trips. His presents were invariably exciting and strange, like the antique windup horses he'd brought back from Spain the year before, or the Mayan goblets for drinking ceremonial hot chocolate he'd produced at Christmas.

"Of course," he said. "We'll have a present-giving ceremony after I've had a shower and a cup of coffee."

They turned toward the back door, and all three stopped as they saw Susan standing there with her arms folded and a tense expression on her face.

"Ah," said Hector. "You go on ahead, Jack and Jaide. I think your mother wants a word."

The twins grabbed the handle of the battered Samsonite case. It was something of a ritual for Jack and Jaide to take it up to their parents' room, and they were happy to get out of the way of the brewing parental argument. Since their mother worked shifts as a paramedic, any unexpected change of schedule (like their father being a day late) wreaked havoc with all the complicated juggling of school, after-school activities, and work.

"It's heavy," puffed Jack when they reached the stairs.

"Our presents must be huge!" Jaide let go of the handle and lifted the suitcase from its base. Together they negotiated the hairpin bend halfway up and lugged the suitcase into their parents' bedroom. The room was decorated with a series of nineteenth-century watercolors by an artist their father had discovered in Paris, depicting small animals and birds all dressed in Victorian costumes.

The twins started to hoist the suitcase up onto the bed, but Jack lost his grip at the last second and Jaide couldn't hold it alone. The case fell back on the floor. Jack leaped aside, and with an almighty crack, the solid outer shell of supposedly indestructible plastic split in the middle and all the contents cascaded out across the twins' feet.

For a second, Jaide and Jack were shocked into silence. Out in the garden, they could hear their mother cry, "But, Hector, you only just got back!"

The twins stared down at the shattered suitcase.

"Dad'll be mad," said Jaide. "What do we do?"

"I can't believe it broke," said Jack. "It must have fallen a million times before."

Jaide picked up the two broken halves of the top of the suitcase and held them up to her brother.

"Look! It's *burned*. No wonder it broke."

Jack came around and saw a jagged scorch mark

running from one end to the other. He sniffed, and smelled the same odd smell that had been on their father when he had hugged them.

"Do you think — do you think he was in some kind of accident, and that's why he's late?"

"I don't know."

Jaide put down the broken lid and looked at the pile of things at their feet. Most of it seemed pretty ordinary, just shirts and socks, underwear and toiletries. But there was a pair of particularly old and tattered corduroy pants that had something sticking out of the leg.

Jaide picked up the pants and an iron rod fell out. Jack quickly reached down to pick it up.

"Ow!" he exclaimed as a bright blue spark jumped to his grasping fingers. He dropped the rod onto the bed.

Both of the twins looked it over, eager to see something special in it. But it was just a two-foot-long length of iron, pitted and scarred, utterly unmarked by rust.

"Not much of a present," Jaide said, reaching for it. There was no spark, but a wave of dizziness rolled through her.

She shut her eyes and waited for it to pass, but instead the feeling got stronger.

"Are you all right?" Jack asked nervously. Jaide had suddenly gone very pale.

"No," she said, and swayed sideways. Jack steadied her and tried to snatch the rod away, to throw it back on the bed. But the moment he touched the cold iron again, a wave of dizziness hit him as well.

The floor sagged underneath them. The ceiling bowed. Every corner curved and twisted, as though they were seeing the walls through buckled glass.

"What's going on?" Jack's voice boomed like a foghorn.

"It's the rod!" Jaide's voice squeaked like fingernails down a blackboard.

"Let it go!"

"I can't!" She shook her hand, but the rod was firmly attached to her palm. "It won't let go of me!"

Jack tried to let go, too, but he was stuck as well.

The angles and lines of the room bent even further, tangling their world in knots. Bile rose in their throats. Jack shook his head wildly and Jaide blinked and swallowed, hoping that this would somehow make things look right again. But it didn't, and they felt a sudden pain in their ears, a pain followed by a horrible, whispering voice that at first was so soft they could only feel it and not understand. But it grew louder and more strident, until it was the only thing they could hear, as if it emanated from inside their own heads.

++Come to us, troubletwisters. Join us . . . welcome, most welcome!++

The twins spun around and tried to head for the door, though now it was only a tiny rectangle at the end of a distorted tunnel of walls. Their feet still moved, but it was no use — the rod was fixed in place above the bed and they couldn't let go.

++We see you! We see you!++ crowed the voice triumphantly. ++So close, so close!++

As the voice spoke, the watercolor animals on the walls twisted and writhed out of their frames, morphing into hideous, three-dimensional shapes with bulging eyes like those of monstrous goldfish, eyes that rotated and shifted to peer intently at the twins.

Even worse than their attention was the fact that the eyes were entirely white, without iris or pupil, and the whiteness was buzzing and blurry, like the worst kind of fluorescent light.

++We see you! We see you!++

Jaide almost yanked her arm out of her shoulder socket as she tried to free herself from the rod. She kept her head down as she struggled, trying not to meet the gaze of those terrible eyes, the eyes that she felt were drawing her in, sucking her into some other place, some other dimension.

Jack, too, averted his eyes, but the room warped and weirded around him even more. He sensed more than saw that there was something behind these impossible spaces, and desperately he tried to look at something that didn't hurt his brain, but there was nothing.

Both twins screamed at the same time.

Hector and Susan Shield heard the scream, and when they whirled around to the house, they were shocked to see its angles shifting. The roof, which normally peaked at a sharp point, was now as flat as the horizon, while the chimney had stretched up a dozen feet.

"Keep back!" Hector shouted to Susan, acting a second before she could. He leaped through a door that had become triangular and ten feet high, and ran up the stairs, becoming distorted himself in the process.

Then he was gone, engulfed by the bizarre geometry.

Upstairs, Jaide could feel a ghastly coldness creeping up her fingers and into her arms. It robbed her of her natural warmth and weakened her muscles, making it even harder to fight. She knew that if it spread much farther, she wouldn't be able to resist at all, and whatever lay behind the voice would get her.

To Jack it felt as though he was being skewered by the multiplying eyes. Each new pair pinned him more tightly to the spot. If he met their gaze, he knew he would be lost. He kept moving his head, shifting his line of sight, blinking, but he knew there were just too many awful white eyes. . . .

"Kids!"

A flash of purple-blue light cut through the mangled angles, dazzlingly bright and refreshingly straight. It struck the metal rod square in the middle. The twins were flung apart by a soundless explosion, even as another bright ribbon lashed out like a whip, gathering up Jaide and Jack and then looping back to the hands that had cast it. Through their shock, the twins recognized their father, but he looked like nothing they had ever seen before. Light rippled up and down his body like a gas flame, concentrating in his open hands. His hair waved like a nest of electric snakes.

Hector Shield grabbed the lightning as if it were a rope and hauled on it as hard as he could, pulling the twins to him. They reeled into his arms, and he took the iron rod from their frozen hands without difficulty.

The white eyes flared brighter.

++No!++ the voice cried. ++They belong to us! They *want* to be with us!++

"Never!" shouted Hector.

He raised the iron rod. Lightning burst from its tip, chain lightning that crackled across a dozen white eyes, bursting them like trodden-on grapes. But more and more eyes kept appearing, and they grew closer and closer despite everything Hector did. The twins clung to him, not understanding what was going on but in no doubt at all that they were in mortal danger.

"Get behind me!" Hector croaked to the children. He held up the rod again, but only a flickering spark jumped out. The eyes were everywhere, drawing nearer and nearer, as if a vast creature with ten thousand eyeballs was peering down at the small, helpless group of humans. The floor beneath their feet was tilting and rising at the sides, turning into a funnel, making them slide forward, and they all had the growing sensation that hidden behind or below the multitude of eyes, there might also be a mouth.

"Get . . . get behind me!" the twins' father called out again. "Then run for the stairs!"

++Come to us!++ countered the voice. It sounded very self-satisfied now, as if Hector's words were a concession of weakness.

The twins disobeyed both instructions. Jack stayed absolutely still, transfixed and paralyzed. Jaide actually took a step forward.

"No!" she shouted back at the great cloud of eyes. "Go away!"

"Jaide! Don't —" Hector yelled, dropping the iron rod and gathering the children in.

A tide of darkness swept over the room, snuffing out the glowing eyes. At the same time, the air became hot and gusted furiously through the room. The wind pulled at Jaide, lifting her off her feet till Jack and Hector pulled her back down.

"I can't see!" Jaide screamed as the wind tore at her again. The darkness was almost worse than the staring eyes, and the wind kept getting stronger, accompanied by terrible crashing noises all around.

"Down!" shouted Hector. He pushed them flat on the floor as something — possibly the bed — flew over their heads and smashed into the wall. Clothes whipped from the wardrobe with a sound like giant birds flapping, and then the wardrobe itself blew into matchwood. Hector started to drag the twins back through the doorway.

The walls screamed as the roof came off and spun away. The twins screamed, too, not knowing what was making the noise.

Then they felt their father's hands on them, pressing them to him, holding them down.

"Calm down, kids. We'll be all right. Take slow breaths. In for five seconds . . . one . . . two . . . three . . . four . . . five — and now out for five seconds . . ."

As he counted, the darkness lifted. Jack found himself following his father's instructions even as his heart pounded in terror. Sunshine slowly filtered in from above, through the gaping absence where the roof had been. Jaide felt her brother grow calm, and that helped her relax, too. The wind slowed to a gentle breeze, and then stopped altogether, to be replaced by an eerie silence, as if they were in the eye of a storm.

Behind the silence, as though behind a pane of glass that could shatter at any moment, the eyes were waiting.

"That's it," said Hector. "Nice, slow breaths . . ."

Jack's eyes shut for a moment. He twitched and raised his head. Suddenly he felt incredibly sleepy, as if he'd been woken in the middle of the night. He looked at Jaide, who was also nodding off.

Both of them slumped in Hector's arms, and he walked them quickly down the stairs, looking anxiously behind him several times. Halfway down, he met Susan.

"Get them outside," Hector said urgently. "Away from the house."

Susan grabbed them, the intense energy of her grasp keeping them just on the right side of awake. They were moving fast, running down the stairs, into the garden, out through the back gate, into the lane, and then several houses down, where Susan propped them against a fence and checked them over.

She had just taken their pulses when an incredibly loud thunderclap made them all flinch. Looking back, they saw a black column, dotted with tiny, bright lights, rising up above the house. Lightning stabbed at the house out of a clear sky, and then all that was left of the building was suddenly sucked up into the column, broken into pieces, and spat back down again in a shower of debris.

"Hector . . ." whispered Susan.

The black column disappeared in a plume hundreds of feet high. Dust rolled out in a cloud down the lane, making Susan and the twins cough and wipe their eyes.

But there, emerging from the dust, was the twins' father. He had blood streaming from a cut above his left eye and his corduroy jacket was ripped to shreds, but he was alive. In his right hand, he held the iron rod.

Jack and Jaide felt an incredible surge of relief. They smiled up at their father, but their eyes were dazed, and their exhausted minds stunned with shock and incomprehension.

"What have you done?" asked Susan.

"Susan, it's not —"

"Not your fault?" She pointed angrily at the metal rod in his hand. "I knew you didn't go by plane. I looked up the arrivals, but I thought maybe — just maybe — I missed one and you had kept your promise."

"I was going to say *it's not that simple.*" Hector knelt by the children and laid the rod down on the road.

Jack blinked up at his father, slowly regaining his senses. Next to him, he felt Jaide shift, and Jack knew that he should say something, but he didn't have the strength to speak.

"Dad," Jaide whispered. It took a great deal of effort to get the words out, so much that she hardly knew if she was saying them right or getting them in order. "We touched the . . . we saw the . . ."

"I know, sweetie," said Hector. "It'll be okay, I swear."

"How will it be okay?" asked Susan. "How will it be okay, Hector? Our house has just been *destroyed.* You and the kids almost died."

"We knew this might happen one day," Hector said quietly. "The potential is there, and one way or another, it will be realized."

"*She* made it happen!" Susan tugged the letter out of her back pocket and flung it at him. "*She* did this."

Hector scanned the five short lines and sagged back on his heels.

Jack didn't know what was stranger — what had happened, or the fact that his parents didn't seem to be as surprised as he was. Jaide, meanwhile, wondered what on earth the card from the mysterious Grandma X had to do with it all.

"There must be a way to make it stop," Susan said, clutching the twins tightly. "There *has* to be."

"She didn't make it happen," said Hector. "The children have to go to her now."

Go to her? Jaide thought. This was all happening too fast.

Susan could barely put her fears into words. "No! She'll want to take them . . . she'll want to use them . . . I won't let them go!"

Jack had so many questions. But he was so tired and shocked, he couldn't even begin to ask them. For now, he just listened. Questions would come later. Plenty of questions.

"She won't use them," said Hector firmly. "The choice will be their own. As it was for me, when I chose you."

"But you didn't stick with that choice," said Susan, her words as sharp as a knife. "Did you?"

In the distance, they heard the sound of sirens cutting

through the howling of dogs and the shrill repetition of car alarms.

Hector looked behind him, and both Jaide and Jack followed his glance. Smoke was beginning to curl and twine out of the shattered walls and rooftop, and little flames were jumping in the shadows.

"They have to go," said Hector. "The twins . . . we might not be so lucky next time. I need you to take them to Mother before their Gifts fully awaken."

"What gifts?" Jaide finally found the strength to speak up. "What's happening?"

Hector looked at both of the twins. "I can't tell you now. But you'll find out soon. All you need to know is that it's very important that you go with your mother. Now."

"You're not giving us any choice?" Jack asked.

"There is no choice."

Jaide still didn't understand. "What about you? Aren't you going to come with us?"

"Yes, Hector," Susan said. "Aren't you going to come with us?"

A flicker of intense pain passed across Hector's features. "You know I can't go with you, Susan. Me being there would . . . interfere . . . as I interfered today."

Susan looked away, back toward the burning house.

"You might as well go now, then," she said.

Hector nodded sadly. He bent down and kissed both the twins on their foreheads, picked up the iron rod, and stood, his glasses askew and misted over.

"I'm sorry," he said. "One day, troubletwisters, I hope you'll understand."

Hector turned to Susan, but she would not look at him, not even as his footsteps slowly receded down the lane. Jack couldn't watch him, either — he felt like something inalterable was happening, and their family was never going to be the same again. Only Jaide managed a small wave as their father left. She had no idea whether or not he saw it.

A minute later, a clap of thunder echoed across the ordinary suburb and a single black cloud slunk off toward the horizon, marking the end of the ordinary life of Jaide and Jack Shield.

CHAPTER ONE

THE HOUSE ON WATCHWARD LANE

Everyone kept telling Jack, Jaide, and Susan how lucky they'd been to survive the explosion that destroyed their home.

"I'd buy a lottery ticket, if I were you," the insurance assessor had said. The fire department investigator had agreed, adding, "A gas main normally goes up all at once, not in stages. You're the luckiest family alive."

But the twins didn't feel lucky. As far as they were concerned, they just got unluckier and unluckier. First their home got blown up, and then they were told they had to move to their unknown grandmother's house, miles and miles and miles away. And yet, every time someone heard their story — like that morning in the latest and hopefully last slimy motel off the freeway — out came that annoying sentence: "You were lucky!"

"Everyone keeps saying we were so lucky," said Jaide as they got back into the car. "So how come we've had to drive for three whole days to some hick town we've never heard of, to see a woman you *clearly* don't like? Dad is who-knows-where —"

"That's enough," snapped Susan. "It's been a long drive, and I need you both to be cooperative. We're almost there. Don't ruin it now."

They drove in silence for a while, Susan fuming to herself and the twins in no better mood. Then Susan quietly added, "Your father will come when he can. He has urgent business. And we *are* very lucky that we're alive and that your grandmother is so keen to have us come to live with her."

Grandma X lived by the sea in a town called Portland — but not one of the Portlands that anyone had heard of. In fact, as Jaide quickly learned on the Internet, this Portland didn't even make the top ten of cities or towns with the name. It was small and old and sounded generally unexciting. There was only one small school, two parks, one part-time cinema (without a 3-D screen), and a main street with a half dozen shops. The nearest mall was a minimum of forty minutes' drive away. To the twins, it might as well have been on the moon, but without the fun of riding in a spaceship to get there.

"Are we going to be stuck here for good?" Jack asked as their mother drove slowly down the main street of Portland, peering at the street signs. Some of them were so faded, they were completely illegible. "I mean, like, for always?"

"No," said their mother. "It's only till the insurance money comes in and our old house is rebuilt."

"Why couldn't we stay in the hotel until then? Or with Aunt Marie?"

"I told you. Aunt Marie has her hands full with Mamma Jane. It's going to take months to rebuild and . . . and I thought we needed a change of scene anyway."

Jaide knew it was pointless to try to pin her mother down any further than this. Clearly, something strange had happened the hour their house had been destroyed. And there was a link between the freaky things the twins had seen, their father's quick disappearance, and the relocation to Grandma X's house. But Susan wouldn't talk about it. Once Hector had gone, it was like the words they'd exchanged had never happened.

There was one question Jaide figured was safe. "Do we have to call her Grandma X?" she asked.

"Just call her Grandma."

"What does the X stand for?"

"I don't know."

"You don't know Dad's mother's name?"

"No," their mother answered with a distracted sigh. She was looking back and forth between the hand-drawn map Grandma X had sent and the GPS screen. With an irritated snort, she pulled over to the side of the road. "I don't understand this. We've just passed Crescent Street and Dock Road. There's no Watchward Lane between them, and it isn't in the navigator database."

"She said to come in from the east." Jaide held up the map, which had some carefully lettered instructions on the side.

"It can't make any difference which way we come from," said Susan. But her voice trailed off, and she made a U-turn. "I must have missed it. We'll have to go back around."

"Why does she call us troubletwisters?" Jaide asked.

"She's old," said Susan. "It's probably some saying from long ago, like a pet name."

"I don't like it," said Jaide. "We're not trouble."

"Yes, you are," said Susan. "Sometimes, anyway."

"And what do her cats have to do with anything?"

Jack glanced out the window and caught a glimpse of a narrow lane between a bookstore and a hardware shop. He blinked and lost sight of it, then spotted it again through the rear window.

"There!" he called out. "We've gone past it! Next to the shop with all the different stepladders out front."

"Well done, Jack!" Susan said. She spun the wheel and executed another U-turn. "There's the wretched lane at last."

The car turned into the narrow, cobbled lane that zigzagged between two blocks and then up a slight hill, ending in a cul-de-sac opposite a high, whitewashed stone wall topped with gargoyle cats and roosters. There was an arched entrance just wide enough for the car, its gate propped open behind it.

Susan drove through the entrance and followed the long circular drive and its companionable line of poplar trees around to the front of the house. When she turned the engine off, they all sat in silence for a moment, looking out.

The house was old and built of once-rosy bricks that had mostly faded to a dull pink. It was three stories high, and in place of a fourth story it had a widow's walk, a kind of veranda that embraced the very steep roof, which was made of pale timber shingles. Several chimneys projected up much higher than the roof peak, and on the tallest, a weather vane in the shape of a crescent moon with attendant stars pointed firmly southwest despite the wind quite obviously bending the tops of the poplar trees from the east.

"I bet it's moldy inside," said Jaide.

"And there's no hot water," said Jack.

"We'll just have to make do," said Susan. "It's not as if we have any choice, thanks to your fa —"

She bit her lip. Jack waited expectantly for her to finish.

Neither Jack nor Jaide bought the official story of a slow gas leak that rapidly got worse and ended in the explosive destruction of their house. The only problem was, they couldn't explain what had happened, either. Jack and Jaide had talked about it between themselves, but all they could recall was taking their father's suitcase upstairs, and they both touched some kind of metal pipe, and then suddenly everything was twisted and staring and exploding. But the only other person who'd seen it was their father, who was gone. It made them think that maybe it hadn't been like that at all. Because it was so unbelievable. Even thinking about the weird white eyes made Jaide shiver.

"What I mean is," Susan said, "we'll have to make do as best we can. And this," she added, looking gloomily at the big old house, "is what's best."

"I didn't know Grandma ran an antiques store," said Jaide, pointing out the window.

"What?" asked Susan. "What are you pointing at?"

"The sign, about the antiques," Jaide replied. "Over the blue door, there."

The house had two front entrances. There was one with four broad stone steps leading up to double doors, right where they were parked, but there was also another one farther along, consisting of three small steps that led down to a sunken door that was painted a lovely cornflower blue. An old, hand-painted wooden sign above the door read ANTIQUES AND CHOICE ARTICLES FOR THE DISCERNING.

"Where?" asked Susan. "Honestly, I don't have time for this, and I doubt Grandma X will appreciate you making jokes about her being an antique or whatever it is you're thinking."

Susan got out of the car and slammed the door behind her.

"You can see it, can't you?" Jaide asked Jack.

Jack narrowed his eyes. He was looking straight at it as far as Jaide could tell, but his face screwed up uncertainly.

"Not really," he said. "At least, I don't think so. . . ."

For a moment everything that had happened in their old home crashed back into Jaide's mind: the darkness, the wind, the glowing eyes, their father fighting to save them from forces she didn't understand. It felt like a dream, a nightmare, and she didn't like the feeling that the nightmare might be more real than the reality before her.

"Are you coming or not?" called their mother from the front steps.

"Like we have a choice," Jaide murmured. She threw

open the door. Her feet crunched down onto gravel, and Jack's followed a second later.

He was glad to stretch his legs. It had been a long and boring drive. The house loomed over them, no doubt full of their grandmother's rules and regulations. He couldn't bear the thought of staying still a moment longer.

"Race you around," he said.

"On three," Jaide told him, then started running immediately, heading counterclockwise along the front of the house.

Jack concentrated on catching up, barely hearing their mother's *tsk* of exasperation behind them. The earth was loose underfoot, even when he crossed the edge of the gravel and hit the garden proper. There was no lawn, just lots of wood chips and twigs and dead-looking weeds. He turned left, hot on Jaide's heels, and saw that there *was* a proper garden behind the house, including a broad lawn that was dominated by a Douglas fir tree that had to be three times the height of the house. Jack wondered why it hadn't been visible as they'd driven in.

Jack had almost caught up with Jaide, as he usually did unless she had a really huge head start, and was about to grab her hoodie and pull her back when a sudden, stern voice above their heads made him stumble.

"You'll be on your very best behavior. I expect nothing less!"

The voice came from a half-open window midway along the side of the house. Jaide skidded to a halt, assuming the telling-off was directed at them. Jack crashed into her back and they both fell over.

"Are you arguing with me?" the voice continued.

The twins disentangled themselves from each other and looked nervously up at the window. But there was no one leaning out, and they realized that whoever the woman above was telling off, it wasn't them.

"Do you think that's —?" whispered Jack.

Jaide shushed her brother even as she jumped up and tried to see inside, hoping for a glimpse of whoever was talking, presumably Grandma X. Jaide was a great jumper and climber, better than Jack. He had the edge in a straight sprint on level ground, but if there was any climbing or scrambling up something involved, Jaide always left him behind.

"I'll keep my side of the compact if you'll keep yours," said the unseen woman.

A deep-toned bell chime resonated through the house. Something clattered inside the kitchen.

"Shhh, they're here."

Jaide managed to pull herself up enough to see over the sill just in time to catch a glimpse of a tall, elderly woman with silvery hair disappearing through a doorway. She wore a long-sleeved black shirt tucked into the top of blue jeans, a belt that sparkled as though it had metal threaded through it, and cowboy boots with silver heels and tips. The sound of those boots on the polished floorboards ricocheted after her, brisk and no-nonsense.

There was no one else there. Grandma X might as well have been talking to the air, or to herself.

Jack pulled himself up next to Jaide just as something leaped onto the windowsill from inside. The twins both fell back in surprise, ending up in a tangle on the ground again.

"Meow?" asked a sturdy ginger tomcat, looking down at them with a quizzical expression.

Jack felt his elbow, which hurt, and laughed in relief. "You gave me a fright."

The cat turned its head to one side, sniffed, and began to lick its paws, totally ignoring the twins.

"Kids? Where are you?"

Susan's voice traveled through the house and around it, ambushing them from all sides.

"On three," said Jack, but he was already moving.

He was well in the lead by the time he reached the next corner. The trunk of the mighty fir flashed by, and he almost stumbled on its roots, which rose like the coils of a serpent out of the earth all around the tree. Those roots were making short work of the yard's stone walls, which stood cracked and tumbled on all three sides. Over the fallen walls, Jaide caught a quick glimpse of the neighboring house. Its windows were smashed and doors boarded up, and there were black marks all up one wall that looked like they were from a fire. It had clearly not been lived in for a long time.

The southern side of Grandma X's house was a feature-less, smooth brick wall with no windows below the third floor. As they skidded around the last corner and came back to the front door, Jack slowed slightly to let his sister catch up, but not enough that she could win.

"There you are." Susan was waiting at the top of the stone steps, speaking cheerfully but with a forced edge that told the twins not to push their luck. "Come meet your grandma."

Jaide joined Jack, breathing heavily. Standing so close they touched shoulders, they walked together up the steps. The door at the top led into a hallway so dark and gloomy that Jack could only make out shapes and Jaide couldn't see anything at all.

"The twins, at last," said the same voice they had heard through the window. Grandma X stepped out of the gloom, her hands outstretched, reaching for the twins as if to grab them and pull them back into the darkness. Jack flinched away, but Jaide didn't move, struck at once by how much Grandma X looked like their father, especially in the eyes. Though hers were as gray as granite and their father's a more kindly brown, they both had the same bright, piercing gaze.

Jack didn't notice her eyes. He was just shocked at how fast she was, as she gripped him by the shoulder and Jaide by her hand and drew them both in to kiss their foreheads before letting them go.

"I knew you'd come one day," she said. "And look at how grown up you are! Already twelve, already troubletwisters."

"What *is* a troubletwister?" asked Jaide.

"That's a story for another time," Grandma X said, putting her arms around their shoulders. "Won't you come inside and see your new home?"

"We won't be staying long," said Susan, following closely behind. "Just until everything's fixed."

Grandma X sniffed. "You are welcome for as long as you need. I have plenty of room."

Grandma X took the twins with her through the door. Jaide stepped hesitantly across the threshold, eyes adjusting slowly to the darkness. Four tall chestnut and mahogany cabinets lined the sides of the front hall, all of them latched shut, the latches fastened with heavy old bronze padlocks. The air smelled odd, a mixture of the thick, damp smell of old wood and something else, something that neither Jack nor Jaide could identify, but made them think of ancient things. This reminded Jaide of the blue door and the weird antiques shop sign. She had been so busy chasing Jack that she hadn't seen it when they'd run around the house, and for some reason it had gone right out of her mind. Now the smell brought back that lost memory, and she wanted to check it out.

"Hang on," Jaide said, pulling free. "I want to get something from the car."

"Hang on yourself," protested Jack. He made a grab at her arm, and she was unable to shrug him off. Together they stumbled back out into daylight. There, Jaide turned to look at the front of the house.

For an instant, both the sign and the blue door were nowhere to be seen. There was only an expanse of weathered, pinkish brick where she thought they'd been.

Then she blinked, and they were back.

"I didn't imagine it," she told Jack. "I knew it!"

Jack stared at the door, and the sign, and the words: ANTIQUES AND CHOICE ARTICLES FOR THE DISCERNING.

"You were right," he said, amazed that what seemed so solid now had been barely visible before. "Why couldn't I see it at first?"

"I don't know," Jaide said. "And why couldn't Mom see it at all?"

"Kids?" came Susan's voice from inside. She sounded cross, and was trying unsuccessfully to hide it. "Come on, don't be rude, please."

"This is weird," Jaide said, more to herself than to her brother.

"*Definitely* weird," Jack responded, and he flashed her a grin that surprised her. "Maybe Portland will be more interesting than we thought."

Something squeaked above them. The weather vane was shifting, slowly and thoughtfully, to point to the south. But the poplars in the drive and the topmost branches of the great fir tree were still bending west in answer to the *easterly* wind that had grown stronger, herding in a huge mass of dark, angry clouds.

Jaide shivered, but not entirely from the coolness of the wind. She pulled her hoodie up and hurried inside, with Jack following closely behind her.

CHAPTER TWO
HERE AND GONE AGAIN

Lounge, drawing room, study, kitchen," their grandma was saying, sweeping down the hallway like a ship in full sail, tapping on doorways as she passed them. The back half of the hall, past the locked cabinets, was dominated by a number of stern-faced portraits that peered down their noses from the walls. Beyond the paintings there were two glass-fronted bookcases that, instead of holding books, displayed a collection of curious trinkets: snow globes, crystalline animals, brass ornaments, and the like, all arranged neatly but with no obvious sense of order.

Jack and Jaide caught up, hurrying lightly on their sneakers, their scuffling footsteps a sharp contrast to the crack of Grandma X's boots. At the very end of the hall, alone on the wall, a tiny silver mirror caught Jack's eye as he was hustled past it to the stairs. He saw his and his sister's faces in it, stretched and twisted into a pair of question marks.

"I've prepared rooms for you on the second floor," Grandma X said as she led them up the creaking steps. The stairwell was as wide across as most rooms, and continued into the shadows far above.

"I'm sorry it's come to this," Susan said, walking one step behind her. "I hope we won't be staying long and —"

"Think nothing of it," interrupted Grandma X. "You are my daughter-in-law, and the troubletwisters are my grandchildren. Blood is thicker than water. *Our* blood, especially."

"Yes, I'd like to talk to you about that." Susan shot a swift glance at the twins. "Later."

"Don't fret, my dear." Grandma X stopped at the first turn on the stairs and looked down at her guests. They stopped expectantly beneath her. The dim light cast deep shadows in her lined face. "Prudence is my middle name."

"What's *prudence*?" asked Jack.

"It means *being careful*," said Susan.

"And it really was my middle name," said Grandma X with a faint smile. "Once upon a time."

"What does the X stand for?" asked Jaide.

Instead of answering, their grandmother continued up the stairs.

Susan put a finger to her lips. Jack nudged his sister, and she nudged him back. They didn't need to put into words what they were thinking, which was that the longer they were in their grandmother's company, the odder she seemed. Her house was odd, too. It wasn't just the mystery of the blue door. Everywhere Jaide and Jack looked, strange details caught their eyes, like the compass wallpaper featuring letters other than N, W, S, and E — they weren't even English letters — and banisters that looked less carved than grown into long spirals. There were more paintings and, on the first-floor landing, the occasional old, silver-tinted photo of a person from ancient times. Some of them had little brass nameplates on the bottoms of the frames. Jack peered closely, wondering if they were related to Grandma X, and therefore to him.

Heinrich Cornelius Agrippa. Ursula Southeil. Lorenzo Ghiberti. Helena Drebbel.

None of the names rang a bell.

"I've put you in here, Susan," said Grandma X. She opened the door to show a narrow, L-shaped room with windows down the long wall that overlooked the old, empty house next door. There was a twin-size bed tucked into one corner and a heavy cupboard looming next to it.

"Thank you," said Susan. She was unable to hide a small sigh in her voice. The twins knew she was thinking of her old bedroom, the one that she had shared with their father. A shiver of memory ran through Jack, of white eyes and bulging animal faces, but he suppressed it. There was nothing here to be frightened of, he told himself. It was just . . . odd. Different. Not home.

Grandma X swiveled on her heel and indicated the door opposite Susan's room.

"This will be yours, troubletwisters."

Jaide and Jack pushed the door open. It was very heavy, and creaked. The first thing both of them saw was a golden chandelier suspended from a dome in the ceiling. It had four points like a ceiling fan, and hung almost as low as Grandma X's silver hair.

The chandelier's metallic angles caught and reflected the light that was streaming through the high windows that faced the front of the house. Strange gleams and shadows flitted across the two four-poster beds, which had curiously patterned brocade curtains. These were drawn back and tied at the posts, but when let loose would make the beds like perfect little tents inside the room.

There were matching wooden chests beside the beds, and another solid wardrobe tucked into the opposite corner. The floor was bare, polished board, like everywhere else they'd seen in the house, but there was a thick blue rug to fill the space between the beds. It had a gold, four-pointed pattern woven into it, a compass symbol very much like the one on the ceiling that rose directly above it, and on the wallpaper from the other room, and on the card their grandmother had sent. It was like a coat of arms, cropping up everywhere around her.

The walls were painted white, giving the room a lightness that ran counter to the gloom and mystery of the rest of the house.

"I get this one," said Jaide, rushing forward to claim the bed on the left. Mattress and posts squeaked as she jumped on it, crumpling the coverlet under her knees. Jack was less enthusiastic. He, too, missed his room back home, just as he missed the familiar streets of his suburb, and his friends, but he was happy enough with the other bed. He bet that if he pressed close to the window from his side he could glimpse the sea.

"I think you'll be comfortable here," said their grandma from the doorway. "Let's go down and have some lunch. You must be tired after the trip."

"What's on the next floor up?" asked Jaide.

"That's where I sleep," Grandma X replied.

"Don't go up there," Susan warned the twins. "We mustn't invade your grandma's privacy any more than we already have."

"It's not an invasion. I've been expecting you."

"That's, uh, very kind. But you don't want these two little whirlwinds going through your things."

"Perhaps you're right," said Grandma X thoughtfully. "In any case, I must ask you to particularly avoid the widow's walk at the very top of the stairs. This is an old house and the roof needs work. I'd hate for you to slip and take a fall."

"Did you hear that, kids? Stay right away from there."

Jack nodded. Jaide made a movement that her mother accepted as agreement, though in fact she was thinking of the here-and-gone-again antiques store. Grandma X hadn't mentioned it.

"Is that the only place we can't go?" Jaide asked.

"Can't go?" said Grandma X. "There are places you should not go, certainly, as I have mentioned. Then there are *other* places to which you may not yet have found your way."

Jack gave Jaide a *what?* look, but his sister was only intrigued. That sounded to her like permission to explore, perhaps even a challenge.

"This house was modernized some fifty years ago," said Grandma X as she led them back downstairs to the kitchen. "It has central heating, electricity, and a telephone. That probably seemed modern enough to the people who owned it back then."

"What about television?" Jack asked.

"I can't abide television, of any sort," Grandma X replied, making both twins' stomachs sink. "If I want to watch a movie, I'll go to the cinema."

"And the Internet?" Jaide added in desperation.

Grandma X looked down at her, and a slow smile spread across her face.

"I have found the World Wide Web useful. I'll give you the password when you're settled in. However, my own computer must remain private, I'm afraid. Perhaps you have brought your own?"

"Thank you," said Susan. "Normal rules apply, guys. You can use my laptop, after everything is packed away."

Their luggage was still in the car. They had brought what little had survived the explosion with them, supplemented by new clothes hastily bought from a department store before leaving the city. Everything they owned in the world was contained in just a few bags.

"You should eat first," said Grandma X firmly. "Lunch is ready."

A platter lay on the chrome kitchen table, protected from more than just flies by a Portland Lighthouse tea towel. The broad-shouldered ginger tom the twins had seen before looked up from its contemplation of the covered food as they entered. Its nose twitched hopefully.

"Not for you, Ari," said Grandma X, shooing the cat away. "That's Aristotle. Watch out for him. He'll take the food out of your mouth if you let him, particularly if Kleo isn't around to keep him in check.

"Where's she got to, by the way?" she added, speaking directly to the cat. "I thought she'd be here to say hello."

Ari jumped onto the sink and flicked his tail.

"Perhaps she will grace us with her presence later," said Grandma X as she handed out plates and swept away the tea towel, revealing a generous spread of bread, cold meat, cheese, and salad. "Do you like lemonade? I'll get us all a glass each."

Jaide and Jack exchanged a glance, remembering the scene they had witnessed in the kitchen earlier, and the letter they had received the day of the explosion. Their grandma talked to cats. Worse, she seemed to think they talked back. That was almost as bad as the house having no television.

They sat at the table, feeling awkward and out of place. The kitchen was probably the most normal room in the house, but here they were subjected to the scrutiny of the cat, Grandma X, and their mother, who was watching to make sure they were on their best behavior. Neither twin felt inclined to cause trouble at that moment. Apart from the faint sound of a clock from elsewhere in the house, it was suddenly very quiet.

Tick-tock went the clock. *Tick-tock*. Then, out of nowhere, *tick-tock-tack*, as though it had improvised a whole new beat, just because it could.

"Help yourself," said Grandma X, and the twins realized that she had been waiting for them to start.

Jack made himself a particularly thick sandwich with lettuce, ham, and tomato, while Jaide made a much neater and more organized version of the same thing. Susan just had bread with butter, while Grandma X made an open sandwich balancing a bit of everything on top of a generous spread of mustard. Ari stuck out his pink tongue as if he could taste it from a distance, and looked as though he was waiting for the first opportunity to pounce.

"You said you wanted to talk to me about something, Susan," Grandma X said.

"Well, yes. Hector says — that is, Hector said —" Again, the twins' mother glanced at Jaide and Jack, as though wishing they were elsewhere so she could talk to her mother-in-law in private, but simultaneously afraid to let them out of her sight. "He doesn't know how long it will take to fix things, to return everything to normal. I'm hoping it won't take long, but —"

"I'm afraid I can't tell you, either," said Grandma X, reaching out to pat her daughter-in-law's hand. "You are welcome to stay here as long as it takes."

"I know, I mean — that's not quite what —" Susan's phone buzzed. She picked it up, but it stopped buzzing even as she looked at the caller ID and pulled a face. "Oh, blast. That's work. I've been waiting to hear from them about getting something temporary while we're up here."

"That's a sensible idea."

She shook the phone. "I'd call back, but I don't seem to be getting any signal now."

"You may have to go out to the road," said Grandma X. "Cell phones don't work well in this old house."

"Okay, I'll be back in a moment," said Susan. She gave the twins a stern *behave* look and headed off down the hallway.

There was a minute's awkward silence, in which Jack's mouthful of sandwich lost its taste and seemed to swell up like a lump of plaster, so heavy and thick it took three tries to swallow it.

"What does a house being old have to do with Mom's phone?" asked Jaide. "It's new, and radio waves either get through things or they don't."

Grandma X beamed at her. "You're a smart girl, Jaidith. I do believe we're going to get on just fine."

Both twins were keenly aware that she hadn't answered Jaide's question, but before they could ask again, Susan came back, looking unhappy.

"I have to start work tomorrow," she announced.

"So soon?" asked Grandma X. "You've only just gotten here."

"They're desperate. Someone suddenly took sick, and there's a shortage of helicopter-trained paramedics nationwide. I'm all they've got."

"I suppose it is fortunate to have skills that are in demand."

"Except this job is out of town, with three-day shifts," replied Susan, running her fingers through her hair.

"That *is* a shame," said Grandma X, glancing at the twins. "But we'll manage, won't we?"

Jack thought about being stuck in the big old house with their strange grandma and his heart seemed to falter inside his chest. He glanced across at Jaide. She was staring down into her lap, a sure sign she was upset. It wasn't their fault the house had blown up, and they hadn't chosen to come to Portland. Now they were trapped, without even their mother around for the first few days.

Jack wished their father would appear and sweep them away to wherever he was, even though he was apparently somewhere incredibly remote, because Susan said he couldn't even call them for a few weeks. So there was no point wishing for something that could never happen, or arguing, either. Their mother had to work, and it was an important job. She saved people's lives, after all.

Susan's expression was a mixture of hope and desperation. "I'll make it up to both of you when I get back, I promise," she told them. "We'll do something fun."

"They'll be all right," Grandma X assured her. "I'll get them settled in. School starts on Monday anyway, so they'll have plenty to occupy their minds."

Jaide groaned. She'd forgotten all about school! They'd had the last week off, but now it was Saturday, and that was already half over. The prospect of starting at an entirely new school only made things worse. Temporary it might be, but they wouldn't know anyone. All their friends were so far away, they might as well not exist.

"I'm not hungry," she said, pushing her half-eaten sandwich to one side.

Jack pushed his aside, too, even though he *was* hungry. He didn't put what he was thinking into words, because if he said "My life sucks," he could say good-bye to any time on his mother's laptop.

"I guess you had those snacks in the car," said Susan with strained goodwill. "Let's get the bags out of the car now and then we can try to relax. We could take a walk along the beach. Would you like that, kids?"

The prospect of getting out of the house helped restore some of the twins' energy, even if it meant they had to unload the car first. There was depressingly little to carry, and they had all their bags inside after just a few trips. While Grandma X went upstairs to get changed, Susan took the twins into her arms and hugged them tightly.

"It's only three days," she said, sounding more like she was talking to herself than to them. "That might be long enough."

"Long enough for what?" asked Jaide.

"You mean for Dad to come back?" Jack chimed in.

"Long enough for *something* to happen, certainly," said Grandma X as she came down the stairs.

The humans' voices faded into the distance. Ari jumped down from the window where he'd been observing their departure, and then up to the table, via a chair, the stove, and the fridge, just for fun. With one sharp claw he snared a slice of ham, which he delicately ate and then chased down with several licks of lemonade from Jack's cup.

The cat purred to himself as he enjoyed the lemonade. Grandma X was never this distracted — and the children had only just arrived! He could hardly imagine what else might be forthcoming when they settled in and discovered what they were.

The faintest noise came through the open window — the sound of a mouse rustling through the dry grass near the front steps. Ham and lemonade were forgotten in the twitch of a whisker. The chase was on! With a sudden leap, straight through the window, Ari was gone.

High above, the weather vane twirled around thirteen times, counterclockwise, in carefree defiance of the prevailing wind.

CHAPTER THREE
ABANDONED

Susan left very early the next morning, and although she looked in on the twins three times to repeat good-byes and apologies, Jack was still only half awake as he watched the car's taillights recede, a mournful red glow bouncing down the lane. So his father was gone, and now, even if it was only for three days, his mother was gone, too.

Jack grimaced and rolled over. His eyes drifted shut, and within moments he was dreaming about rats. Thousands of rats, lifting him up and carrying him on their backs, kind of like how he imagined crowd surfing at a concert. Only furry. It was quite nice, really, though even in his dream he knew he should be disturbed by this.

Jaide was a deeper sleeper than her brother. She had barely stirred when her mother had said good-bye, but once she was awake, she was wide awake and unable to get back to sleep. The floorboards creaked as she slipped out of bed and put on her father's old dressing gown. Surprisingly, it was one of the few things that had survived the explosion. It was brown and the hem had frayed where it dragged behind her, but she wouldn't wear anything else.

Tiptoeing lightly, she ran to the bathroom, a cramped arrangement of sink, counter, and toilet, all in a sickly yellow next to a white enameled metal claw-foot bath. Flushing the toilet made pipes bang and shudder seemingly miles underground, and Jaide held her breath until the echoes faded away.

She left the bathroom and crossed to the stairs, hesitating on the landing as she thought about going up to see what lay on Grandma X's floor.

"What're you doing?" asked a voice from behind her.

Jaide spun around to see Jack standing in their bedroom doorway, rubbing his eyes.

"You gave me a fright," she said, putting a hand to her chest.

"Yeah, you really jumped!" Jack grinned. "What are you up to?"

"Just looking around."

Jaide glanced up at the next landing, the gateway to their grandmother's domain, but instead of going that way they went down the stairs together.

"Remember the blue door?" Jaide asked. "It must lead somewhere."

"I bet it goes to a cellar." Jack shivered as he thought of what unknown terrors they could encounter down there.

"There might be another way in, from inside the house," Jaide said. "Let's see if we can find it."

First they went into the lounge. It was crowded with three well-worn leather couches, two long, glass-fronted bookcases, and no fewer than four coffee tables. If there was a cellar entrance there, it was hidden by a thick rug that could not be moved without completely removing all the furniture, which was beyond the twins' strength and inclination.

A connecting door of etched and colored glass led into the drawing room, which contained a locked rolltop desk, more bookcases, and an antique globe of the world that sat in one corner on three scaly, reptilian bronze legs that ended in silver-washed talons. The twins pressed various countries on the globe in the hope that there might be a secret switch to a door leading to the cellar below, and Jack pulled at every talon, but they were solid metal, not hidden levers. The twins even stamped on the floor, but heard no telltale echoes or loose boards.

The study door was tightly locked. The kitchen's floorboards stretched unbroken from wall to wall, with no faint lines to indicate a hidden trapdoor. The walls were solid, without interesting echoes when they knocked, even on the side facing the study.

There *was* a cupboard under the stairs, but that held only mops, brooms, and buckets.

Momentarily frustrated, the twins stood in the hallway, surrounded by their grandmother's odd collection of trinkets and portraits. Blank eyes stared at them, making Jack feel faintly queasy. That could have been hunger, though, and he pushed the thought firmly from his mind.

"Looking for something?"

The amused voice came echoing from the very summit of the house. Grandma X was watching them, looking down the center of the stairwell. Her gray hair hadn't been brushed, and stuck out in odd clumps and streamers.

"We're just exploring," said Jack, hoping that was okay.

"Very good. I'll be down in a second to make us some breakfast."

The wild-haired head disappeared.

"Quick," said Jaide, tugging at her brother's arm, "while we still have the chance."

"What?"

"Outside! We'll try the door itself and see if we can get in that way."

The door was exactly as it had been when she'd seen it the day before: bright blue and three steps down from ground level. Or perhaps not exactly as it had been, for she thought it had possessed a handle or doorknob, but now it was completely featureless, solid wood. And the sign they had seen, which had said something about antiques, was gone.

The twins went down the three stone steps side by side and pressed their hands against the door, dislodging some remnant drops of dew. They pushed as hard as they could, but the door didn't move. Jaide ran her hands around the edges, feeling for the hinges, while Jack pressed every faint whorl or discoloration in the timber, hoping for a secret catch. Neither approach worked. The door wouldn't give up its secrets.

"I think it's going to rain today," said Grandma X.

Jaide and Jack spun around, but their grandmother wasn't visible. It sounded as though her voice had come from the front door, just out of sight.

Instead of replying, Jaide put a finger to her lips and pulled Jack away from the door.

"Where —?"

"Shhhh!"

They ran around the house a second time, this time

peering at every vent and chink in the house's brickwork. There was no other hatch or entrance to any underground spaces, but there *was* a shuttered window on the southern wall that certainly hadn't been there before. Unfortunately it was too high up for even Jaide to get to without a ladder or a convenient drainpipe to climb. They stared up at it, trying to see through. The glass reflected thickening clouds and revealed nothing of what lay within.

"There *must* be a way inside," hissed Jaide. She didn't like mysteries she couldn't solve.

"In where, dear?"

This time Grandma X's voice came from right behind them, impossibly close. Jaide jumped again, and for an instant it seemed like she was literally airborne, she felt so startled. She hadn't heard her grandmother's boots on the gravel. How could an old woman move so *quietly*?

A hand came down on both twins' shoulders, pinning them to the earth.

"Uh, nothing?" said Jack, glancing in disbelief at his sister. When she had jumped it seemed she had *really* jumped, higher than was possible without a trampoline.

Jaide felt light-headed but recovered quickly.

"Do you have a cellar?" she asked, turning to face her grandmother, who had her hair back under control and looked quite severe.

"A house this size," said Grandma X, "you'd expect so, wouldn't you?" She smiled, but it wasn't a comforting smile. "Come on in and get dressed. I'll make you some breakfast."

She pushed the twins ahead of her with irresistible strength. They stamped reluctantly up the stairs to their room while she banged and crashed in the kitchen.

"She doesn't answer any questions," Jaide whispered. "Have you noticed?"

"I know. Not much we can do about it now, though."

Jaide went to the tiny bathroom, slipped out of her father's dressing gown, and got into some of the new clothes their mom had bought her before leaving for Portland. Meanwhile, back in their room, Jack put on the same clothes he'd worn through the long road trip. He liked them; they felt reassuringly familiar.

"You probably want to explore Portland," said Grandma X when they reluctantly traipsed downstairs, "but I fear we'll be stuck inside today, once it starts raining. Do you know how to play cards?"

The twins nodded slowly, even though the thought of playing cards with her didn't fill them with overwhelming excitement.

"What about the cellar, Grandma?" pressed Jack.

"What cellar is that, then?" she said, bustling past them. "How about toast, or cereal? Or both?"

Jack's stomach rumbled, making him miss Jaide's frustrated look.

"Toast and cereal, please," he said.

"Just cereal, I guess," said Jaide. "What about the cellar, though?"

"Let's sit down and eat our breakfast," said Grandma X.

Jaide frowned in a way she normally only used with her mother.

Jack sat with his sister at the table and watched Grandma X's back as she put the kettle on the stove and lit the gas with a very long match that he wasn't entirely sure he saw her strike. As he stuffed cereal in his face, he could tell that Jaide wasn't going to be distracted by anything as trivial as food.

"Grandma," Jaide started to ask, her cereal sitting ignored in front of her, "I really need to know about the —"

"The blue door," said Grandma X. She turned back from the stove and looked at Jaide. "You can see it, can you?"

"Yes! So can Jack. But is it really there?"

"Of course, dear. If you can see it, it must be."

"I knew it!"

Jaide thumped her fist on the table, sending the milk slopping from side to side in her bowl. "But why can't Mom see it? When we pointed it out to her, she just told us off."

"That's one of the mysteries, dear," said Grandma X, and blew out the match. The smoke from it wound once around her head and then went out the window.

"One of *what* mysteries?" Jaide persisted. Grandma X's lack of straight answers was utterly infuriating her.

"You'll have to be patient, Jaidith. There is a time for the telling of these things, and a natural order to be maintained. Some doors are not meant to be opened before their time. Rushing things would be . . . ill advised. Here, have a cup of hot chocolate. The day doesn't start until I've had one, and I love the smell it gives the place. What do you think?"

Jack looked up from his cereal. Grandma X had a cup of hot chocolate in each hand. But she'd only just lit the stove for the kettle, and she hadn't even gotten out any milk or anything. Or had she?

Steam swirled up from the mugs into the twins' nostrils, and they breathed in its velvety scent. It filled Jaide's mind with a warm, caressing breeze, and Jack's with a comforting, companionable darkness. Breeze and darkness did their work, and all the twins' thoughts ceased for an instant.

When they started again, neither Jaide nor Jack could remember what they had just been talking about.

CHAPTER FOUR
TRIALS OF THE
TROUBLETWISTERS

Cards," said Grandma X firmly. "You said you can play. How about you show me after breakfast? I have a deck I save for special guests. We can have a game or two in here, then see if the weather is going to clear."

Jack felt as though he'd forgotten something, but the aroma of the hot chocolate reminded him of what was really important. He raised the mug to his lips and sipped. It was absolutely delicious. If every day in Portland started with hot chocolate, he was going to like it here very much.

Jaide's frown hadn't completely faded, but she did the same as Jack, telling herself that she was worried about nothing. *If it's important, it'll come back*, her father was always saying. Hector was notoriously absentminded, another Shield trait Jaide hoped she wouldn't inherit.

After their hot chocolate, Grandma X served the twins thick slices of toast spread with real butter and her own homemade gooseberry jam. They had just finished clearing up when a slender, blue-gray cat came through the window, landed elegantly on the table, and immediately jumped to the kitchen bench and paraded along it like a model to receive a pat from Grandma X.

"Kleo, at last," said Grandma X. "What kept you? These two troubletwisters, as you no doubt already know, are my grandchildren, Jaidith and Jackaran."

The cat rubbed her chin under Grandma X's hand, then turned and meowed at Jack and Jaide.

"She missed breakfast," said Jack, remembering Ari's hungry eyes. "Can I get her a snack?"

"She's fed well enough already where she lives."

"I thought she was your cat," said Jaide.

"If Kleopatra here belongs to anyone, it's to David Smeaton, who runs the secondhand bookstore around the corner. She just likes to visit, when it suits her."

Kleo meowed again, defensively.

"Rubbish!" said Grandma X. "Ari is always happy to see you, whatever his other . . . ah . . . engagements. Wait here and I'll get the cards."

Kleo inclined her head in regal agreement and turned her attention to the twins. She watched them and the children watched the cat until, one after the other, they found Kleo's cool blue gaze too unnerving. Surely cats weren't supposed to look people in the eye, Jack wondered, or engage them in staring contests?

"Uh, can I pat you?" asked Jaide.

"Rowr," Kleo acquiesced. She lay down and allowed herself to be stroked.

Grandma X bustled back into the room, holding a rather large pack of cards.

"Who wants to deal?" she said. Instead of waiting for an answer, she continued, "You try it, Jack. Five cards each, facedown, just like poker."

Jack took the deck from her and almost dropped it, surprised by its weight. The cards were more square than rectangular, and though at first he had thought they were gilt-edged, by the weight alone he realized they were actually thin plates of gold that had been enameled with colorful designs, the diamond pattern on the backs a rich green and red, reminiscent of a tartan.

"Deal Kleo in, too," Grandma X added as Jack tentatively shuffled the metal cards. "She can sit in this round."

Mad as a meat axe, Jack thought, using a phrase his father sometimes employed to describe very rich people who paid millions for paintings they didn't like but whose artists were famous. It was bad enough that Grandma X talked to cats as though they could understand her. Now she expected them to play cards as well!

Odder still was what he saw on the cards when he picked up his hand. Instead of the usual suits and numbers, there were illustrations in red and green lines of enamel on the first three cards: a cave mouth in a mountain; a crescent moon; and a wave that reminded him of a famous Japanese woodcut of a tsunami. Even stranger, the last two cards were blank, just burnished gold, without enameled illustrations.

Jaide was puzzling over her cards, too. She had been dealt an old-fashioned sun with long, wavy streaks of fire around a disc; a bird in flight, its wings outstretched, with more wavy lines that she supposed represented the wind underneath; a half-shut human eye with very long lashes; and she also had two cards of plain burnished gold.

"Let's see what I've got," said Grandma X. She laid her

cards on the table, but stacked so only the topmost card was visible. It was a crescent moon.

"As one might expect," she commented. Quickly she flicked over her other cards. The next three were all also crescent moons. The fifth card was the same eye Jaide had, only instead of being half shut, it was open and staring.

Jaide and Jack looked at each other and knew they were thinking the same thing: What kind of game was this, when Grandma X showed her hand at the start?

Instead of explaining, Grandma X pointed at the five cards sitting in a stack in front of Kleo, who was sitting up again and had one paw sitting on them as if she actually did know how to play. "Do either of you know what cards Kleo has?"

"How could we?" Jaide asked. "We can't see them."

"Well, if you don't know, perhaps you can guess. Let's see if, between the three of us, we can get all five by guessing two each. That gives us one spare guess. I'll go first: a tree and the hanged mouse. Now you guess, Jaidith."

"But the only cards I know in this weird deck are yours and the ones I have!" Jaide protested.

"That doesn't matter," said Grandma X with a wink. "Perhaps this deck contains anything you can think of."

"Uh, if you say so. . . ." Jaide looked at Jack, who shrugged, and then said the first things that fell into her mind. "A house and the number two."

"Jackaran?"

Jack scratched his nose.

"Um, I guess . . . a nose . . . and a . . . donut."

Grandma X reached over and Kleo delicately withdrew her paw. Her blue gaze was curious as Grandma X turned over the first card. It showed a mouse hanging upside down in a snarl of threads.

"The hanged mouse!" said Jack. "How did you know?"

Grandma X just smiled mysteriously and turned over the remaining four: an acorn; a barbed arrow; a gutted fish; and an oak tree, her first guess.

"No correct guesses from the troubletwisters," said Grandma X, with a rueful look for both of them. "Perhaps we shall see something from the other perspective. Show me your cards, Jackaran."

"Okay," said Jack. He folded his cards into a stack and put them in front of him, as she had done. The first he turned over was plain burnished gold, and the second was, too. But so were the third, and the fourth, and the fifth. The illustrations were gone.

"But . . . but there was a wave, and a cave, and . . . uh . . ."

"Not unexpected," said Grandma X, "and not terribly helpful, either. What about your cards, Jaidith?"

Jaide laid her cards down and turned them over one by one. Four of hers had become blank, too, but the fifth card still showed the wavy lines of a breeze supporting a bird caught in midflight.

"How can they change?" Jaide asked. "What's going on?"

Grandma X swept up the cards in one smooth motion and clicked her fingers. The click echoed through the room, and with its echoes, Jaide and Jack felt the warmth of the hot chocolate rush through them again, and they forgot the card game completely.

"Here we are, I've got the cards," said Grandma X. "Not the usual type. These are more fun. Before we play, who thinks they can flip a card into that bronze bowl in the corner?"

Jack took a card and was surprised by the weight and the fact they were metal, and by the strangest sensation that he had handled cards like this before.

"I'll try," he said, but when he flicked the card it missed by several inches.

They all had several goes. Grandma X missed most times. Jaide missed her first two attempts, but then got the knack of it. Four out of her last five went in with resounding clangs of metal on metal, and Kleo came to sit at her side, as if the cat was a prize that Jaide had won.

"How are you doing that?" asked Jack, growing frustrated. He had missed every time, and even managed to lose one of the cards in the process.

"Oh, it's easy," she boasted, and perhaps became a little overconfident, because her very next attempt ricocheted off the lip of the spittoon and whizzed about their heads like an excited hummingbird before finally embedding itself in the side of a loaf of bread. Kleo yowled and ran out of the room with her ears flat to her head.

"All right, that will do." Grandma X picked up the cards and shifted the spittoon out from the wall. "Well done, Jaidith. Don't look so glum, Jackaran. We'll try something else you might be good at next. First, though,

I'd like to find that missing card. Will you help me look? It must be in here somewhere."

They turned the kitchen inside out, looking in all the obvious spots first, then opening drawers and even shifting the fridge to see behind it. There was no sign of the card anywhere.

"Hmm," said Grandma X, putting her hands on her hips and staring at Jack as though he had lost the card deliberately. "Let's see if you can find something else instead. Before I went to bed last night, I hid six coins in the lounge. Think of it as a treasure hunt. But remember, everything else has to go back in its place afterward. No permanent mess, please."

"Why?" asked Jack, feeling uncharacteristically rebellious.

"Why no mess? I had enough of that with your father —"

"I mean, why find the coins? If it's a game, it isn't a very good one."

"How about if I say what you find, you keep?" said Grandma X. "There's a sweet shop on the main street. They make their own licorice and lollipops. I'll take you there when it stops raining."

Jaide and Jack exchanged another look. Homemade licorice and lollipops were not something they could get excited about. While Jack liked food, he didn't have a sweet tooth, and Jaide didn't have the patience for anything that took too long to eat. A lollipop would just annoy her.

Still, money always came in handy. They didn't have to spend it on candy. The twins loped off to search, riffling through books, upending cushions, and scrabbling around on the floor to see under the couches.

The coins were: (1) under the corner of the rug; (2) on the windowsill behind the velvet curtains; (3) behind an antique clock that had long lost its tick; (4) tucked out of sight beneath the easy chair; (5) sitting out in the open on the mantelpiece; and (6) between pages sixty-four and sixty-five of *Travels, Travails, and Toilets of Tibet*, about a man and his pet pig who visited that country in the 1930s.

The twins returned with three coins each, somewhat reassured that the exercise hadn't been a complete waste of time.

"Look what turned up while you were distracted," said Grandma X, pointing.

Right out in the open, where the shadow of a chair cut an elongated line across the floor, lay the missing card.

"How did we miss *that*?" asked Jaide, amazed.

"Good question. Can you guess the answer?"

Jack studied his grandmother closely, wondering if she had placed the card there herself in order to trick them. Why would she do something like that? He didn't know, and the uneasy feeling grew stronger.

"You're testing us, aren't you?"

"Yes, but not in the way you think."

Grandma X snapped her fingers again. The smell of chocolate was fading, and the effect it had on the twins was weakening with it, but Jack's brow smoothed and he looked around, wondering momentarily what he was doing.

"Here you go," he said, picking up the card and giving

it back to his grandmother. "It should go with the others, shouldn't it?"

"Yes, dear," she said, slipping it onto the pile. "All things have their place. Sometimes you just have to look a little harder to find it."

Jaide was staring at the coins in her hand, wondering where they had come from.

"Were we going outside somewhere?" she asked.

"I had hoped so," said Grandma X. "But the prospect of lollipops seems more remote than ever."

One glance out the window confirmed that impression. What the clouds had threatened earlier had finally arrived in full force. The rain was falling in steady sheets.

Jaide's spirits immediately fell, too. She liked bright, warm days, and hated winter. Jack was the opposite. He loved dim, cloudy weather and disliked the heat and glare of high summer. Jaide's idea of a perfect afternoon was to be at the beach under a hot sun. Jack preferred the dusk of a cool evening, or a still night with just a sliver of a moon.

"Still, there's lots to do in here," their grandmother said. "Come into the drawing room. I've got a bunch of . . . interesting objects . . . in there that you might like to see."

Puzzled, the twins followed her into the drawing room and watched as she unlocked the desk and rolled back the cover to reveal all manner of contraptions. There was a spark gap generator that sent a bright blue jolt of electricity shooting between two metal points, especially when Jaide pulled the trigger. An old compass spun wildly as they passed it from hand to hand, pointing every direction other than north. There was a small box that Grandma X assured them was an old camera, with no LED screen and a shutter that clicked solidly behind the lens's glass eye. When Jack clicked the button, he saw people and places from long ago, but all Jaide saw was her brother in the drawing room, pulling faces.

Grandma X watched them as they played their way through the odd collection. Sometimes she wrote in a pink leather notebook she had produced from a drawer. Once she even took a magnifying glass out of her pocket and studied the top of Jack's and Jaide's scalps, as though looking for head lice, but didn't seem to find what she was looking for. She put the magnifying glass away and lit some old lanterns that stank of kerosene and cast a lovely warm glow over the room.

As the last lantern wick flared, Kleo returned, and her eyes caught and reflected the flame. She meowed and jumped up to sit like a sphinx on a straight-backed chair, as if waiting for something interesting to happen.

"What's this, Grandma?" Jaide asked, pulling a strange contraption from behind the desk.

"A pogo stick, dear. Have you never seen one before?"

Both twins shook their heads, then gasped with surprise as Grandma X demonstrated it for them. The floor and the furniture shook as the elderly woman in her silver-tipped cowboy boots climbed onto the crossbars and took two spring-fueled bounces across the drawing room. A cloud of dust rose up, Kleo fled again, and Grandma X climbed off and hurriedly opened the windows to let some fresh air in.

"They were all the rage when I was a girl," she said, looking slightly pink in the face. "Why don't you have a go?"

"Really?" asked Jack. "In here?"

"Outside isn't an option with all that rain coming down."

"All right." He took the device from her and pointed it spring down toward the floor, glancing around at all the fragile-looking things in the room. "Mom would never let us do this."

"Guess we'd better not tell her about it, then," said Grandma X with a wink. "Go on. Let's see who can bounce the highest."

That was all the encouragement the twins needed. Jaide took the pogo stick from her brother and immediately mastered it. She laughed and felt as light as a feather, bouncing around the room. Vases danced and books swayed on their shelves, but she bounced with total control and only reluctantly handed it back to let Jack have a go.

Jack lacked his sister's easy grasp of the art of pogoing, and distantly, distractedly, he was sure this wasn't the first time that day he had missed out on something fun, although he couldn't quite remember what else there had been. He watched himself in the mirror above the mantelpiece in the drawing room trying to do everything Jaide had done, exactly as she had done it. The daylight from the window, although grayer than it normally would have been, cast a dazzling silver halo around him, and he bounced to his right in order to see himself better. But the moment he was away from the window it seemed that he faded into the heavy folds of the curtain and his reflection disappeared from the mirror entirely.

Suddenly disoriented by his lack of reflection, Jack mistimed his next bounce, careened into the desk, ricocheted off it, and fell over, smacking his temple on the cushioned front of a chair as he went down.

For an instant, the world went black. He hadn't knocked himself out. He hadn't even hurt himself very badly, apart from feeling as though all the air had been sucked out of him. But somehow all the light around him vanished, and he was falling through an empty void. Empty, that was, apart from distant white points that looked at first like stars, but soon revealed themselves as eyes, rushing rapidly closer —

"Jack!" Jaide was crying out as she knelt down next to the fallen pogo stick. "Jack! Where are you . . . oh!"

"I'm here," answered Jack crossly. "Where else would I be?"

Jaide shook her head in bewilderment. She was sure that Jack hadn't been there, that he'd disappeared as he hit the floor, vanishing into the shadow of a chair. The fear that he somehow might have gone for good slowly ebbed, but the memory of that sharp stab of fear remained. He was her *brother*. Sure, he annoyed her sometimes — but what would she do without him?

A sudden gust of wind made the window rattle like a drum, and both twins twisted around, startled by the noise.

"I think that's enough bouncing for now," said Grandma X, helping Jack up.

"Are you sure you're all right, Jack?" asked Jaide.

Jack glanced at the mirror and saw himself, perfectly visible again, as he should have been. But he was distracted by a sound from outside, something rising above the sounds of the rain and wind.

"What's that noise?" he asked. "Is that someone shouting?"

Jaide squinted through the rain-swept glass and gasped. There was a man being blown like a leaf up the drive, his feet never quite touching the ground, his mouth open and bellowing.

"Oh, dear," said Grandma X. "That isn't right."

CHAPTER FIVE

THE OTHER PORTLAND

The twins followed Grandma X as she rushed to the front door, threw it open, and ran outside. The wind howled and roared almost loudly enough to drown out the shouts of the man who was caught in its grip. He was in his fifties, heavily mustachioed. He wore jeans and cowboy boots very similar to Grandma X's, and was waving an umbrella around and around his head.

He spun and tumbled toward them, somehow managing to always get back upright despite the intensity of the wind around him. It swept him right up to the front door, spun him around in a tight circle, and dumped him in the gravel by the steps. He landed on his bottom with his legs in the air, but he was still waving his umbrella.

"Yee-ha!" yelled the man, and only then did the twins realize that his shouts were of excitement, not fear.

The small tornado rushed back toward him, whipping up a cloud of wet gravel as it came. But before it could get hold of the man again, Grandma X stepped out and raised an admonishing finger.

"Stop this at once!" she commanded.

The hair on the backs of both the twins' necks stood up at the whipcrack of her voice, and they felt a strong compulsion to stay completely still.

The wind must have felt it, too, for the tornado fell apart. The gravel dropped straight down, and the air was suddenly quiet and still, apart from the rain, which continued to fall in a steady stream.

The man picked up a handful of stones and threw them over his head like confetti.

"That was great!" he cried. "Just delightful!"

"Are you okay?" Jack asked, hesitating only slightly before rushing forward to help him up, with Jaide a step behind him.

"Better than all right, young fellow, young lady — why, thank you. I feel quite enthused, as a matter of fact. That doesn't happen every day."

"It shouldn't happen at all," said Grandma X in a warning tone, coming up beside the twins with her arms folded. "How did it start?"

"Well, I'd just ducked out of the shop to see where Kleo had gotten to when the wind snatched me up. I've never felt anything quite like it. A most amazing ride!"

"Weren't you frightened?" asked Jaide, gazing up at his ruddy, beaming face.

"Not at all. Why would I be?"

Because it isn't normal, she wanted to say, but the words died on her lips. Very little about Grandma X, her home, and now her friends struck Jaide as remotely normal. That they seemed to like it that way only made them weirder.

The man thrust out his hand to her.

"David Smeaton's the name, but you can call me Rodeo Dave."

He shook hands with both of the twins as they introduced themselves in turn. His hand was calloused and very strong, and his good mood infectious. Jack, who was normally reticent around strangers, found himself laughing at a slightly off-color joke about wind.

"You're obviously all right, then, David," said Grandma X, not quite smiling. "Kleo is here, so the wind brought you to exactly the right place. Shall I call her?"

"She'll come home when she wants to, I expect. I'm just glad she's found a safe port in all this weather, and some new friends to play with, to boot. Better get inside before you're soaked right through," he added, his mustache dripping. "Come and visit any time you want, young Jack and Jaide. Adieu!"

With that and a brisk wave over his head, Rodeo Dave walked back along the drive to Watchward Lane. A steady chuckle was audible in his wake.

Despite her earlier misgivings, Jaide found herself wishing that she had been caught up in the wind, too. It did look like fun, and a lot easier than walking everywhere.

That reminded her of something from the night before — something about flying . . . or something *like* flying — which in turn reminded her that there was something else she had been trying to remember, something important. . . .

"Why is he called Rodeo Dave?" asked Jack. "I thought you said Kleo's owner ran a bookshop."

"I did. He does. But he didn't always run a bookshop."

"Was he a cowboy before that?" asked Jack, his imagination full of wild horses and lassoes.

"I'll let him tell the story when he's ready," she said. "I must confess I am curious to visit your school. I don't believe I have been inside since your father was a student there."

Grandma X turned to Kleo, who was peering warily out from the drawing room. "As for you," she said, "make yourself useful and catch me a mouse."

The schoolteacher, Mr. Carver, was a towering beanpole of a man, with a kindly smile and just a fringe of hair around his otherwise bald head. He smelled faintly of incense, wore his linen shirt untucked, and had plastic sandals on his feet.

"Call me Heath," he told the twins, shaking each of their hands enthusiastically in turn. "I'm sure we're going to be marvelous friends."

"Uh, thanks," said Jack. At the twins' old school, the teachers wore suits and ties and were called "sir" or "ma'am" — the concept of teachers and students being friends would have been met with more than surprise on both sides. Jaide was struck dumb by the man's overbearing good nature. She simply didn't know what to say to this kind of adult.

Grandma X had done her hair up in a tight gray bun before leaving the house, and it had made her look quite severe — even before she saw the changes at the school, like the cushions on the floor instead of desks, and a motto on the blackboard in rainbow chalk that read *Harmony, Sharing, Discovery.*

"My daughter-in-law would like to know what materials Jackaran and Jaidith will need for their first day, Mr. Carver," said Grandma X.

"Oh, do please call me Heath!" exclaimed the schoolteacher. "And, of course, Mrs. Shield, if you —"

"I'm not Mrs. Shield," said Grandma X.

"Oh, I do apologize, I presumed . . . your son being one of our past top pupils, his name on the old honor board . . ."

"My name is —" said Grandma X, but whatever word she said was simply incomprehensible to the children's minds, and obviously to Mr. Carver's, too, because he goggled at her for a moment before resuming what seemed to be his trademark half smile.

"Indeed, Mrs. Xantho . . . er . . . Xeno . . . Xerxes . . . that is . . . ma'am . . . regarding materials, there's no need to worry about anything like that. Here at the Stormhaven Innovative School of Portland, we help students through the educative process by encouraging them to study at their own pace, in their own special way."

"What exactly does that mean?" asked Grandma X. Her lips had become surprisingly thin and her eyes had narrowed.

"That we don't treat our children like battery hens," explained Mr. Carver. He clasped his hands together and leaned down to look directly into the twins' faces. "Bring as much or as little as you want, Jack and Jaide, and we'll make of you what you will."

The gummi bear that Jaide had been chewing dissolved in her mouth, forgotten. "We don't have to bring any books?"

"Not unless you want to." Mr. Carver beamed as though he'd won a debate with Albert Einstein. "Would you like a run around the playground while you're here?"

"Good idea," said Grandma X, surprising the twins. "Run along now while I talk to Mr. Carver."

The twins bolted through the classroom and out the school's back door. For such a small school, it had a very large oval with some play equipment tacked onto one side, almost as an afterthought. Presumably the playing field was shared with the town for sporting events and fairs. Jack raced Jaide right around the oval, winning by a comfortable margin despite the sludginess of the grassy ground beneath their feet. The rain was holding off for the moment, although the clouds, if anything, had thickened.

"Stop!" called a woman's voice as Jaide rushed up the ladder of a slippery dip and prepared to whoosh down the other side. "Hold it right there!"

Jaide froze, poised between standing and sliding with both feet out in front of her. The voice had come from inside a wooden fort. A tall woman in overalls crawled out of the fort's child-size gate and pointed emphatically with a wrench.

"It's broken! Get down or you'll hurt yourself!"

Jaide's face flushed, partly from embarrassment at being yelled at by a stranger and partly out of annoyance. She could see nothing remotely wrong with the slippery dip.

"How do you know?" she asked.

"Because I'm here to fix it," said the woman. She stood up and indicated the base of the slippery dip, where Jack was standing. "I was going to work on the slide next."

"She's right, Jaide," said Jack, pointing. The slippery dip's legs had rusted right through and would have collapsed under Jaide's weight. From where he was standing he could see it clearly. "You're lucky she saw you in time."

Slightly mollified, Jaide retracted her legs and climbed back down the ladder. The woman came around to meet her, her expression less severe now that she saw Jaide was safe. She reminded Jaide of her mother whenever one of the twins had a close call, going from terror to telling-off to apologies in a matter of seconds.

"Sorry I gave you a fright," the woman said, slipping the wrench into a pocket and wiping her greasy hands on her overalls. "You're all right?"

"Yes," said Jaide, coming around the slippery dip to find solidarity next to her brother. "Thanks."

"Oh, no bother." The woman waved cheerfully, although there was a sadness to her eyes that Jack couldn't decipher. "I'll have it shipshape by the time you come back tomorrow. Wouldn't want to let the little ones down."

She took a step closer, as though she wanted to keep talking, but the twins said thanks again and hurried back inside, made nervous by the presence of yet another stranger. There had been so many in the last twenty-four hours that they were beginning to feel overwhelmed.

Mr. Carver and Grandma X were engaged in a lively discussion on the proper education of children.

"The mind of a child is the most precious thing in the universe," Mr. Carver was saying. "It's our job to encourage them to grow!"

"It's a teacher's job to make sure they grow *in the right way*. How does letting something run wild achieve that?"

They broke off on seeing the twins, Mr. Carver with visible relief.

"Ah, yes, here you are. Did you meet Rennie? She's the town's odd-job woman. If you ever need anything done up at your house, she's the one to call."

If Mr. Carver was trying to make amends, he failed in the face of Grandma X's determined disapproval.

"My house looks after itself perfectly well," she said. "And rest assured that we will continue this conversation another time. For now, we're going to take a walk through the park."

"Be at one with nature, yes, that's a lovely idea, good. Well, it's been nice meeting you both." Mr. Carver shook the twins' hands again, meeting their eyes meaningfully and sincerely. They both noticed the dampness of his palm. "I'll look forward to getting to know you better tomorrow."

"Uh, sure," said Jack. Grandma X's grip on his shoulder was tight as she led them out the front of the school's sole building. From the direction of the sea came the smell of fish. They had passed the fishing co-op during the short trip from Watchward Lane, and a trawler was off-loading a big catch of something.

"I suppose the school is at least *convenient*," said Grandma X, screwing up her nose at yet another apparition of rainbow paint, this time along the fence, a mural of many children holding hands and smiling exaggerated smiles.

"Where else could we go?" asked Jaide.

"Nowhere close," replied Grandma X. "I don't believe a long train trip each morning and afternoon would improve your minds very much." She peered at the clouds. "There'll be time for that tour I promised you, I think."

Grandma X's car was a canary yellow 1951 Hillman Minx, with bulging leather seats and a steering wheel as big as a truck's. It was Jack's turn to ride shotgun, and he paid more attention to the car's wood paneling and ancient accessories than to the places he was taken in it. There was no CD player or MP3 plug. The radio had only one dial. When Grandma X changed gear, the whole car vibrated, as if the gear change required the effort of the entire vehicle.

The park she had mentioned to Mr. Carver was on the other side of the iron bridge that crossed the wide, lazy river and its attendant swamps, leading to the town's main street. Jaide had expected the usual trees and shrubs in the park, but found instead a large, carefully mown lawn with a bizarre centerpiece: an oval-shaped garden of cactuses growing out of weirdly placed stones. One cactus in particular stood up like a long, skeletal hand, pointing straight up into the sky. Others puffed and prickled in the breeze, looking various degrees of dangerous. They seemed very out of place in the rain.

"Why cactuses, here?" asked Jaide. "I thought they only grew in the desert."

"They require careful tending," replied Grandma X. "But they have been here since the town was founded. In fact, your great-great-grandfather — my husband's grandfather — planted them, I believe out of a hankering for a former life in more arid parts."

When quizzed about which parts, exactly, Grandma X was vague. The twins trailed after her as she looked at each cactus carefully, even getting out a pair of brass opera glasses to peer at the flowers atop the largest and presumably oldest cactus, which was well over thirty feet high.

But when she had finished, she summoned the twins with a clap of her hands.

"Not a moment to lose!" she exclaimed, even though she'd been the one staring at the plants. "Not if we're going to see everything. Time is of the essence!"

"Why?" asked Jaide. "We're not in any hurry."

"The rain, dear, the rain," Grandma X said.

From the cactus park Grandma X took them past the hospital and police station, but not, unfortunately, to the beach they had visited the day before. Grandma X parked on the edge of the coastal reserve and peered through the trees at the ocean. She fiddled in her bag and produced the opera glasses again, which she focused on Mermaid Point. She hummed and tutted for a moment, then passed the glasses to Jack.

"Tell me what you see," she said.

"Just rocks. Big black ones."

"Now you, Jaidith. Anything unusual?"

Jaide squinted down the unfamiliar instrument. "The rocks look like a giant, curled up into a ball."

"Let's see," said Jack, taking the glasses back from her. "Where?"

"Look for the shoulders. Once you see them, you can see the rest."

"Oh, yeah," Jack exclaimed. "I see him!"

"Her," Grandma X corrected, without further explanation.

Jaide assumed they were going home — Portland was very small, after all, and they had already seen most of it — but instead of turning up Parkhill Street, Grandma X headed out onto the headland visible from the opposite side of the bay.

There they found an old church and cemetery, and a lighthouse, all under the shadow of Portland's most striking geological feature: the Rock.

The Rock was a hill of gray stone that speared up out of the ground fully four hundred feet high, providing numerous rookeries for seabirds on its steepest side and some precarious perches for clumps of pandanus trees and other small plants on the other.

The view from the top would be fantastic, thought Jack, and it didn't look too hard to climb. In fact, he could see the beginning of a path, and a sign that looked like it marked the start of a trail. But his hopes of climbing it were temporarily dashed when Grandma X parked the Hillman at the base of the lighthouse and peered up at the tapering white column through the opera glasses.

"What are you looking for?" Jaide asked her. She was getting bored of sightseeing, particularly when she didn't get to look through the opera glasses.

"Oh, nothing, dear."

"Then what are we doing here?"

"You can live somewhere all your life and see it afresh every day," Grandma X said. "It's all in how you use your eyes . . . how attentive you are to *changes*."

It didn't look to Jaide like the town had changed in at least a generation, maybe two, and she could tell when she was being fobbed off. She folded her arms and huffed back into the seat, despairing of ever seeing or doing anything that interested her.

"How long *have* you lived here, Grandma?" Jack asked.

"Hmmm?"

"Were you born in Portland?"

The glasses came down. Grandma X's expression was distant, as though seeing something very far away.

"Oh, no, I grew up on the other side of the world, almost. It was your grandfather who came from here. He was a clock maker, and a very good one, too."

"What happened to him?" Jack asked, thinking of the broken clock in the lounge, and the other one that went *tick-tock-tack*.

"He died a long time ago." Grandma X sniffed, and turned her steely gaze back to the twins. "Things have changed an awful lot since his time. Schools, for instance."

"Can we go for a walk?" Jack asked.

"I'm sure you can," Grandma X said, "but *may* you? That's the question."

Jaide had heard that line from her father. "*May* we go for a walk, Grandma? It looks like the sun is coming out."

Grandma X raised the opera glasses once more, but not

to look at the clouds, which were parting a little. Instead she focused the glasses at the top of the lighthouse.

"I suppose the . . . conditions . . . are not unfavorable," she said slowly. "Stay within sight of the lighthouse, keep well away from the rocks at Dagger Reef, and be home before dusk. That is very important. Do you understand?"

"Yes, Grandma," they both said. They already had their car doors open.

"You do remember the way home from here, don't you? Go back down Dock Road and left at Parkhill. If you reach the iron bridge, you've gone too far."

"Yes, Grandma."

"If you're not home in an hour, I'll come looking for you!"

The twins slammed the doors behind them, making the car's heavy body rock from side to side. They didn't need to discuss where they would go first. Gravestones beckoned by the church.

Maybe their grandfather lay under one of them.

CHAPTER SIX

IN THE SHADOW
OF THE ROCK

Jaide and Jack raced across the parking lot and around the lighthouse. Jack relished the feel of the pavement under his sneakers and of holding back as he always did at the end, to let his sister catch up a little, but not too much. When he reached the first of the headstones, he slowed to an amble in order to read what they said.

"Look," said Jaide, pointing. "This guy died when he was ninety-eight!"

"Well, this whole family died in the same year."

"Was there a plague?"

"Maybe an accident."

Jack hoped their father was okay, wherever he was. "Look for Shields. Dad's dad came from here, remember?"

They separated in search of their family history. Quite a few of the gravestones had become illegible with the passage of time, the carved letters eroded beyond any possibility of puzzling them out. Despite this, several Shields stood out, notably a Giles Chesterton Shield, who had died thirty-three years ago and lay buried alone in one corner of the cemetery. There were no words on his headstone, apart from his name and the date, but there was a compass-shaped insignia carved into the marble, which looked markedly less weathered than the stone around it.

"I guess this must be our grandfather . . ." said Jack. He felt like he should take his hat off, but he wasn't wearing one. Instead he bowed his head a little bit and felt solemn.

Jaide looked behind them to see if Grandma X was watching them from the car with her opera glasses. But the old car was gone.

Jaide felt free, as if relieved of some constraint or leash. Though she was curious about this whole new branch of her family tree, the prospect of endless pots of plastic flowers, worn granite, and dead, dusty things faded in comparison to the much more interesting places to explore nearby.

Especially the great hill of stone that loomed up so very close to them.

"Race you to the top," she said, pointing at the Rock. "There's a path, look!"

"I already saw the path," said Jack, but he hesitated. "Do you think Grandma X would let us?"

"It's in sight of the lighthouse," replied Jaide. "Well, the top is, anyway — and she didn't say we couldn't."

"Or *shouldn't*," said Jack with a grin.

They ran to where the sign advertised the start of a walking trail, by the rear of the old church. The trail wasn't paved; instead, numerous feet had cleared the way of weeds and pounded the dirt to something like concrete. The way was easy at first, but it grew steadily steeper, winding back and forth around sudden rocks and promontories, with the occasional bench for people to catch their breath. The twins were the only two on the track. They quickly climbed to a height where the path narrowed and hurrying seemed unwise, so they settled into a more cautious, steady plod upward.

The higher they got, the stronger the wind became. Jack hugged himself tightly against its bite. It was so strong, he had to brace himself when they reached the top. From the summit, as they stood next to a small stone memorial with a metal plaque, Portland was entirely revealed to them, as though they were looking at a model.

The bay swept in an almost complete circle from Lighthouse Park to Mermaid Point. There was a break-water on the south lip, protecting the angular marina from the open sea, though today the swell was massive, and the spray from the breaking waves was carrying well over the huge stones. A smattering of shops served the marina on that side of the bay, mostly old buildings but all sport-ing some form of renovation or extension. On the northern side of the bay there were sand flats and a dredger bobbing wildly, even in the partially sheltered waters.

The red roofs of newer houses stretched inland, roughly following the river, which had swampland bordering it, particularly on the northern side. To the west there was a smaller version of the Rock, which a railway tunnel ran through like thread through the eye of needle.

Along the coast to the south there was another beach, less hospitable than the one they had visited the previous day, with forests of seaweed crowding close to the shore. Jaide's eyes were drawn to it. She wished the weather would clear up so they could go for a swim. A bit of seaweed didn't worry her.

A particularly strong gust of wind pushed both of them back, and Jaide suddenly felt herself becoming weightless for an instant, as though she might be lifted up and off the Rock — and then she *was* rising up into the sky, and Jack only just managed to grab her by the ankles. For a second, Jaide thought they were both going to be blown away, and then the lightness inside her vanished and they tumbled back down.

"Wow," she said.

"You were about to take off, like Rodeo Dave!" exclaimed Jack. "Don't do it again!"

"It wasn't on purpose," said Jaide. "I just . . . got really light."

. She laughed uneasily. She had felt as light as a feather, light enough to be blown away, to go flying across the sky in the grip of the wind. But why her and not Jack? They weighed exactly the same, despite their slight differences in height and build.

"I think we should head down now," said Jack firmly. "The path keeps going down the other side, and then we can cut straight across toward Grandma's house."

Jaide looked along the zigzag way on the other side, up to where the path disappeared from sight. She figured Jack was probably right. If they followed the path, they would come out on the southern side of Watchward Lane, near where the decrepit house abutted Grandma X's property. Though it was hidden by the fir tree, she could see part of her grandmother's house itself, with its widow's walk, pointed roof, and spinning moon-and-star weather vane.

Jaide peered closer and frowned. The wind was strong and mainly coming from the east. It was difficult to see, but she was fairly sure the weather vane was pointing directly at the Rock, which wasn't east at all.

As she stared, eyes blinking against the breeze, a lost memory suddenly returned. Jaide remembered that this wasn't the first time she'd seen the weather vane behaving oddly. When they'd arrived, it had displayed a life independent of the elements, as though it was pointing to something other than the source of the wind. But what could that be? What use was a weather vane that didn't pay attention to the weather?

Her frown deepened. There were other things she knew she'd forgotten and couldn't quite retrieve. But they were coming back now, becoming less dreamlike and more concrete, as if the wind was clearing cobwebs from her mind.

"The door!" she cried.

"What?"

"The blue door!"

Jack stared at her blankly, a puzzled look flickering across his face. Then he knuckled himself in the side of the head.

"Of course! How could we have forgotten?"

"I don't know."

Jaide thought back to that morning, but everything was still a little blurry. They had been looking for a cellar, hadn't they? She was sure of it. Grandma X had said something about it, then they had had some hot chocolate, and after that it had just been playing around with golden cards and other odd things, and Grandma X's fingers clicking loudly. . . .

She was suddenly afraid, although she didn't know exactly what she feared. It wasn't only the wind almost taking her up, or the weirdness of everything to do with their grandmother, or even the uncertainty surrounding their move from their old home. There was something else, a chill that came not from the wind alone.

"Let's go down now," she said, suppressing a shiver. "She'll be looking for us if we're not back soon."

The downhill path was rougher and steeper, and they had to proceed much more slowly than either of them would have liked. Both of them felt an urgent need to get off the Rock, to get out of the wind, especially as the sky grew darker and spots of rain dotted the gray boulders around them.

Jack concentrated carefully on putting his feet down safely, and as a result didn't notice when the path turned, putting the bulk of the Rock between them and the lighthouse.

The moment the lighthouse was out of sight, a swarm of tiny flying insects — midges or sand flies — fell upon them. Buzzing almost inaudibly, they numbered in the thousands, it seemed, and Jack waved a hand in front of his face to keep them out of his eyes and nose, but they were impossible to deter. The air was full of little specks with wings. He could feel them wriggling into his hair and tickling into his ears. He waved more furiously and was conscious of Jaide doing the same beside him.

"Yuck!" she cried, then spat and spluttered as a dozen midges shot straight into her mouth.

The swarm followed the twins as they inched down the side of the Rock, slowing them down even more than the difficulty of the path. Blinking, gasping, flailing, it was all they could do to keep moving.

Then, as quickly as it had come, the swarm disappeared, leaving Jack feeling as though he had stepped out of a cloud of smoke.

"What was that?!" he asked, wiping his eyes clear with the back of his hand.

"At least they weren't the biting kind," Jaide said as she combed midges out of her hair with her fingers.

She'd barely said those words when a big, fat, green-backed fly flew onto the back of her hand and stung her. It wasn't a bad bite, just annoying, but the shock of it made her cry out.

"Ow!"

Before Jack could say anything, a second green-backed fly got him on the back of the neck. He swatted it, but there were more of them on the way, dozens of them, barreling in with the wind, aiming for the twins' hands and faces. Where they landed, they bit.

"Get off!" shouted Jack, wildly batting at the air with his open palms, like a kung fu maniac. The midges had been insubstantial, but these flies were solid lumps . . . with a bite.

To Jaide they felt like fuzzy little hailstones dropping out of the cloudy sky. Each individual impact was barely noticeable, but added together the swarm was like a barrage of tiny missiles. And then there was the biting. The flies were voracious and seemed intent on stinging every exposed part of her.

Together the twins raced down another ten yards or so, constantly slapping their own faces and necks and clapping their hands, leaving a trail of dead flies behind them.

Then there were no more green-backed flies. Like the sudden onset of the midges, the assault of the flies was over as abruptly as it had begun.

"We must smell good . . . or something," said Jaide. Both of them were thinking not very happy thoughts about what the "or something" might be, given all the other strange stuff that had been happening.

The twins warily descended another ten steps before they heard the deep chorus of thousands of bugs suddenly start up, and saw the next onslaught of insects gathering just below.

"You're kidding," said Jack as a dense, dark cloud of crickets boiled up the Rock toward them in a tide of tiny legs and antennae. He looked back the way they'd come, as if hoping for some secret line of retreat to suddenly reveal itself. But the fog of flies was standing firm. "This can't be happening!"

"It is," said Jaide. The swarm of crickets would be on them in a moment, hopping, scratching, staring at them with their wild insect eyes. "We've got to run through them! Go!"

They broke into a sprint down the treacherous path. Even though the slope was starting to flatten out, the path still doglegged back and forth as it descended, and there were many dangerously steep spots. Jack went first, wind-milling his arms in front of him, running headlong into the mass of crickets.

The hard-shelled insects pummeled the twins at first only from the front but soon from all sides. The swarm followed them as they ran, swooping back to make multiple attacks, chirruping and clicking all the way. The noise was deafening, drowning out all attempts by the twins to talk to each other. Even Jaide felt her confidence weaken at that. There was definitely something sinister in the insects' united determination. First midges, then flies, then crickets —

All of a sudden, they burst out of the swarm. The cloud hung behind them, but the crickets did not pursue.

"Yee-ha!" shouted Jack in victory. He slowed down and glanced back. Crickets started to fly off in all directions, the horde suddenly disbanded.

But even as he shouted, he heard Jaide gasp, and he whipped back around to look ahead.

A living, moving, three-inch-thick carpet of cockroaches was coming up the path, a great roiling mass of big brown bugs that extended for a dozen yards or more.

Jack didn't waste any more time shouting, and neither did Jaide. They ran quickly down the hill, lifting their feet high and half running, half jumping, crunching up hundreds of cockroaches as they went. But for every hundred they squashed, there were hundreds more, and with every step, cockroaches latched on to their shoes and ankles and started to climb up their legs.

The twins jumped higher and ran faster. Both of them instinctively knew that the cockroaches were trying to drag them down. If enough of them got a hold, they might even be able to do it. . . .

It was the strangest, grossest thing Jack had ever experienced — the *squish*, the *splat*, the oozing guts, and the terrifying attack of legs, legs, and more legs. Cockroaches on his skin. Cockroaches in his hair. Cockroaches climbing into his sleeves. All he could do was run faster. Harder. He had to breathe through his nose so the cockroaches wouldn't get in his mouth. But his ears — they were attacking his ears. He swatted at them. Stepped on them. Pushed himself, with Jaide right next to him. Then they broke through — once again, the cloud had passed, but this time there were still bugs all over them. The twins slowed a little and bent over to smash cockroaches off each other's legs, while continuing to stumble forward like crazy clowns.

"Let's stop and get them . . . get them all off!" shouted Jack.

"No! No time!" yelled Jaide. "That'll do! Run!"

She started off straight ahead, but Jack pulled her back.

"Not that way!" he yelled.

There were dozens of horrible, jar-size things sliding down invisible webs from the branches of the trees uphill from Grandma X's house. As they hit the ground, their eight legs uncurled, and they began to scuttle toward the twins, moving with alarming speed.

Spiders. Jaide couldn't stand spiders.

The twins ran from the spiders to dive frantically through a hole in the fence of the derelict house, sprint across the empty garden, and duck down the long-abandoned drive. At the front of the house there was a van with REPAIRS & ALL MAINTENANCE painted on the side, and the odd-job woman they had met at the school that morning was sitting in the front eating a sandwich. She didn't look up as the twins dashed past and onto the cobbled street.

Ahead of them, at last, Jaide saw the arched entrance to Grandma X's yard and slowed down. But from behind them came the throaty snarl and scrabbling paw-steps of a large, angry dog.

Jack didn't bother to turn around. He grabbed his sister's arm and put on a last desperate burst of speed. Together they rocketed through the gates, skidded on the gravel, and fell over in a tangled heap. Behind them, with a yelp, the dog also skidded to a halt. Farther down the lane, a few remnant spiders were seeking the shadows of the drain. They didn't look as big as they had only a few moments before.

Hearts pumping, Jaide and Jack rolled over, hands raised to fend off a dog attack.

But the heavyset pit bull terrier was still on the cobbled street, not quite under the arch of the gate, staring at them with its piggish, deep-set eyes — eyes that were entirely white and shiny, without any trace of a pupil. Its flanks were heaving and its chops dripped spittle, but it wasn't following them anymore, or growling. It paced back and forth just outside the gate, shaking its head and snapping at the air.

"Hello, puppy," Jaide said. She tried to sound the way her father had taught her to talk to dogs, without fear or submission. Like a friend. An out-of-breath friend. "You don't want to eat us, do you?"

The dog turned its head toward her, and all of a sudden the milky cloud left its eyes, like a mist being blown away by a sudden breeze. It yawned and licked its chops with a great lolling tongue and then, with one allover shake, it turned and trotted off.

"How did you do that?" asked Jack. "I mean, with its eyes and everything?"

"I didn't do anything," said Jaide. "As far as I know —"

Something dropped to the ground behind them, and Jack whirled around in fright, thinking of the spiders.

"Ari!" he exclaimed in relief as the ginger tom slid up to him and did a quick back-scratching circle of his leg. "Was it you who scared the dog away?"

Ari looked up the lane and performed a very human-like shrug.

"Me? Scare that great beast away? I was hiding up the tree, like anyone sensible should have been."

Jack stared at him, unable to believe what his ears told him. Cats didn't talk. It simply wasn't possible.

"Did you . . . did you hear that?" he asked Jaide.

"Hear what?"

Jaide hadn't reacted to the cat at all. Perhaps he had imagined it.

"Uh, nothing, I guess," he said.

Ari stared at him, and gave one slow, deliberate wink.

"If you can hear me, that ugly mutt is the least of your problems."

With that, the cat sniffed and began to lick his paw.

Jack opened his mouth to ask Ari another question, but before he could talk, Jaide grabbed his arm.

"The blue door," she said, pointing excitedly. "It's still there — and the sign, too! Let's check it out!"

Jack wasn't so keen. He looked around again, but there was no sign of any further attentions from the insect or animal world. Even the wind had dropped away.

"I guess we're safe here," he said tentatively.

"To a certain degree," said Ari quietly. He stopped licking his paw and stalked off toward the front entrance.

Jack stared after the cat and wondered if he was going mad.

"I'm sure we're safe," said Jaide. She *was* sure, though she couldn't have said why she felt so confident. There was something about the house itself, looming over them, that gave her a sense of protection. "Come on!"

"I really don't know," said Jack. He just wanted to go inside and stick his head under a pillow until all the rampaging insects and talking cats went away.

"Come on!" repeated Jaide.

She dragged him over to the blue door. It was as solid as it had been that morning, and as they hammered on it they slowly remembered their earlier efforts to get it open, the memories drifting back like a forgotten dream recaptured days later.

With a strong feeling of déjà vu, Jaide ran her fingers around the jamb, looking for a hidden catch. When that failed, she stepped back to peer up at the hand-painted sign. The words had changed since yesterday. Now it said TEMPORARILY CLOSED FOR BUSINESS.

"How could we just forget?" she asked her brother. "And how could the sign be there, then not be there, then come back later saying something different?"

"It didn't go anywhere," said Grandma X.

The twins jumped, their hearts pounding again, and backed up against the door. She was standing right behind them, and once again they hadn't heard her boots on the gravel. It was like she had materialized there, out of thin air.

"Maybe you're seeing it differently now, don't you think?"

Grandma X smiled and tilted her head, waiting for them to answer.

"But . . . but . . . Mom couldn't see it, either," Jaide said, just to say something, to try to get everything back to a more normal situation.

"She sees what she wants to see, and understands what she *can* see entirely her own way."

Grandma X bent down and peered closely at Jaide's head.

"You have dead crickets in your hair, green-backed fly bites all over you, and mashed cockroaches do not make a tasteful addition to even modern footwear. What happened? Tell me everything."

There was no resisting that tone. Jaide stammered out an explanation, with Jack filling in details she had forgotten. Talking about it made it all seem unreal, like a story they had made up. The panicked horror she had felt was becoming distant, as though it had happened to someone else.

When they had finished, Grandma X's eyes narrowed and she looked past the twins. First she gazed toward the town, then she turned completely around and looked toward the lighthouse. The twins shifted nervously during this strange rotation. Finally she stopped and, facing them again, took Jack's hand and sniffed it.

"That wretched handmade soap I put out for you," she said. "I thought your mother would like it, but it must have honey in it, and perhaps some of the more unusual herbs. That's what attracted the bugs." Her words sounded forced. "I'll get you some store-bought stuff and clean you off before you go out again. And I'll talk to Old Mac about that dreadful dog of his, too: Luger is not normally unchained. What a terrible scare he must've given you!"

Under other circumstances, Jack and Jaide might have been satisfied with Grandma X's explanation — or satisfied enough to leave it alone. But there were too many mysteries mounting at once, and too many questions that needed answers. There was something in her eyes that told them both there was a *lot* more to worry about than she was letting on.

Which reminded Jack that this was what Ari the cat had said.

"What's *really* happening, Grandma?" he demanded. "And why is it happening to us?"

Grandma X put her left hand on his head and smoothed down his hair, a delaying tactic they were familiar with from their father. Hector must have learned all his shilly-shallying and covering up techniques from his mother.

"I promise you, Jack, when the time is right, I'll tell you. For now, let's just go inside and get you cleaned up. Then you can finish unpacking and we'll talk about dinner. Would you like a hot chocolate to warm you up?"

Jaide and Jack both shook their heads firmly. Every time they pressed Grandma X for an explanation, that hot chocolate made an appearance.

Not this time. A quick, shared glance confirmed that the twins were thinking the same thoughts. They knew each other's faces better than anyone else, and right now they had exactly the same expression: a look of deep suspicion coupled with a determination that they would discover what they needed to know.

If Grandma X wasn't going to tell them the truth, they would find another way to discover it. Later that night, perhaps, when everything was quiet. There were probably all kinds of clues hidden inside the house.

"I think you can leave your shoes outside," said Grandma X. Her attempt to sound casual was spoiled by her looking around again, scanning every part of the horizon, her eyes narrowed and her face anxious. When she led them inside, it was at a pace so fast, they almost ran up the steps.

CHAPTER SEVEN

PRISONERS OF THE WITCH

Grandma X insisted they both have another shower and thoroughly wash their hair. Jaide could still feel a thousand little legs tickling her skin, so despite her reservations, she didn't put up much of a fight. When she was done, she slipped out of the hot water, smelling of soap and shampoo, and wound herself up in a thick, prickly towel that was still slightly damp from earlier. The bathroom was dense with mist. There was no sign of Grandma X.

"Where is she?" she whispered to Jack, who rushed into the bathroom as soon as she was done with it.

"Washing our clothes," he reported.

Jaide remembered seeing an ancient washing machine in the laundry downstairs. She could hear it through the floor, rattling and thumping like it was a cage with a wild creature inside.

The second-floor landing was empty. Only the blank eyes of the photographs and paintings watched her as she ran to her room. There she found new clothes waiting for both of them on their beds and all their mess cleaned away.

Jack followed suspiciously quickly, looking as though he had barely washed his hair beyond wetting it and giving it a bit of a shake.

"What's she doing in our *stuff*?" he whispered, taking everything Grandma X had put away and pushing it back into his suitcase. He felt happier with it in there, and less trapped.

Jaide put a finger to her lips, listening. A moment later, silver-tipped cowboy boots thudded across the kitchen floorboards below. She nodded, and the twins had a hurried, whispered conversation while they had the chance.

"Is this really happening?" asked Jack, thinking not just of mad swarms of bugs and rabid dogs, but talking cats as well. Either he was going crazy, or Portland was.

"Of course it is," said Jaide in the bossy voice that reminded him of their mother. "And whatever it is, Grandma doesn't want us to know anything about it. That's why she made us forget."

"How?"

"The hot chocolate. It must have been. Just thinking of it makes me feel dizzy." She passed a hand across her eyes and pressed on. "We've got to make sure it doesn't happen again, Jack. We have to remember, and we have to find out what she's up to. Don't let her give us anything that could make us forget."

"But we have to eat and drink," said Jack. Lunchtime felt like days ago already. "How do you know it's her making us forget, anyway? It could be someone else."

"Yeah, right," said Jaide. "Like who?"

"Uh, the cats?"

"How could it be the cats?"

"I don't know. Maybe someone's controlling them," he said, flailing for an explanation that wouldn't sound mad. Clearly Jaide hadn't heard Ari talk, which meant he probably *was* mad, after all. "The same someone controlling the insects and the dog."

An idea went off in Jaide's head like a firecracker. "What do you call the pets that witches keep?"

"Familiars." Jack's eyes widened. "You think Grandma X is a *witch*?"

"Have you got a better explanation? She's up to something, and we've gotten in the way by coming to live in her home."

Jack frowned. He didn't like this explanation at all. If Jaide was right, it could be the gingerbread house all over again, and mad or not, he didn't fancy being Hansel. . . .

"But she's our grandmother," he said weakly. "I mean, she's Dad's *mother*. . . ."

"Dad isn't exactly reliable himself, is he?" said Jaide bitterly.

"Troubletwisters!" came their grandma's voice from the ground floor. "Come down for dinner!"

Jaide checked her watch in disbelief. "It's only five o'clock!"

"Old people always eat dinner early," said Jack, hoping the stab of fear he felt wasn't warranted. The hunger he had felt a moment ago had quite evaporated.

"Troubletwisters?"

"Don't ask any questions or act suspicious," Jaide reminded him forcefully. "I guess we'll have to eat what she gives us, but *don't* drink any more of her hot chocolate, no matter how much you want to."

Jack swallowed his concerns and nodded. As Jaide left the room and he got dressed, he realized the mystery of Ari would have to wait. If they didn't survive the night, it would be irrelevant, anyway.

Dinner was laid out on the table for them: two innocent-looking hot dogs each with equally innocent-looking buns and a selection of decidedly non-suspicious mustards and ketchups. The smell made even Jaide's stomach rumble, but she forced herself not to eat too much, and to carefully examine every mouthful before she swallowed it. She had never before paid such close attention to the inside of a hot dog, and immediately wished she hadn't.

"What's the matter?" asked Grandma X, watching them pick their slow and painful way through the meal. "I thought all children enjoyed hot dogs."

"Uh, we do; it's just, we've been thinking about becoming vegetarians," Jaide improvised. It wasn't entirely untrue, thanks to a particularly large piece of gristle caught between her front teeth. "We were learning about it at school back home, you see. . . ."

"You didn't mention it before. And yesterday you ate a ham sandwich. Still, it's not a bad philosophy, as long as we make sure your diet is balanced." With a heavy silver spoon, Grandma X indicated the bowl in front of her. It contained a strange-looking broth of lumpy green and orange vegetables, to which she now added a further layer of pungent herbs. "Lately I myself have been . . . not at my best . . . and I am hoping this will help."

"What do you call your diet?" asked Jaide in as innocent a tone as she could manage.

"Nothing in particular, dear. There are simply occasions when certain foods are beneficial, particularly for cleansing the mind. Would you care to try some?"

Both twins quickly shook their heads.

Grandma X smiled as though she rather enjoyed their reaction. "No, I didn't think so."

Jack tried his best to smile back, thinking that at least Grandma X wasn't turning into a Hansel-and-Gretel type of witch. Or at least not yet. He couldn't help glancing at the big old oven, though. It was huge, much larger than any normal person could need, particularly if she lived alone.

A child could fit in that oven. Even two children, in a pinch.

Jack shuddered and looked away. What was he doing? Staring at ovens, talking to cats —

Grandma X burped with surprising volume and waved her hand rapidly in front of her face.

"Pardon me!" she exclaimed. "I'm very sorry about that. Well, if you're not going to eat any more, you can dispose of your leftovers and clean up your plates. And then, if you like, I've fished out a stack of your father's old toys for you to play with. They're in the lounge, by the ottoman."

Jack didn't know what an ottoman was, but the thought of toys his father had owned as a child was very nearly sufficient to drive all his anxieties from his mind. He raced through his chores, then hurried to the lounge, Jaide hard on his heels.

What they found, next to a bursting footstool, was a pile of dusty old board games. They browsed disappointedly through them, recognizing titles like Scrabble, which Hector notoriously beat everyone at, but finding many others they had never heard of. What their father had seen in them, Jack didn't know.

"I'll just be in here, tidying up, all right?" called Grandma X from the drawing room.

Conscious of her proximity, the twins settled in for a game of Park and Shop, which proved to be no more exciting than its name suggested. As Jaide moved her token listlessly across the board, from Bakery to Women's Wear via something called Hay Grain Feed, she saw the old lady fiddling with the compass she had brought out the previous day, turning it from side to side and holding it upside down above her head. Whatever Grandma X was doing, it didn't look like tidying.

As the twins played, the cats moved restlessly through the house, padding softly up and down the stairs and peering closely into every room. To Jaide they seemed to have a purpose of some kind. They were patrolling, or searching for something. Or maybe, she thought, they were like guards in a prison, doing the rounds. And if that was the case, then she and her brother were no doubt the prisoners. . . .

Every time Kleo looked at Jack, he twitched guiltily back to the game. Luckily, however, neither Kleo nor Ari said anything more comprehensible than a meow the whole evening, and by the end of it he was convinced that he must have imagined Ari talking before. Maybe it had been oxygen deprivation from running so fast, Jack thought. His brain had become starved of air and had started hallucinating.

Then, as Jack and Jaide were packing up the game, the cats came back with something that indicated they had been on another mission entirely: Kleo strolled into the lounge with an apparently unharmed mouse wriggling about in her mouth.

Jaide ran forward in interest, trying to see how the cat was holding the mouse without killing it. Jack stayed back and watched from a distance.

As they studied it, Grandma X loomed up behind the cats.

"What is it?"

"A mouse!" Jaide pointed at the tiny creature in Kleo's mouth. It was staring around, obviously terrified. "Make her let it go!"

"You're not frightened of mice, are you?" asked Grandma X.

"No, but Kleo shouldn't play with it. That's torture."

"Take it from her, then. Kleo will give it to you. You can wash your hands afterward."

Jaide pulled a face. "Can't she just drop it outside?"

"I'll take it," said Jack. He came forward and crouched down and held his hands under Kleo's mouth. She blinked up at him and opened her jaws. The mouse fell into his hands. It lay there for a moment as if stunned.

"Hello," said Jack softly. He didn't close his hands for fear of crushing the tiny animal. But the mouse wasn't quite as shocked as he thought, and with a sudden twitch and twist, it leaped from his hands and scurried rapidly off.

As Jack grabbed at it, the cats tried to pounce, and they all got in one another's way. Grandma X stood in the doorway, her feet planted wide apart, and the mouse ran straight between her heels and crossed the hall like a rocket into a tiny hole at the corner of the stairs.

"Interesting," said Grandma X, dusting her hands on her jeans. "I had thought you might like mice more than Jackaran, Jaidith, but I see it is quite the opposite."

Next she turned to address Kleo. "You were also rather late. I asked you for a mouse hours ago."

Kleo's only answer was to raise a paw, lick it, and begin cleaning her face. This was clearly the equivalent of a shrug.

Jack had forgotten that Grandma X had asked Kleo to catch a mouse. Jaide had to be right, he thought. The cats *were* Grandma X's familiars, and that meant she really was a witch. He looked at Jaide. She lowered one eyelid slightly, a sign to be cautious.

The ring of Grandma X's phone sounded from the drawing room. She marched out to get it, and they heard her answer with a brisk, "Hello?"

"I'm not frightened of mice," whispered Jaide. "I just don't like the cats playing with them."

"I know. What do you think that was about? Do you think she's going to send an army of mice to get us?"

Before Jaide could speculate, Grandma X returned, holding the telephone handset out to them.

"It's your mother, troubletwisters."

They scrabbled for the phone, each wanting to be the one to tell her what had been going on and each wondering how to do it without making themselves sound crazy.

Jaide won. "Mom!"

"Hello, dear girl. How are things going? Your grandma tells me it's been raining."

"Is that really all she said?"

"She said she took you for a drive and that you've been playing all evening. It sounds like you're having fun."

Of course Grandma X would make it sound like that, Jaide thought. "You have to come back, Mom —"

"I can't, Jaide. One of the helicopters is out for heavy maintenance, we're short two paramedics, and it's a very busy time. But I'll be back on Wednesday, I promise. Is Jack there?"

Jack was bouncing around Jaide, trying to get at the phone. His sister reluctantly handed it to him. Maybe he would have better luck.

"Hello, dear boy. I just want to say a quick hello before you go to bed. Are you being good for your grandma?"

"Yes, but . . ."

Jack wanted nothing more than to tell her everything that had been happening, but Grandma X was in earshot. He moved up the hallway and whispered into the phone, "Mom, everything is weird here."

"Don't worry, Jack. You'll get used to it soon enough."

"That's not what I —"

Jack stopped. Kleo had come out and was stalking toward him, her ears rotated forward to catch everything he was saying. He retreated to the kitchen.

"If you get a good night's sleep, everything will seem better in the morning."

"But —"

Jack stopped again as Ari came out from under the kitchen table and Kleo appeared at the door. Jack despaired of finding anywhere he could talk unheard.

"Jack, I really need you and your sister to —"

A chattering bell in the background of the call drowned out whatever his mother was saying, and Jack heard someone shouting, "Sue! We're rolling!"

"I have to go now," said Susan very quickly. "Lots of love to you and your sister."

"No, don't —" shouted Jack.

But it was too late. There was only the dial tone in answer. Despondently, Jack took the phone back to his grandmother, who returned it to its cradle.

"How nice to hear from your mother," she said. "Now, it's getting late. There's time to read in bed, if you like."

"Late?" said Jaide. "It's not even eight thirty."

"It's a school night, and you've had a long day. I have some work to do. If you go to your room, I'll come and turn the light out in half an hour."

For a moment, Jaide thought about refusing to obey, just flat out rebelling against her grandmother. But there was something in the old woman's gaze that said this would be a very big mistake.

The twins had no choice but to trudge up the stairs and

do as they were told. They both had reading lamps on flexible metal arms that snaked out from behind their beds, lamps that cast misshapen shadows across the walls and ceiling when they were switched on. Jack settled back to an adventure novel with a plot he had trouble paying attention to, while Jaide picked up her illustrated book on whales. She was very interested in marine life, but now, with the events of that day turning over and over in her mind, and the thought of school on top of all that, she could barely concentrate.

The strange sounds coming from the ground floor didn't help. There were clicking footsteps, doors opening and shutting, and clanks and clunks, as if Grandma X was moving furniture back and forth. Whatever she was up to, it kept her so busy, she didn't come to say good night until almost ten o'clock.

Jaide was already asleep, and Jack wasn't far off. He closed the book he hadn't really been reading and switched out the light. Grandma X stood in the doorway for a moment, her face hidden. He thought she might be about to say something, but then she left and pulled the door shut behind her.

It was very dark in Portland compared to the city, but after a minute or two his eyes adjusted, and Jack found that he could see pretty well. He looked out his window and counted the regular flashes of the lighthouse's beacon, warning ships away from the perils of Dagger Reef. Twenty-three was the last number he remembered before he slipped into a dream about giant spiders swarming out of the cactus garden and tying a dog up in their webs. He twitched restlessly, but didn't wake up.

Jaide was dreaming about spiders, too, only she was the one in danger from them. She had been flying again, this time on her own, without a magic carpet, and had blundered into a giant web. The sticky strands wrapped themselves around her face and hands. No matter how she tugged she couldn't get free, and she couldn't call for help because her mouth was glued shut. At the far edge of the web, something dark and red-eyed moved closer. . . .

A roaring sound woke both twins at precisely the same moment. Their beds were shaking and their sheets were whipping around them. It sounded like a storm had burst through the windows and was turning the room inside out, but there was no rain, just wind. Jaide fumbled for the switch of her reading light. It didn't come on the way it was supposed to. The filament glowed feebly, as though something was sucking the light out of the wire.

By the faint, flickering glow, Jack saw a whirling funnel of dusty air spinning in the center of the room, sucking up all their clothes and books and whipping the chandelier around in tight circles. The wind was so strong that he had to hang on with both hands to stop himself from being sucked in as well. Frenzied eddies swirled around the room, dropping books and clothes on every horizontal surface, including the twins. The curtains flapped like sails, and the noise they made was so deafening, he couldn't hear himself or his sister shouting for help.

Then the darkness came. The feeble electric light was snuffed out, and the window went dark. The howling, tortured air began to smash things, and all of it was much too much like the terrible day the twins' house had exploded.

Only the awful, staring eyes were missing, and Jack found himself whimpering at the thought that they would soon be there. He could almost see one already —

With a bright, metallic ping, both lamps and the overhead light suddenly flashed back into full life. The darkness was whipped away like a magician's cape, revealing Grandma X in the doorway, her arms upraised and the sleeves of her white dressing gown bunched up over her elbows. She brought her hands together, and as her palms touched, the crack of their meeting resounded through the room. Instantly the tornado collapsed like a water balloon that had been squeezed too hard. A few whiplike wisps of wind scattered around the walls, like snakes trying to escape from a barrel, and vanished.

When the air was still, Grandma X surveyed the mess with a severe eye.

"You should be asleep," she said sternly. "All aspects of you."

She seemed to be talking to someone else in addition to the twins.

"What was it?" asked Jaide. "Where did it come from?"

"Is it going to come back?" Jack added. "Will . . . will the eyes come?"

Grandma X looked directly at Jack and Jaide and continued in gentler tones.

"There's nothing you need to worry about, troubletwisters. Go back to sleep."

She accompanied the instruction with a wave of her hand, like someone smoothing down a sheet. With her words and the wave, the twins felt suddenly tired again, the adrenaline of waking in fright entirely dissipating. They lay back on their pillows and shut their eyes.

Grandma X swept out the door.

Her footsteps had barely reached the stairs when Jack forced himself awake. It was like swimming to the surface from a long way down, requiring enormous effort. But finally he got his eyes open and managed to swing his legs out of the bed and stagger over to his sister.

It took quite a few vigorous shakes, but eventually Jaide came awake, too. She yawned widely as Jack said, "Did you see that whirlwind? Did you see what she did? She tried to make us sleep again, too. She *is* a witch!"

Jaide was much less happy with her theory now. It was all very well to speculate about the supernatural when the sun was up. At night, believability was a *bad* thing. The similarity between the whirlwind in Portland and the explosion in their home had her wondering exactly how they had come to be here, and why.

"What should we do?" she asked her brother.

"Follow her," Jack said. "Find out what she's up to. Stop her if it's something bad."

"How?"

"I don't know. We'll think of something when we know more about it — her — everything!"

Jaide thought about this as she slowly came fully awake.

"All right," she said with a shiver. "Hang on. I'm cold; I need my dressing gown."

Jack opened the door a crack and peered through. They heard Grandma X moving about on the floor above, then moving back to the stairs to go even higher, up to the widow's walk, the balcony on the dangerous rooftop.

Jack slipped out into the darkened hallway and peered up the stairwell. The sleeve of Grandma X's robe was just visible, so white it seemed to be glowing in the gloom. Gingerly, mindful of even the slightest noise, he put a foot on the first step and began to climb.

Jaide finally found her father's old dressing gown in the mess. Out in the hallway, she looked around for her brother but couldn't see him.

"Jack," she hissed, "where are you?"

"Up here" came the answering whisper out of the shadows, and suddenly there he was, crouched at the top of the first rise of stairs. Jaide had been looking right at him. "Come on!"

CHAPTER EIGHT

MACHINATIONS BY MOONLIGHT

Jaide blinked and rubbed her eyes. Jack disappeared again for a moment, then became visible, almost as if he had momentarily become part of the shadows.

She kept her eye on Jack as she followed him upward, but he didn't disappear again. The stairs creaked under their weight, but luckily the floor here was carpeted, which muffled their footsteps, and the house was making plenty of other noises to cover the sounds. The wind outside — completely outside now, thank goodness — was rattling the window frames, and the old house creaked and groaned like a ship tossed at sea.

From far above came the clank of a bolt being pulled back, followed by the thud of a door — or a hatch — opening.

Jack's hand found Jaide's in the gloom, and they went up together, turning once to the right, then turning again. Seven steps later, they were on Grandma X's floor. Three shut doors greeted them, one of them presumably to her bedroom. Instead of paintings or photos on the walls there were masks, strange masks of different people with varied expressions. Some were smiling and happy, some frowning, some screaming, mouths stretched open. More than a dozen pairs of empty black eyes stared at the twins as they tiptoed by.

Jack resisted the urge to run. The next set of steps was bare wood, without the carpet, so any footsteps would be much louder. The air also felt colder and the creaking of the building sounded clearer and alarmingly alive, as if it was a living organism complaining about the wind.

Jaide was acutely aware of how high they were. The house seemed to contract around them, becoming all angles and strange intersections as they passed into the roof cavity. The ceiling was barely as high as their heads. Cobwebs swayed against their faces. All about them was the smell of dust.

Directly above the last step was the hatch they had heard closing from below.

Jack reached ahead to fumble one-handed with the bolt. Jaide kept a tight grip on Jack's free hand, because unlike him she couldn't see a thing.

Grandma X had already drawn the bolt, so all Jack had to do was push open the hatch. He did so cautiously, and a coil of icy wind came through and whipped around them. Jaide was relieved that enough starlight came in for her to see. When Jack pushed the hatch completely open, she saw the wooden rail of the widow's walk ahead, with the night sky beyond.

Jack put a finger to his lips and they crept out onto the walk, under the stars and into the wind.

They had emerged from the western side of a strange vertical construction in the middle of the walk that stuck up very much like a submarine's conning tower. The moon was partly obscured by cloud and was still rising, but it was bright enough for Jaide to see. There was no sign of Grandma X, at least on this side. The twins huddled together, looking out.

By the increasing moonlight, the view from the widow's walk was almost as good as the one from the top of the Rock. They could see across the bay, all the way out to sea. To the south, the Rock itself was clearly visible above the tower door. The stately fir tree swayed back and forth with the stiff breeze, its needles making a sound like a crowd whispering. Below that, Jaide could hear something else — an unpleasant hissing noise that she couldn't immediately identify. It sounded a bit like a big water sprinkler, but no one would have one of those on after all the rain.

The wind plucked at her, and once again Jaide felt that feeling of weightlessness, as if the breeze might pick her up and fly her away, off into the night sky. The sensation was not welcome, and Jaide felt a stab of fear.

"She's not here," Jaide whispered to Jack. "Maybe we should go back down."

Jack pointed with his thumb, indicating that they couldn't see the other corner unless they moved, and he started to inch around the conning tower. Jaide reluctantly followed him, keeping a firm grip on his hand.

They only had to go one step before they saw Grandma X standing in the southwest corner of the widow's walk. She was leaning over the railing, staring at something on the ground in front of the house.

The twins hunkered down. If she turned around, she'd see them at once.

But Grandma X was totally intent on whatever lay below. Suddenly she raised her right arm to point to the south. Something flashed on her finger, and she shouted five words loud and sharp enough to make the twins flinch.

"Do as I have commanded!"

The weird hissing noise grew louder. Grandma X straightened and took a deep breath. She gripped the railing tightly with both hands. Her back arched and her eyes closed.

She became very still.

The twins broke from cover and ran to the other end of the rail. They didn't dare breathe as they leaned out over to catch a glimpse of what Grandma X had been talking to — and then, when they *did* see, they couldn't breathe at all.

A writhing, wriggling horde of black rats surrounded the house, thousands and thousands of them, all staring up at Grandma X and the twins. The rats' eyes were bright white, just like the dog's had been, far too bright to be just the reflected moonlight. The ghastly throng moved as one, surging against the base of the house like a horrible sea that spoke with one great voice, a squeal that issued from thousands of rat mouths, either in salute or defiance.

The squeal faded as a slender column of glowing light appeared in the middle of the pack. The rats closest to it squeaked, suddenly separated from the mass, and jumped and tumbled away, biting one another in their efforts to escape. Once far enough away, they calmed again and moved with the tide of the horde.

But there was now a clear circle in the mass of rats, with the column of light gently pulsing in the middle, the exact same color as the moon above. As Jack watched, transfixed, the column slowly took the shape of a woman.

She stood straight and tall, with long, silver hair and a robe of shimmering starlight. On her right hand there was a ring that shone brighter than any star. Her beauty took Jaide's breath away. Standing next to her brother, whipped by the relentless wind, she felt that she had never seen anyone so strong, so wonderful, and so . . . luminous before. She had to be a ghost, or even some kind of goddess.

"Do as you have been bidden!" commanded the silvery apparition.

Jaide was shocked to hear what was recognizably her grandmother's voice, though it was infused with a power that she could physically feel as a deep vibration through the air. She was also shocked by the sudden realization that the apparition *looked* like her grandmother, though fifty years younger.

"At once!"

The horde of rats exploded as if a bomb had been dropped among them. Rats jumped into the air, climbed fences, dived through bushes, ran over one another, all squeaking and scratching in their panic to obey the ghostly figure.

The moon went behind a cloud, and the glowing woman faded and was gone. Grandma X stirred as though waking from a deep sleep. Jaide and Jack retreated to the doorway and peeped around.

"We should go *now*," Jaide whispered, and tried to pull Jack back to the door.

He shook off her hand and edged forward. He loved being out at night, and he wanted to know more about what was going on. Had Grandma X summoned the rats to tell them what to do, and the twins had just witnessed her sending them off? That fit in with the theory that she was an evil witch, and the rats were servants like the insects that had plagued them on the Rock. But a nagging doubt lurked in the corner of Jack's mind. Grandma X clearly had magical powers, but what was she using them for?

At that moment, Grandma X started to turn back from the railing. Jack froze in panic. She would see him for sure — but she paused to wipe her forehead with a large and very white handkerchief that came out of her sleeve.

In those vital few seconds, Jaide pulled at Jack again, and this time he didn't resist. They ducked back through the door and went straight down the hatch. Jack whipped it closed behind him and the twins hurried down the stairs as fast as they could.

But they were in too much of a hurry, and Jaide was in front and couldn't see. She miscounted the stairs and thumped down hard on the third floor landing. The dull thud seemed horribly loud in the darkness, echoing up the stairwell.

"Who's there?" called Grandma X, frighteningly close above them.

Jaide thought fast. She couldn't run — that would be far too noisy. But she certainly couldn't tell the truth about where they'd been.

"It's us, Grandma," she said, the tremor in her voice entirely real. "I . . . we . . . woke up when we heard a noise outside. I called but you didn't answer, so we came up here to find you."

Grandma X came down through the hatch. Jaide flinched as she heard the boots coming closer, with a threatening *tap . . . tap . . . tap*. Even when her grandmother stopped, it was too dark for Jaide to see her, so she couldn't tell whether she looked angry.

"I'm sorry I didn't answer, Jaidith," said Grandma X. Somehow she found Jaide's shoulder in the gloom and gave it a squeeze. "You need to go back to bed now. We'll talk more in the morning. Where is Jackaran?"

Jaide opened her mouth and shut it again. Jack had been behind her coming downstairs. Grandma X should have run into him. . . .

"Uh, he must have gone back to bed," she said weakly.

A very soft footfall to her left and below her suggested that this was not true. Jaide tried to look without turning her head, but couldn't see a thing.

"I'll turn on the light," said Grandma X. "I don't want you to break your neck. Unless you can see in the dark?"

"No, I can't," said Jaide, though she had a very strong suspicion that Grandma X could see quite well. But if that was so, why hadn't she spotted Jack?

"I'll only be a moment," said Grandma X. Jaide heard those boots tap-tapping up a few steps. At the same time, she heard the faintest of footfalls going the other way. Then there was the click of a switch and all the lights on the stairs came on.

"No more wandering about," said Grandma X. "Come with me, and I'll tuck you in."

Jaide looked down. Was that Jack, there in the shadow at the turn of the stairs?

"Grandma," Jaide said in a desperate bid to give Jack more time, "is this house haunted?"

Grandma X stopped on the step above and looked at her granddaughter.

"Not as such," she said. "Why? What have you seen?"

"That wind . . . the weird noises . . ."

"There's nothing to worry about, Jaidith. You and Jackaran are completely safe in this house. Now, to bed."

They walked down together. Grandma X took Jaide's hand, and Jaide was surprised that she'd never noticed the ring the old lady was wearing before. It was reversed with the stone on the inside, so Jaide couldn't see it clearly — but it had to be the same one she'd seen shining on the hand of the apparition that had sent the rats off on their mission.

At the door to their room, Jaide pretended to stumble. Grandma X helped her up immediately, but it gave Jack a few more seconds, and when they finally did get into the bedroom, her brother was back in his bed, pretending to be asleep.

"Hop into bed now and shut your eyes."

Jaide climbed into bed and shot a glance over at Jack. He didn't open his eyes, but she knew he was awake. When Grandma X was gone, they could discuss their close call and decide what to do next.

That was the plan, anyway. But as Jaide pulled up the covers, Grandma X went across to Jack and patted him gently on the head. Moonlight spilled from her palm, and Jaide saw her brother twitch, the reflexive shudder of someone falling instantly asleep.

"Sleep tight," said Grandma X, and took the few steps back to Jaide, her hand coming down to the girl's head.

No, not again! Jaide thought. *I must resist! I have to stay awake! I have to —*

But she couldn't resist. Moonlight washed across Jaide's face, and she fell into a dark, dreamless sleep.

CHAPTER NINE

JAIDE TAKES CHARGE

The sun woke Jaide early. She opened her eyes very slowly, fighting a mental fog that threatened to drag her back down into sleep. Cats, rats, and cockroaches? Her thoughts wouldn't line up straight, and neither would her memories. There had been a ferocious wind, and darkness, just like when their house exploded. . . .

Jaide's heart suddenly hammered fast and she sat up, her eyes wide open as she looked around in panic. But it was daylight, and there was no whirlwind, and the bedroom was perfectly tidy. Everything was neatly packed away in the wardrobe, and their empty bags were zipped up tightly in the corner. The curtains hung straight and even their bedclothes were orderly, as though she and Jack had hardly stirred all night — as though everything hadn't been upended by a tornado.

And Grandma X had been standing there, Jaide remembered. *She* must have sent the wind and caused the darkness, for reasons Jaide still didn't understand.

Understanding wasn't important. Jaide *knew*. She knew that things weren't right in Portland, and hadn't been from the start. And if tidying everything up was Grandma X's attempt to make her think it had all been a dream, she wasn't going to fall for it.

Jaide swung her legs off the bed. An unexpected crinkling of paper stopped her from going any farther. There was a note attached to the front of her pajamas by a hat pin shaped like a peacock's feather. The note had been composed on an old typewriter and the letters had drifted up and down from the horizontal as Grandma X typed them.

> Jaidith,
> I don't want you to go to school today.
> Better to stay here, where I can keep an
> eye on you. If I'm asleep when you wake
> up, help yourself to breakfast. There's a
> pot of hot chocolate on the stove.
> Love, X

Jaide snorted and stuck the pin deep into her pillow. She felt much more clearheaded now. Whatever had woken her, she wasn't going to miss the opportunity that being up so early gave her.

She crossed to Jack, who was drooling onto his pillow. There was an identical note fixed with an old sapphire and gold tiepin to his T-shirt. She unpinned it and rocked his shoulder back and forth.

"Jack, Jack, wake up," she hissed in his ear.

Jack didn't respond. He was breathing all right, but no matter how she shook him, he didn't stir out of his unnaturally deep sleep.

"You better stay here, then, I guess," said Jaide hesitantly. "I'll get help."

On bare feet, she crept to the bedroom door and tried the handle. Her fear that it would be locked was unfounded: It opened smoothly and with barely a squeak. She peered out into the hallway, and neither saw nor heard a living soul. In sharp contrast to all the creaks and groans of the night before, the house was so quiet now it, too, seemed to be under a spell.

As lightly as a cat — the stairs hardly complained beneath her at all — Jaide went downstairs and checked out the situation. The kettle was cold; the front door was locked. Grandma X was almost certainly asleep, two floors above, and couldn't possibly hear her use the phone. At least Jaide hoped she couldn't. She wasn't sure of anything about Grandma X anymore.

The phone was on its cradle in the hallway, on a small wooden table with animal feet. Under the table, Ari was curled up in a tight ginger ball. On tiptoes, Jaide approached close enough to reach out and gently lift up the phone. Ari's whiskers twitched, and his tail lashed out once, but his eyes stayed closed. Jaide retreated, hardly daring to breathe.

Susan had long ago made the twins commit her phone number to memory. Jaide took the handset into the cupboard under the stairs, shut the door, and tapped out the familiar digits in the dark. Only the voice mail picked up. Her mother had to be out on an emergency call.

But Jaide felt there was an emergency going on here as well. Only it wasn't something she could put in a message.

She hung up, then sat in the cupboard for a while, thinking furiously, full of hurt and anger and indecision. She was absolutely sure of one thing: There was no way she was going to wait for whatever Grandma X came up with next. She and Jack had to get away.

If she could wake her brother up . . .

Very carefully, she slid out of the cupboard and walked on tiptoe back down the hall. She was about to replace the phone when she noticed Ari was no longer under the table. Jaide's head whipped from side to side, trying to locate the cat. She couldn't see him, but that only made her more fearful. Dropping the phone back on the cradle, she ran for the stairs. Halfway up, she saw Ari waiting at the top, and froze.

The cat looked at her and yawned, showing all his very sharp teeth. Jaide stood absolutely still, wondering what she should do. Part of her was thinking, *He's only a cat*, but another part of her was thinking, *He's a* witch's *cat*.

Ari yawned again, then turned away and slowly padded up the next flight of stairs.

Gone to tell on me to Grandma X, thought Jaide. She jumped up the next three steps and ran.

In the twins' bedroom, Jack rolled over and his hand touched the glass of the window. A moment after he did so, a moth with long, feathery feelers flew up and landed on the other side of the window. There was a faint crackle, a flash of silvery light, and the moth fell to the ground. It was immediately followed by another, which suffered the same fate. But a third moth did not touch the glass. Instead it hovered in place, and only its feelers ever so gently brushed the window.

At that very instant, Jack's sleep was disturbed by a feeling that someone was trying to get through to him, to tell him something. The voice was far away, and its words unintelligible, but the speaker was insistent, and he found himself straining to hear. Very slowly, a couple of words became clear, as they were repeated over and over again.

++We want . . . we want . . . we want . . .++

"*We want* . . ." whispered Jack, still asleep, just as Jaide came rushing into the room. "*We want . . . we want . . .*"

"What?" snapped Jaide. She took him by the shoulders and shook him much harder than she had before. His face was very pale, and his lips were moving very strangely, almost as if someone else was trying to speak through his mouth. "Jack, who are you talking to?"

"*We want . . . we want . . .*"

"Jack!" shouted Jaide, and she slapped him across the face.

"*You,*" said Jack's mouth, and then his eyes flashed open and in his normal voice he said, "Hey! What'd you hit me for?"

"Are you all right?"

Jaide looked worried and annoyed, both of which surprised Jack. He was the one who should be annoyed. His cheek was burning — it felt like she'd left her fingerprints there.

"I was asleep! What are you playing at, waking me up like that?"

"No time for that now," said Jaide. She was somewhat reassured by his perfectly ordinary irritation, and certain that if only they could get away, all the strange happenings would stop. "Get up and get dressed. We're running away."

"We're what?"

"You heard me," she said, flinging back the covers. "Come on, before Grandma wakes up and stops us."

"Hang on," said Jack. "I mean, I know there's weird stuff going on, but do we have to run away? Besides, we don't have anywhere to go."

Jaide thrust a note into his face. He blearily focused on the words his grandma had typed.

"So?"

"If she doesn't want us to go to school, that's the first place we *should* go. And Mr. Carver will help us, I'm sure of it. He seemed nice, didn't he?"

Jack was having trouble keeping up.

"No, he didn't. He seemed like an idiot! Besides, you want to run away to *school*? Shouldn't we try to get the bus over to Mom's work instead?"

"We don't even know if there is a bus," said Jaide. "Besides, I called Mom and couldn't reach her. It's up to us now." She gripped her brother by the shoulders and turned him so he faced his wardrobe. "Just get dressed. I've decided we have to go."

"Oh, well, if you've decided!" said Jack sarcastically as he forced his sluggish limbs to obey him. "Hang on! In the night . . . there was a wind, and it got dark, just like . . . just like at home —"

"Yes!" exclaimed Jaide.

Jack stared at the tidiness of their room. Nothing was broken and everything was in its place.

"Are you sure?"

"Yes! Grandma X did it, and now Ari's probably waking her up and reporting me, so get a move on!"

Jack's forehead wrinkled. Unlike Jaide, he wasn't completely sure Grandma X was behind all the bad stuff, or whether she was working with the rats or against them. But either way, she was a witch . . . so the sooner they got away from her, the better. He agreed with his sister on that point.

But when it came to actually going out the bedroom door, Jack hesitated.

"We should leave Mom a note," he whispered.

"Why? We'll call her from the school. And what if Grandma X reads it? She's the last person we want to know."

"All right," he said. "I guess."

Impatience had made Jaide cross. "You don't have to come if you don't want to. Stay here alone if you like."

Jack vigorously shook his head. *Alone* was something the twins rarely were, and Jack didn't like the thought of it at all. Besides, he wouldn't truly be alone: He would have Grandma X to answer to when she woke up.

"All right, then," Jaide said with her hand on the doorknob. "Let's go."

CHAPTER TEN

WHAT THE CAT SAID

Jaide led the way down the stairwell, shushing Jack as they reached the last wind of steps. She peered over the banister to see if Ari was around, but she couldn't see him.

"What?" Jack whispered into her ear.

She shook her head. Maybe Ari was still waking up Grandma X, or she was giving him instructions. Moving quickly now, fearing that something or someone might catch them on the brink of freedom, she ran to the door and turned the big, old key. It clicked, but not too loudly, and the door was open.

They hurried out into the yard and froze at the sudden sound of voices. But it wasn't Grandma X. It was some people in the yard next door. Even though it was still early, not much past six o'clock, there were workers there and one of them was complaining about a bulldozer that was running late.

The twins didn't stop to listen further. They hurried along the fence line, bent almost double, and ran out the gate into Watchward Lane. Jaide didn't dare look back. She felt the presence of the house like a physical weight, with its windows like piercing eyes tracking her every movement. She wanted to get as far as possible from that terrible gaze.

As the twins ran, they saw evidence of the previous night's rodent assembly. The ground was scuffed by thousands of tiny feet and dotted with droppings. The air had a musty smell. Some of the trees had been gnawed at ankle height, and here and there were spots of dried, dark blood. Jaide shuddered, remembering the heaving mass of rats. She hoped they were all well away from Watchward Lane now. . . .

As she thought of the rats, she noticed a tiny movement out of the corner of one eye. She whirled around, but there was nothing there.

"What?" asked Jack. He was spooked as well. A moth was fluttering around his head, determinedly batting at his face and eyes, and he feared that at any moment a whole swarm of them might descend upon them, like the midges and crickets. "What is it? What did you see?"

"Nothing. . . ."

"Are you sure?"

"Let's keep going."

They reached Parkhill Street and turned right, cutting quickly past Rodeo Dave's bookshop. It was shut, of course, like all the other shops at this time of the morning; there were few cars on the road, and no pedestrians at all. Portland wasn't like the city, where no one ever seemed to sleep. Their father had often told them how much he wished the city would just stop for a while and give everyone a moment to think.

Both twins at that same moment felt a pang of longing for their absent father. If he had been there, he would've known what to do. Grandma X was his mother, after all.

The smell of the fish co-op grew stronger as they approached Dock Road. Jack's head was cold and he wished he'd thought to pack his cap. Jaide's red hair kept being blown into her eyes by irritating gusts of chill wind. But at least they weren't trapped in the house anymore.

Jaide had just started to think they had made it when all of a sudden Jack stopped and grabbed her arm. An orange shape jumped out of a hedge, landed in front of them with a yowl, and raised one white-mittened paw very like a policeman directing traffic.

"You're making a big mistake," Ari said.

Jack couldn't help but reply. "Be quiet! You're on *her* side."

"You speak like you've never met a cat before. There's only one side — my own."

Jaide looked at Jack in alarm. Ari was sitting in front of them yowling and meowing, and Jack was talking back?

"Jack?" Jaide was tugging his arm. "Jack, what are you doing?"

"But that doesn't mean I don't look out for friends," continued Ari.

"By spying on us, you mean?" said Jack, shrugging off Jaide's attempt to drag him past.

"I'm just trying to help. You're protected in the house. You should go back."

"At least no one's going to shove us in an oversize oven out here."

"Shove you in . . . an oven?!" Ari's tail twitched for an instant, either in amusement or surprise. "I think you are somewhat confused."

"Can you really understand what he's saying?" asked Jaide.

"Yes!" snapped Jack. "Obviously!"

"Well, don't listen!" Jaide snapped back. "It . . . it isn't right. You shouldn't be able to talk to cats, or think you are! It's part of everything that's wrong here! Come on!"

She pushed him again, and this time Jack didn't resist. Stepping around Ari, he followed his sister. But Ari followed, too, and began to weave in and out of Jack's legs, slowing him down.

"I don't know what's so wrong about talking to me," said Ari. "Like I said, we're friends, and as a friend, let me repeat: You should go back home now."

"Are you sure you can't hear him?" Jack asked anxiously as they rounded the corner.

"Of course I can't," said Jaide. "Ari's just a cat. He can't talk."

Ari looked heavenward and sighed.

"The words *just* and *cat* were never meant to go together," said the ginger tom to Jack. "Tell your sister she could hear me if she listened properly. Maybe I could talk some sense into *her*."

"He says —"

"I don't want to know!" Jaide put her hands over her ears. "Whatever he's saying to you, it has to be a trick. Ignore him before he talks you out of escaping!"

"Ah, the foolishness of the troubletwister," sighed the cat. "Remember that I tried to warn you."

The cat angled away from them, slinked between the shops on Dock Road, and swarmed up and over a fence.

"He's going to tell Grandma X where we are," said Jack.

"Was that what he said to you?" asked Jaide. She might have protested otherwise, but she did believe Jack had talked to Ari, and she didn't like it. She was worried, too, that Jack was beginning to doubt her plan. She couldn't see it through without him.

"No. He said that we should go back to her house, that we're not safe out here. I'm sure he'll tell her, though."

"Then we'd better hope Mr. Carver gets to work early," said Jaide. Her eyes flickered as she spoke. There was something in the corner of her vision again, something that was moving with them, that she just couldn't get a good look at.

Please, please make all this weird stuff stop, she thought. *If we can just get to school, I'm sure we'll be okay.*

The school was on the elbow formed by Main Street and Dock Road, but the entrance was from River Road, which defined its northern edge. The river was sluggish and wide where Main Street crossed it via the old iron bridge. A steep bank sheltered by willows led down to the water opposite the school. Birds squawked and argued in the hanging branches as the twins turned left off Main Street and hurried toward the front gate of the school.

"We're going to make it!" said Jaide happily, a microsecond before she saw the first rat.

It shot out of a roadside drain and came crawling directly toward them with its nose upraised. Its eyes were the same horrible, shiny, milky white as the eyes they had seen in their old home.

Instinctively Jaide stopped. The rat looked at them with those hideous white eyes for two very long seconds, then it turned and fled, its pink tail whipping behind its fat, black-furred body. It ran up the path and ducked through a hole in the school wall.

A moment later, it reappeared atop the wall, and it wasn't alone. Dozens of rats slowly spread out along the wall, every one of them looking at the twins, every one of them with those same milky, staring eyes.

"They're all around the school," said Jaide grimly. "That cat must have told Grandma X already."

Jack's face was pinched and pale. "What do we do now? We've got nowhere else to go!"

"Troubletwisters!"

The call came from behind them, but it wasn't Grandma X's voice. This was a softer, straining kind of whisper.

"Young troubletwisters, come closer."

"Who's there?" Jaide called out. She and Jack edged nearer to each other, both of them peering around in all directions.

"Look under the trees. Come to us and we will help you. We are your friends."

Jaide and Jack took a step back, paused, and looked across at the school. The rats' heads tracked their every movement.

"Let's look," Jaide whispered. "But be ready to run."

The twins warily crossed the road and looked down the slope, through the gnarled branches and misshapen trunks to the river. But they couldn't see anyone — or any rats — which was a relief.

"Where are you?" called Jaide. "I can't see you."

"There," said Jack, pointing.

As if he had made the person appear, Jaide now saw a solitary human figure standing under one of the twisted trees, wrapped in shadow.

"We are your friends," the whispering voice repeated. "Only we can save you from the witch. Come."

There was something fascinating about the voice. The twins took a step closer without even thinking, and would have taken another step, but the voice was interrupted by a car that drove across the bridge to their right. The iron bridge hummed with its passage, and strange, rhythmic echoes spread across the water.

"Who . . . who are you?" Jaide called.

"You do not know us yet, but you will. It is time. We will tell you *everything*," the figure said. It thrust out an arm in a jerky, peculiar wave. "Come with us. Hurry."

Jack started to head down the slope, moving like a sleepwalker. Jaide made a grab for him but missed.

"Jack, wait!"

"We will tell you the truth," said the voice. The figure stepped partly out of the shadow of the tree, legs jerking like a puppet's. Jaide hesitated, then jumped down the slope after Jack.

"Jack! Come back!" she shouted. "Something's wrong!"

"We want only to help," said the figure soothingly. "Come to us, troubletwisters. Quickly!"

Jack moved faster. Jaide slipped in the mud and fell on one knee.

"Jack! Stop!"

The figure under the tree reached out, as if in welcome, but its arms were too long. A cat yowled somewhere in the distance behind them.

Jack started to run toward that strange embrace.

"Yessss," said the voice. "Welcome!"

With that last word, the figure fell apart, white-eyed rats cascading off a decaying, scarecrow framework of sticks and black cloth, the illusion of a person completely gone.

In that same moment, the ground in front of Jack collapsed. His balance went, and he fell backward, twisting around as the earth carried him down into a sudden sinkhole.

Jack slid down, down, down, the loose soil carrying him deep underground. Desperately he tried to scrabble and claw his way to the surface, but there was nothing to hold on to, and nothing solid under his feet.

He sank deeper, gulping one desperate breath before the earth closed over above his head.

CHAPTER ELEVEN

THE TWINS APART

Unlike her brother, Jaide did scream as she tried to stop herself from being swallowed up by the hole as well. She was already sliding in the mud, slipping inexorably toward the patch of turbulent earth, which was moving as if in answer to strong currents below the surface. But at the last second she managed to grab a tree trunk, forcing her fingernails into the bark so hard, they broke. She came to rest with her feet in loose earth up to her ankles.

"Jack!"

There was no answer.

"Jack!"

This time Jack did not answer, but something else did. There was a flicker of movement in the hole. Jaide pulled herself back with a shriek as thousands of red ants boiled up out of the earth.

But the ants didn't attack. They were busy filling in the hole, burying her brother. Jaide scrambled upright and put her back to the tree, just as a dozen milky-eyed rats poked their heads out of the roiling mix of dirt and ants. The rats turned as one and opened their mouths, speaking together.

"Come! Come to us, troubletwister!"

Jaide screamed again and went up the tree faster than she had ever climbed before. The rats watched her, their horrible eyes moving in unison, and then a great column of white-eyed red ants swarmed out of the dirt and came straight to the tree, climbing in an incredibly fast swathe of red and black and white.

Twenty feet up, Jaide looked down, just for a moment. The tide of ants was almost upon her, and the rats had disappeared back under the loose earth. There was no sign of Jack at all.

The vanguard of the ants reached her foot. Jaide shut her eyes and jumped toward the river, her arms outstretched in the approved safety-jump style.

The wind shrieked across her face. Light spun around her. River, sky, and sun dazzled her as she braced herself for the sudden impact of the water.

But there was no impact. Jaide felt something cold under her hands and she instinctively gripped an iron rail. She opened her eyes, utterly disoriented as, far too close, a car honked its horn.

She wasn't in the river. For a moment Jaide feared that she might faint, but she couldn't do that. Jack needed her, and the rats and ants might be coming for her at that very moment. She needed to do something!

Jaide's vision cleared, and she looked in wonderment around her. She was on the bridge.

Below her, the trees whipped and swayed. She was high above the bank, at least momentarily safe from what she knew lay in the shadows.

I flew, Jaide thought. *The wind took me here!*

"Are you all right?"

Jaide felt a hand on her shoulder and gasped with fright. She pushed herself away, but it was only a portly man in a baseball cap, who had just gotten out of the car that was stopped close by in the middle of the bridge.

"I didn't see you at first," said the man. He held up his hands to show that he meant no harm. "I didn't . . . I didn't hit you, did I?"

"My brother," said Jaide, pointing frantically over the safety rail. "My brother!"

"It's all right, Alf," said a familiar voice. "She's with me."

All the blood drained to Jaide's toes. She didn't need to turn to know that Grandma X was on the bridge, too — with her hair wild and her slippers showing from under her hastily donned coat. Her expression was furious and her eyes bored into Jaide's.

"I'll take care of her."

Jack's chest was burning and he was desperate to breathe, but he didn't dare open his mouth. Then he felt himself fall again, the earth giving way completely, and he landed heavily on his backside.

He instinctively took a breath, a breath that turned into a series of sobs and coughs. But at least he *could* breathe. More dirt rained down on him and he quickly scrabbled backward to avoid being buried under a miniature landslide.

The shower of earth stopped. Jack brushed himself off and looked around, his eyes slowly adapting to the darkness. He was relieved to find that he could see as well as breathe, even though there was no visible source of illumination. He guessed there must be daylight leaking in somewhere.

He was in a dimly lit tunnel that might once have been some kind of sewer. It was circular, wide enough to stand up in, and made out of concrete. A jagged hole had been smashed in the ceiling, through which he and a small mountain of dirt had just fallen. Dozens of tiny red ants crawled across the ground, waving their angry feelers at him.

Thin, white tree roots stretched like harp strings across one end of the tunnel, to his right. He couldn't see what was at the other end, but for the moment his thoughts were directed above the ground.

What was happening to Jaide?

Jack picked himself up and started to dig at the ceiling with his bare hands, but as fast as he tried, more earth fell down on him. Ants followed, scrambling into his clothes and biting him. Then a big lump of concrete missed him by an inch, forcing him to stop.

He told himself to stay calm. He was scared, he was covered in matted earth, there were ants crawling all over him, but at least he was alive. And he could see, too, which was a great relief — although he still couldn't work out where the light was coming from.

Then he heard the voice. A soft, slurring voice that did not sound at all human.

"Troubletwister . . . Troubletwister . . ."

Jack looked up. Directly above him, a great mass of white-eyed ants was hanging down like a swarm of bees migrating from a hive. The ants moved as one, tens of thousands of them working together. As Jack watched, a large and very dead rat was pushed to the front of the mass, and then the ants pulled and pushed the mouth and inflated the dead rat's chest.

The voice came out of this dead rat's mouth.

"So good you have come at last, troubletwister!"

"Oh, I didn't see you there. . . . Good morning."

"Not to worry, Alf. I appreciate your stopping. There's some traffic building up now. Best you be moving on."

"Right you are."

Alf nodded to Grandma X, almost bowing, and hurried back to his car. A truck and two other cars were queued up behind him, as close to a traffic jam as Portland ever saw. Their drivers watched curiously, wondering what an old lady and a young girl were doing in the middle of the iron bridge.

Jaide opened her mouth to call for help, but at that moment Grandma X's ringed hand came down on her shoulder and the girl could neither move nor speak. Jaide was locked into her body as though it were a coffin.

Grandma X waved with her other hand as Alf drove away and the backed-up traffic began to flow again. Jaide found that she could move her eyes, but looking at Grandma X didn't help. The old woman had the air of someone dragged backward out of bed, and she wasn't happy about it at all.

"When I take my hand off you, I want you to tell me where Jackaran is," said Grandma X calmly. "It's vital you do so without delay."

Jaide couldn't nod or shake her head. All she could do was stare in frustrated silence and wait for her chance.

"Don't run, Jaidith," said Grandma X, as though she could read her mind. "I don't know what on earth you think is going on, but I am not your enemy. Your brother needs help, and only we can give it to him."

The spell came off. Jaide pushed herself away and immediately tripped over Kleo, who yowled and retreated behind Grandma X. Jaide landed on her elbow. The pain was sharp and startling. Tears sprang to her eyes.

Grandma X showed little sympathy as she hauled Jaide to her feet.

"Every second counts, Jaide. Tell me what happened to Jackaran."

Jaide clambered to her feet, very confused. She'd thought the rats and ants and everything else worked for Grandma X. Surely the woman already knew what had happened to Jack?

"We were going to school, but the rats were there . . . your rats . . . then someone called to us from the trees and it was . . . it was like we couldn't resist . . . or Jack couldn't. He went first and . . . he fell into a hole that swallowed him up and there were ants and I climbed a tree and jumped and . . . then I was here, I don't know how."

"Show me where it happened," said Grandma X urgently. She pushed Jaide into movement and followed closely behind. "There were rats, you say? White-eyed rats?"

"Yes, at the school and then . . . the person, the one calling, he . . . it . . . was just all rats as well," Jaide said.

"Look, under that willow with the two branches in an F, the clear patch of dirt. That was a hole and Jack went in it! Your rats and ants have probably got him right now!"

"They're not my rats and ants," said Grandma X. She was peering at the bare patch of ground and fumbling with something in her bag.

"Who do they belong to, then?" Jaide asked weakly. She recognized the feeling that was starting to spread through her, underneath her fear for Jack. She didn't want to acknowledge it, but she recognized that Grandma X was speaking the honest truth — and that was accompanied by the dawning, awful realization that she had made a bad mistake.

"I will explain everything as soon as I can. Right now we need to rescue Jack."

Grandma X strode down the slope to the bare patch where Jack had disappeared. The live ants were gone, but when Jaide got closer she could see quite a number of dead ones sprinkled around.

"Be careful," said Grandma X, waving her back. "That's how he was taken, through unsound soil."

"Taken where?" Jaide still wasn't sure about Grandma X, but she didn't know who else she could turn to, to get help for Jack. The police or the fire department certainly wouldn't listen if she showed them apparently solid ground and said that Jack had been taken down into the earth.

"Probably into an old drain. The town is crisscrossed with them. We had a very energetic engineer for several decades back in the nineteen hundreds."

Grandma X looked up from her examination of the soil. "Did you see any other creatures apart from the rats and the ants?"

Jaide shook her head. "No. Does that matter?"

"It gives us . . . and Jack . . . a little more time. Let's go!" Grandma X started up the hill.

"But shouldn't we stay here . . . and dig or something?"

"No. Jack won't be directly underneath anymore. Come on!"

Grandma X was already halfway back up to the bridge. Jaide hesitated, then hurried after her grandmother.

"Where are we going?" she gasped. "What are you going to do?"

"The first step is to find out exactly where Jackaran is, and to do that I must get inside, out of the daylight."

"Why?"

"Because my Gift is tied to the moon, and the sun interferes with it," said Grandma X.

"What Gift? What are you talking about?"

"This is part of a greater explanation, which I have been waiting to give you. Suffice it to say that each of our kind is different in his or her own way. Your Gifts appear to be of the sun and air. I think your brother's are of night and darkness. I have learned that much about the two of you in the short time you have been with me."

They turned onto Parkhill Street and hurried toward Watchward Lane. Grandma X was moving very fast for an old lady, and Jaide had to jog to keep up.

"My Gifts? Our kind?" asked Jaide. "What do you —"

She was interrupted by Kleo, who ran up from behind

them carrying a long-tailed rat that, while still alive, hung limply in the cat's mouth, Kleo's teeth firmly fastened in a fold of fur behind the rat's head. The rat's eyes were only partly milky, the white cloud swirling around like milk going down a drain.

"Good work, Kleo!" exclaimed Grandma X. "Very good work indeed! That's exactly what we need."

As they hurried up the drive to Grandma X's house, Jaide saw that the blue door was completely visible now, as was the sign. Now it simply said: KEEP OUT!

High above, the moon-and-star weather vane was pointing fixedly to the northwest — toward the iron bridge. Jaide hesitated on the steps, remembering the efforts she and Jack had made to escape, and the certainty with which she had decided that Grandma X was a witch who was out to get them. But that certainty was completely gone now, and in its place was the knowledge that Jack was in terrible danger . . . and Jaide felt that it was all her fault.

They ran straight into the drawing room. Grandma X took down a bell jar and held it upside down so Kleo could deposit the rat inside. Then she slapped on the lid before the rodent could escape.

"Now. Let's find out what this thing knows. Jaide, give me your hand."

Jaide let herself be gripped tightly by her grandma's strong fingers. She could feel the impression of the stone set in the ring. It was smooth and oval, and weirdly cold.

Grandma X placed her left palm against the bell jar. Instantly the cloudiness in the rat's eyes stopped swirling and settled into a band across the middle. The rat thrashed around, as if it had been struck, then its head went up as if caught in an invisible noose. It squeaked piteously, and slowly and reluctantly turned to press one pink ear against the side of the glass, against Grandma X's hand.

As it did so, something very strange shot into Jaide's arm, into her mind. It was the rat's thoughts, tiny and petty and focused on smells and tastes and food and its kind.

Jaide gasped.

++Don't distract me,++ said Grandma X. Her mouth didn't move — the words came directly into Jaide's mind. ++I need some of your strength to do this in daylight, and you need to see what we're dealing with. Be calm and let me do the work for you.++

Jaide nodded through her disorientation. The rat's thoughts rose up to overwhelm her; within them, she was surprised to find the thoughts of other creatures, too, tinier appetites that tasted of dirt and decay and family. She squirmed, thinking of insects. Was this what it was like to be a cockroach or a fly? And if so, what were such experiences doing in the mind of a rat?

Grandma X probed deeper. Something dark lurked in the rat's thoughts. She seized upon it and pursued it deeper still. Jaide felt as though they were following a lightless tunnel down into the heart of the earth, where creatures lived that had never seen the light of the sun, or the moon, or the stars. It was like being at the bottom of the ocean. And still they went deeper, following a tendril of darkness that never seemed to end.

Down, down, they went, silently, stealthily, hands clasped tightly as they searched for Jack.

++Help me,++ Grandma X said into Jaide's mind. ++You're his twin. You know him best of all. Conjure him in your thoughts so we can find him, together.++

Jaide struggled to comply with the request. She felt as though the blackness was sucking out her very life, like an oil slick creeping across a shore. Jack was a fading memory that took some reviving. He was four minutes younger than her, and looked more like their father than like their mother, with brown eyes, darker skin, and black hair. And although he could be annoying sometimes, Jaide didn't know what she would do if he never came back.

++That's it,++ Grandma X communicated. ++That's good. I can feel him now. We're getting close. Hold on!++

CHAPTER TWELVE

ALONE IN THE DARK

Jack paused, panting, at a Y intersection. The pipe he was following split into two, and he couldn't tell which looked lighter to his eyes. Left or right? Behind him the whispering of the ants grew louder. He had to choose quickly.

++Come back, troubletwister!++

The voice was faint, but not as faint as it should have been, given the distance he'd come. Jack had a horrible vision of the ants moving together, the bloated, speaking rat riding on their backs like a boat on a wave . . . following him wherever he went.

He went right. The decision was random. He had been running for ages and had seen no increase or decrease in light, whichever way he went. Just the same gray view everywhere and still no visible light source. He had begun to think he wasn't seeing by light at all — but how was that possible? How could anyone see, except by light?

The pipe he had chosen was starting to get damp and cold, and he could smell the salty odor of the sea, combined with the far less pleasant stench of rotting seaweed. That was encouraging, for if the pipe ended at the beach, it would be a short walk from there to the police station. He had already decided that that was where he should go. The school was infested with rats, and Grandma X's house wasn't safe. He hoped Jaide would come to the same conclusion and meet him there. Even though the police wouldn't believe him about the rats and the ants and everything, they would at least call his mother.

Jaide would be freaking out, Jack thought, if she hadn't been caught, too. He really, really hoped she hadn't been captured . . . because if she was free, there was a chance she could get help. Though he wasn't really sure what kind of help you could get for the trouble he was in. . . .

Jack bit his lip in frustration as the pipe ended in a mossy iron grille that wouldn't budge no matter how he pushed and tugged at it. He could hear water dripping farther down the pipe, but he had no choice but to turn back.

++Why are you running, troubletwister?++

Jack stopped in sudden fright. That voice wasn't from the rat. It was closer, and different. He looked wildly around, but all he could see were the crumbling walls of the pipe.

Then he realized that he wasn't actually hearing it. The voice was inside his head.

"Who are you?" he shouted. "What do you want with me?"

++We have many names, troubletwister,++ came the answering whisper. **++Just as you have, Jackaran Kresimir Shield.++**

"How do you know —" Jack started to say, but he stopped. Maybe if he didn't talk to it, the voice would go away.

I have to get out of these tunnels, thought Jack. *I have to get away!*

++We have been waiting for you, Jackaran Kresimir Shield. Soon we will meet, oh, yessss. . . .++

Jack shuddered and ran faster. If the ants hadn't reached the Y intersection, he might be able to take the other tunnel. It had to lead to safety!

++Come to us, Jackaran Kresimir Shield. Be with us. Be one of us!++

Jack stopped. While the voice was inside his head, he'd heard something else with his ears. A nasty shuffling sound from the tunnel ahead of him, a sound that was rapidly getting louder.

Then he saw what was making the noise. A long, low, lumpy shape, kind of like a really big, undulating worm. It rose and fell as it moved along the tunnel — and then it split into two at the Y intersection and continued to slither up the two different tunnels.

Jack had passed a tiny alcove in the sewer wall several paces back. Now, almost without thought, he raced there and folded himself into it. He felt every ragged line of the old bricks as he tried to press himself farther back. Then he tried to keep absolutely still, not even breathing, as the thing came closer and closer.

It was like a giant worm, only it was made up of rats and cockroaches and red ants and other nameless insects, all with white eyes and all stuck together, crawling and writhing like a single creature. The sound it made as it moved was a ghastly mixture of every rat and insect noise ever made, combined with the slithering of its strange flesh upon the tunnel.

As its head passed him, something heavy and dark pressed against Jack's mind. He felt it in his thoughts, a presence even worse than the physical presence of the creature. It threatened to overwhelm him, to suck his mind away and combine him with what it had already gathered. But at the same time it offered peace, a certainty that if he did give in, it would take away his fear, just as it would take away every other emotion, along with all his memories, everything that was him. If he let it in, he would disappear forever.

++We see you, Jackaran Kresimir Shield!++ said the voice in his head. **++We see you!++**

The worm's head turned to Jack and reared above him, all its component rats and insects swirling and wriggling to create a vast but toothless maw.

"No!" Jack screamed. He ducked and dived forward as the clumsy worm-mouth struck into the alcove where he'd been. Before it could pull back, he jumped onto it, kicking and flailing, smashing his way through rats, ants, and cockroaches, which flew in all directions.

The worm temporarily collapsed as Jack rampaged along it, desperate to reach the intersection. But even as he smashed his way through its component parts, he felt its tendrils clutching at his mind, sapping his will, making him slower and more stupid, so that every step he took got more difficult, and the worm was beginning to re-form around him. It was like fighting through quicksand and —

I'm not going to make it, Jack thought, sharp panic fighting back against the relentless pull of the creature's mind.

++You can't escape us, Jackaran Kresimir Shield! You can't escape!++

But Jack was suddenly through, running as fast as he had ever run, and the worm shrieked in fury and broke apart, sending thousands of rats, ants, spiders, and crawling horrors after Jack. No longer constrained by moving together, they were at his heels within seconds.

Far off in the distance, Jack caught a glimpse of light, real light, and he ran toward it, hoping against hope. It led him to a wider tunnel, one lined with brick rather than concrete. Rusted iron grilles blocked off several tunnels leading elsewhere.

Jack ran to the tunnel's end, where he found a vertical shaft leading up into darkness. There had once been a ladder, but it had pulled away from the wall and only a twisted length of rusted metal remained to show where it had been. There was no way for him to climb up.

But the light didn't come from above. It was emanating from a luminous, cylindrical cloud that was swirling slowly around underneath the vertical shaft, blocking the way up.

Jack wondered if it was marsh gas. He'd read about it in an old book once, how it could choke you to death, or explode. Jack looked at it, then back at his pursuers. They had slowed and were grouping together again. They were rebuilding the worm-creature, and he could feel its mental pressure growing, trying to break into his head.

Jack lifted the bottom of his T-shirt up to cover his mouth and nose, and walked into the shining cloud.

Instantly, the mental pressure ceased. Behind him the worm-creature screamed with all its rat mouths and rose up, drawing in more and more rats, ants, and insects as it surged forward to overwhelm him.

The cloud of light moved forward to meet it, leaving Jack behind and growing brighter as it went. Jack backed up to the tunnel wall and watched in amazement as the cloud coalesced and took on a human form, a human form that he instantly recognized.

Hanging brightly in the darkness of the tunnels, as cool and beautiful as the full moon, was the ghostly form of the young Grandma X.

Jack pressed harder against the tunnel wall, thinking that he had been caught by the witch and her minions, and that he had come to the end at last.

The radiant image of Grandma X raised her right hand, and there was a flash of intense light. The worm-creature charged, sending shadows writhing across the walls of the tunnel.

Grandma X and the worm-thing met in a blaze of light and darkness, sending Jack flying under a shower of rats, ants, and bugs.

In the darkness of the rat's deepest thoughts, Jaide suddenly saw a light bloom, a light that also brought Jack into view. He looked frightened and dirty, and he was backed up against a brick wall that curved over his head. He seemed to be staring right at her.

"Jack, it's me! We're coming to get you!"

Jaide's voice echoed back at her from the walls of Grandma X's house. She didn't know how to speak with her mind as Grandma X did, so she was just speaking aloud — but something *did* hear her nonetheless, something heavy and dark and terrible that crashed over them and said in a voice that tried to drag her down into the darkest halls of memory —

++We see you, Jaidith Fennena Shield. We see you!++

The light flared. The darkness struggled against it, briefly but intensely, then abruptly snuffed out the light, taking Jack with it.

"No!" Jaide recoiled, tripped, and landed on her backside in the drawing room. Spots of black danced in her eyes. Above her, Grandma X quickly snatched her hand off the rat. Kleo jumped up onto the desk and butted her head against the woman's side.

All traces of the darkness vanished with the breaking of that contact.

"It is already so strong!" exclaimed Grandma X, wiping her hand across her brow. "But at least we know where Jackaran is now, that he has managed to evade it so far, and my . . . our . . . intervention will have given him some more time. Where the shadows are darkest, light burns most brightly. If only he can keep away from it . . ."

Jaide got to her feet and clutched at Grandma X's arm urgently, adding emphasis to her question.

"What is *it*? And what does it want with Jack? With *us*?"

"It wants you for the same purpose it wants every living thing in this world: to absorb you and make you part of itself. As to what it is, well, no one knows exactly where it comes from, and it has no name in any human language. It just *is*."

"You must call it something."

"We do," said Grandma X gravely.

She looked older and wearier than Jaide had ever seen her before.

"We call it The Evil."

CHAPTER THIRTEEN

WHERE THERE'S LIFE, THERE'S . . .

The Evil.

The name filled Jaide with images of vampires and were-wolves and horrors she couldn't find words for. *The* Evil had to be more evil than any of them, or perhaps all of them combined. And it was down in those tunnels with Jack!

"We have to rescue him; we can't leave him alone!"

"Of course we will rescue him," said Grandma X. She tapped the last two fingers of her right hand on the desk, her forehead deeply creased in thought. "But it is more easily said than done. Even if it does catch him, it will . . . it will take some time to subdue his will, before it can . . . absorb him."

Jaide recoiled, shocked at the thought of Jack being absorbed by something. She couldn't get that glimpse of Jack's terrified face out of her mind, and she didn't want him to be in danger for a second longer than he had to be.

"Can't we just go down there and get him?"

"I am not strong enough in daylight to confront this manifestation of The Evil directly, and your Gift is neither fully revealed nor even partially under your control. We'll have to find a less direct way to get him out."

Kleo meowed. Grandma X looked down at the cat and sighed heavily. "Yes, The Evil has caught us napping. Caught *me* napping, I should say. It should not be here, not so strong. The wards should have stopped it, but somehow it's getting through. . . ." She rested her head in her hands for a moment. "I've been so weary and distracted. . . . I've not been thinking clearly for days, ever since the cats sensed your awakening Gifts."

"If we can't directly rescue Jack," Jaide said, "can we *help* him escape? We can't just sit here and do nothing. You have to tell me what we can do."

Grandma X looked up and surprised Jaide by slapping herself on the cheek and shaking her head wildly from side to side and up and down, like a horse getting ready to run.

"You're a very smart girl, Jaidith Shield. Jackaran has managed to get away from The Evil so far. . . . Perhaps if we helped him find a way out . . . Let me see. . . . Moonrise is at ten minutes past eleven. . . ."

Jaide remembered what Grandma X had said about her Gift being tied to the moon.

"Will the moon make you stronger?"

"Yes, even if it is not visible. The tide will be coming in, too," said Grandma X. "But I'll need your help. Let me gather a few things and we'll get started."

Jack shielded his face with his arms. He had fallen onto his back, and prickly legs ran all over him as the insects and rats scurried about the tunnel. Not in a panic, but desperate to regroup and attack the glowing figure swaying with arms outstretched among them. Wriggling, dark shapes spun in midair around the image of Grandma X, as though floating in free fall. Jack could feel the black mass of thought swirling around him, struggling to bring its ghastly composite creature back together. He could hear its wordless call and struggled to resist it himself.

When that call took on words, he found a strength he had never known he had.

++We see you, Jaidith Fennena Shield. We see you!++

Suddenly he was on his feet, brushing off debris and throwing himself bodily into the mess of creatures, squashing those that were squashable and tossing aside those that weren't.

"You!" he shouted. "Leave! My! Sister! Alone!"

The creatures were taken by surprise, but only momentarily. For every one he dispatched, two more took its place. He felt himself grow heavy with accumulated bugs and rats. They clung to his clothes, to his hair, to his ears and fingers. He flailed and whipped his head from side to side, fighting once more for his own life.

The light flared again, and in that split instant of the brightest possible light, he glimpsed how his shadow looked against the wall of the tunnel. His arms and legs were rippling with the creatures trying to bring him down . . . but even worse than that, the shadow looked deep, and dark, and enticingly safe.

A rat crawled up over his head and its snout thrust against his left eye.

He shut his eyes, and in the darkness found a new strength.

This is it, Jack thought. *They've got me now. But I'm not giving up.*

He stopped thrashing about and stood absolutely still, though it took every ounce of self-control that he possessed, as the rats and bugs squirmed all over him, noses and paws and feelers and legs thrusting at his ears and eyes and the corners of his mouth.

"You'll have to kill me," he said quietly and with great certainty, spitting out a cockroach that swarmed across his lips. "Because I am not joining you, not now, not ever!"

No more bugs crawled into his mouth or nose. A rat squeaked and stopped probing at his eyes with its nose. Then all at once, the mass of creatures fell away. He heard the sodden, rolling thuds as thousands of soft bodies hit the floor of the tunnel. He heard their squeaks and chitters of complaint, individual again, not a massed noise.

He felt, more than heard, a roar of frustration off in the dark, and he braced himself, ready to defend himself against a renewed attack.

But no attack came. Slowly Jack opened his eyes.

The worm-thing was gone. The rats and insects that had made it up were scurrying away, back up the tunnel, or into cracks and holes.

The shining figure had also disappeared. Several last wisps remained, gleaming off the damp bricks and mortar of the tunnel. Like the last of the insects, they soon faded.

Then the underground world was dark, and Jack was alone.

He looked down at his feet, able to see well enough — somehow — to know that he wasn't standing where he had been before. He was under the broken ladder now, whereas before, he was sure, he had been farther along the tunnel, where he had been thrown when light and darkness had first met. Something had moved him away from the creatures that had attacked him — or he had moved himself. . . .

"Jaide," Jack said in a hesitant whisper. "Are you here?"

If the worm-thing had seen his sister, he was thinking, perhaps she was in the tunnels with him.

But there was no answer, only the scurrying sound of retreating rats.

At least he was being ignored for the moment. Whatever had happened, it had deflected everyone from looking for him. The bugs were gone, presumably searching elsewhere, and the ghostly Grandma X was gone, too.

He didn't know how to feel about her now: He was supposed to think that she was an evil witch, as Jaide did, but instead he took a kind of comfort that someone was looking for him. He hadn't been forgotten.

"Jaide? Come back! Please!"

Silence.

He knew he couldn't stand there all day, calling helplessly into the shadows. While the rats and bugs were busy getting themselves together, he had to take the chance to make another run for it, even though that meant backtracking the way he had come.

There had to be a way out of these tunnels.

He ran back, following what he hoped was a faint smell of the sea. A slight downward slope was also cause for optimism. As he ran, the tunnel widened and others joined it. The smell of salt and seaweed grew stronger while the sound of the rats and insects behind him grew fainter. If only he had followed this tunnel originally, he thought, he could have been out ages ago!

A new noise reached his ears — the booming of waves, surging and thundering against the shore. He began to run faster along a lazy bend to the left, certain now that he had found a way to freedom.

The pipe straightened, and he saw what truly lay ahead.

Water. *Sea*water, rippling and foamy. The pipe was submerged in the ocean, and he had no way of telling whether it came back up into the air or not. He could either swim for it and hope for the best, or turn back and try to find another way.

But the . . . the . . . whatever it was that controlled all the rats and insects and everything in the tunnel . . . was behind him. Turning back wasn't an option.

Jack splashed into the salty water. It rose steadily up his legs as the pipe angled downward under him. When it reached his waist, he held his breath and ducked under.

There was no light at the end of this tunnel. Just more water as far as his eyes could see.

For a moment, Jack seriously considered swimming as far as he could, and he would either get lucky . . . or drown. But the moment passed.

"Where there's life, there's hope," muttered Jack after he broke the surface and took a deep breath. It was one of the sayings his father used, and it made him feel both slightly better and intensely alone. If only his father was with him now!

A tiny wave slopped across his ankles as Jack retreated

out of the water. He looked behind him and saw another slowly rolling in, and noticed that the water level was rising. The pipe did lead to the sea, and the tide was coming in. Soon the whole maze of pipes would be full of seawater.

"I really *have* to get out," Jack muttered.

He didn't expect an answer, but he got one.

The voice, the dark, insidious voice, was back inside his head.

++Jaaackaaaraaannn.++

"Leave me alone!" Jack shouted. He clenched his fist and, unable to hit anything else, punched the palm of his other hand.

++Come back, troubletwister,++ said the voice. **++We don't want you to drown.++**

"So show me the way out!"

++Join us, and we will show you everything.++

"I already told you, I'm never joining you!"

++Never say never, troubletwister,++ whispered the voice in his head. **++Sometimes you need to change your mind. Remember, we will tell you everything you need to know. All knowledge will be yours.++**

"Yeah, right," Jack said. "What do you really want?"

++Only to protect you, Jackaran. Only to make you safe.++

"From who?"

++From the witch. From the Wardens. They are tricking you. Turn your back on them and join us instead. We will tell you nothing but the truth.++

Jack stood shivering at the edge of the water in wet, heavy clothes. If the mental voice had found him, he was sure the worm-creature wouldn't be far away. A second later, he saw the first white-eyed rat, sneaking along, leading a line of others, all marching in step.

"I don't know what you're talking about," Jack shouted. "I don't know who the Wardens are or who you are. I just want to find my sister and go home!"

++Your sister is with us. Come, join her. We do not mean you harm. We will be home to both of you.++

The chill Jack felt came from more than just the cold. The darkness pressed into him again, and he ground his fists into his eyes to keep it out.

"I don't believe you! Go away! I . . . I *refuse* to listen to you! I'm not . . . I'm not here!"

Bright lights flashed behind Jack's eyelids. His voice echoed wildly in the tunnel. The invasion of his mind reached a peak, and then suddenly it fell away. When the last impressions of his cries faded, the tunnel was silent. The rats were still there, but they were no longer marching in step. They were scrambling about in confusion, turning their heads from side to side, staring blindly in the gloom.

++Ah, you see, your powers grow,++ said the voice. **++But we can teach you more than simple tricks with darkness. Far more! She will never tell you who you really are. But we will.++**

Jack almost answered, but just in time shut his mouth very slowly and quietly as the rats continued to look around, staring in all directions, sometimes even straight at him, but without any sign of recognition.

They can't see me, Jack realized. *They can't see me!*

He remembered the way Jaide had looked right through him on the stairs the previous night, and how he had seemed to disappear from the drawing room mirror while playing with the pogo stick. He thought of how well he could see in the dark, when there was no light at all, and how he had escaped the creatures before, when the light had cast such dark shadows across the tunnel. And there was the whole talking-cat thing.

Powers, thought Jack. *It says I have powers . . . so maybe I do!*

It wasn't such a weird thought. Since coming to Portland, he had seen far weirder things. And if it meant that the voice couldn't get inside his head, and the rats could no longer see him, he was more than happy to accept it without explanation.

Jack slipped off his sneakers so they wouldn't squelch, and tiptoed up the pipe. The rats grew excited as he came nearer and they raced about sniffing — but he edged past without alerting any of them. Farther along, there were great mounds of ants and cockroaches, the building blocks of the worm-creature. But he got past them, too, holding his breath and creeping as silently as he could manage.

Now I've got to find a better tunnel, he thought. *One that goes uphill.*

He chose one and started along it, pausing to stifle a yawn. It was only then, the energy lent by fear fading from him, that he realized he was very, very tired. Whatever he was doing to keep himself hidden was also wearing him out.

At the back of his mind whispered a very small voice, his own, warning him that he was running out of the frying pan and into the fire. If the voice was right, and Grandma X was evil, escaping from the tunnels might be the very worst thing he could do. . . .

Once at home, Grandma X appeared older and more exhausted than ever, but Jaide, still feeling hot blood burning in her face, felt the need to defend herself.

"Look at it from our side," she said. "The bugs — the hot chocolate — the cards —"

"Yes, yes," said Grandma X. "I understand. I would have told you everything earlier, but too much foreknowledge can send a troubletwister's Gifts astray. Even more astray than normal. Obviously, I misjudged that. When this is all behind us, I hope you'll give me the opportunity to make it up to both of you."

"Okay . . ." said Jaide reluctantly. She wanted an apology less than she wanted answers. "But what about —"

"No time for that this second. Come on. We have work to do! I'll explain what I can as we go."

With renewed energy, Grandma X hurried her out to the car, which had somehow started while they were in the house and was waiting with its front doors open.

"It can't drive itself," Grandma X said. "But sometimes inanimate objects gain a certain liveliness when they are long associated with one of us."

"One of what?" asked Jaide. "A witch?"

"I am not a witch!" exclaimed Grandma X. The car's wheels spun as they exited the gravel drive and shot out into the lane. "The proper name for what I am is a Warden. I was born with a Gift that I have spent my entire life trying to control. You'll be a Warden, too, one day, if you can get your Gift properly under your command."

"How do you know that?"

"Because it's hereditary, Jaidith dear. Your father is a Warden, I'm a Warden, my mother was a Warden, her father was a Warden . . . and so on unto antiquity."

"But Mom's not one, is she?"

Grandma X's foot went down on the accelerator and the car rocked as they hurtled around the corner of Watchward Lane and Parkhill Street.

"No, she is not. It is one of the trag — difficulties of a Warden's life that we must marry non-Wardens in order to have the chance of Gifted children. It can make life very . . . tricky."

"Oh," said Jaide thoughtfully. That explained a lot about her father. Knowing Jack would be really interested to hear this, she felt yet another pang of fear for her brother.

"Where are we going, Grandma?" she asked, realizing they were heading away from the place Jack had been captured, not toward it.

"To the lighthouse."

"What are we going to do there?"

"We're going to raise the tide rather more than usual and flush The Evil out of the old tunnels, into the open, and Jackaran with it."

"But what if Jack is trapped? He'll drown!"

Grandma X glanced at her as the Hillman shrieked past the cemetery. "Don't worry. The Evil won't let your brother drown. It needs him alive to get at us."

"Why?"

"If The Evil takes over Jackaran, it will use him to attack us. Troubletwisters are particularly vulnerable to The Evil, and particularly prized by it, because if it succeeds in taking one over, then it can take over his or her Gift as well."

"Why do you call us troubletwisters?" asked Jaide. "Mom thinks it's just an old word."

"It is a very old word, Jaidith, and a meaningful one. Young Wardens just coming into their Gifts are often unconscious causes of magical trouble, and they twist and complicate any existing trouble as well. And believe me, there's always trouble *somewhere*."

"You've been fighting The Evil a long time, haven't you?" said Jaide with sudden insight.

"All my life," said Grandma X. "Ever since I was a troubletwister like you. The Wardens are the enemy of The Evil. We stop it from getting into this world, and we have done so for centuries. If we ever weaken, all that we hold dear will be destroyed. We cannot let The Evil win, no matter what the cost. Do you understand?"

Jaide sat up straighter.

"Yes," she said in a small voice. She knew very well what Grandma X was saying. They were going to try to save Jack, but his life was less important than stopping The Evil in its tracks. If Grandma X had to choose between them, Jack would lose.

CHAPTER FOURTEEN

THE RISING TIDE

The car skidded to a halt in the lighthouse parking lot. Grandma X turned off the engine and pulled on the hand brake before leaning over to cup Jaide's chin in one old hand, just for a second.

"You're a brave girl, Jaidith, and one day you'll make a good Warden. Remember that, no matter what happens here."

Then she was sliding out through the car and waving for Jaide to follow. Long brass rods had been rattling around inside the trunk like giant toothpicks, and it took a moment to gather them.

A restless wind sent Jaide's hair dancing, and she felt the urge to jump up into it, up into the sky with its scudding clouds, to join a solitary seagull that was struggling to maintain a stationary position as it looked for food among the jagged rocks of the reef.

But the moment passed, and the seagull dropped down on a fish or crab with a predatory *keee!*

"Bring as many rods as you can carry," Grandma X told Jaide, who briefly wondered if they had also come there to fish. "We have to stick them in the ground between the lighthouse and Dagger Reef in this shape."

Using the tip of one of the rods, she drew a *U* in the ground with a vertical line down the middle:

$$\Psi$$

"This side," she said, tapping the open end of the *U*, "points out to sea."

"What's it for?" asked Jaide.

"A spell, I suppose you could call it, that speaks to the ocean, asking it to bring in a storm surge of wind, wave, and tide."

"Isn't this going to look weird to normal people?" asked Jaide as she hurried around the base of the lighthouse, loaded with rods.

"There will be no 'normal' people about," said Grandma X with great certainty.

"Okay." Jaide still felt like someone was watching her, even though she couldn't see anyone, not even when she looked up to the top of the lighthouse and the observation rail around the light at the top.

The door at the bottom of the lighthouse was padlocked three times on the outside, so no one could be inside. Jaide wondered if anyone ever did go in, except for the workers who looked after the automatic light. It wasn't open to the public, like some other lighthouses she'd visited.

The ground was soft after the rain of the weekend, so sticking in the rods wasn't difficult. Jaide and Grandma X put in nine, then ran back to the car to get more. Even with only half of the trident shape completed, Jaide could see it starting to have an effect. Out to sea, the water was growing dark as the wind came, and a line of black clouds was rolling in from the horizon.

By the time the next lot of nine rods was in place, great booming green waves were smashing into the reef below, sending plumes of spray high enough for the rising wind to blow them across the lighthouse, thoroughly saturating Jaide.

"Go wait by the car," shouted Grandma X, even her powerful voice barely audible over the wind and crashing surf. "I have to go do something. Think heavy thoughts!"

Jaide went back to the car, fighting with every step to stay on course, not to be picked up by the wind despite her thinking extremely heavy thoughts. She was shivering and wished she'd brought her coat. But it was undoubtedly colder where Jack was, and soon would become a whole lot wetter, so she told herself not to complain.

The seagull that had been fishing at the reef was sheltering in the lee of the car. She didn't blame it. Inside the car, Jaide wiped the condensation off the window so she could see what Grandma X was doing. The old lady was standing at the closed end of the trident symbol they had made out of the rods, one hand raised up to the sky and the other holding one of the rods. The spray from the waves below whipped around her, almost like a tornado, and the first, heavy drops of rain came spearing down, as if aiming right at Grandma X's head.

A booming roll of thunder came from the open sea. Grandma X lowered her hand and let go of the rod, then hurried to where Jaide was waiting in the car. With a rumble, the engine started of its own accord again.

"I hope that works," said Grandma X. She slumped back in her seat and shut her eyes for a few seconds.

"Are you all right?" asked Jaide.

Grandma X opened her eyes and gave Jaide a rather forced smile.

"Yes, dear. I'm just a little tired . . . and rather perplexed. The Evil is far stronger than it should be."

She looked around through the windshield, each side window, and the rear window, before adding, almost under her breath, "Yet all four seem to be in place, so far as I can tell. . . ."

"All four what?" asked Jaide. She was getting a bit concerned about Grandma X. She needed the old lady to focus on helping Jack, not sit here in the car mumbling. "What do we do now?"

"Now we go home," said Grandma X, suddenly decisive again. She put the car in gear and reversed with a screech of wet tires suddenly finding their grip. "We watch the storm rise, and see what The Evil does in response."

"How will it know we had anything to do with this?" Jaide said. "This could just be an ordinary storm."

"It would know soon enough in any case. It would feel the difference, as I would feel its interference with any natural force. But it already knows this is no normal storm. It saw us calling it."

"How?" Jaide swiveled in her seat to look back at the receding lighthouse, remembering the feeling that she had been watched the whole time they were on the shore. "I didn't see any bugs or rats or dogs."

"You saw the gull, didn't you?"

"Yes, but . . ."

"The Evil works by taking over small things, like midges and ants, then moving up to steadily more complex creatures, like rats, birds, dogs — and people. Then, as it draws upon the power of its collective life forces, it can do other things . . . but it isn't always obvious and it can disguise itself and its actions. You need training to recognize its presence. That gull was an agent of The Evil, all right, and what one of its creatures sees, it sees."

"That's how you found Jack," Jaide said with sudden understanding. "You got into the mind of that rat and followed it back to The Evil."

"Exactly."

A violent gust of wind shook the car as they pulled up in front of the house.

"I'm hoping the storm will distract The Evil sufficiently for us to repeat the trick and find out where Jack will pop up."

However, the rat was dead, lying on its back in the jar with eyes normal but blank and legs curled tight. Grandma X looked accusingly at Kleo, who shook her head and trotted out the door, presumably to find another rodent hostage.

"Well, that's disappointing, but not entirely unexpected. The Evil can will its creatures to death, though it is always loath to lose even one of its conquests, no matter how small it is. Particularly when the battle has barely begun."

Grandma X scooped up her opera glasses. "Let's go up onto the roof and see what we can see. Not forgetting our coats on the way. I would suggest an umbrella, but with this wind . . ."

They climbed the stairs to the top of the house. Opening the hatch let a great gust of cold air in to howl down the stairs. Jaide tightly gripped the edges of the door as she stepped outside, and she had to jump to the rail, where she hung on for dear life, feeling as though she might fly away at any moment. All around them, treetops swayed and groaned, and the branches of the tall fir leaned over so far, they tapped on the house's angular eaves. The sky was as dark as dusk, and the world had been leached of color. To the east, the horizon was ribboned with lightning.

Grandma X swept the town with her opera glasses. Then she put them down and turned the ring on her hand around so that the stone was clearly visible to Jaide for the first time. It was a large, oval moonstone.

"I will be . . . absent . . . for a few minutes," said Grandma X.

She closed her eyes, leaned against the rail, and became very still. Slowly, the moonstone ring began to glow with a soft internal light.

Jaide wondered if Grandma X would teach her the trick of it when all this was over. She imagined thousands of uses for leaving her body, such as sneaking into the cinema without paying, spying on her parents, or even visiting her friends back in the city.

A gust of wind broke into these thoughts. The house creaked, and the first heavy drops of rain struck the widow's walk. Jaide pulled the hood of her coat up over her head and reached out to do the same for Grandma X, but just at that moment an extra-strong blast of wind blew straight in and lifted her right off the ground.

Suddenly Jaide was upside down, clinging with one hand to the rail as she desperately scrabbled for a hold with the other.

"Grandma! Help!"

Grandma X didn't move. Jaide whipped back and forth like a flag in the growing storm. If she let go, she'd be blown halfway across the town — maybe farther! She closed her eyes tightly, afraid to look at the ground, and called for her grandmother's help again.

"Grandmaaaaaa!"

Grandma X didn't answer, but there was a long, shrieking cry out in the wind, immediately followed by a lone seagull that flew straight at Jaide, smashing into her face. She screamed and almost lost her grip, and tried to butt the seagull away with her head. Somehow she connected and the seagull was thrown against the rail. There was a flash of pale light and the bird tumbled to the ground far below, a lump of dead feathers.

But there were more seagulls swooping in. With a wild lunge, Jaide got a grip on the rail with her other hand as well. Gasping, she pulled herself closer to Grandma X, hoping her touch might bring the old woman back.

She was almost there when three more seagulls crashed into her, this time aiming at her hands. Beaks tore at her skin and knuckles, sending lances of pain up her arms.

"Leave me alone! Go *away*!" Jaide screamed.

Out of nowhere, a violently spinning vortex of air swept sideways across the widow's walk, against the main body of the wind. It picked up the birds in a tangle of legs, beaks, and feathers and hurled them into the trees. Jaide had time only to note that it looked very like the one that had trashed the twins' room before it spiraled off into the sky and disappeared.

Gasping for breath, Jaide resumed her painful creep along the rail. Every time she slid her hands along, she thought she was going to lose her grip, and the rain was making everything slipperier and slipperier. Finally she got close enough to make a desperate, pinching grab at Grandma X's elbow with one hand.

The old woman's gray eyes flickered open at Jaide's touch.

"Oh, dear Jaidith — I'm so sorry! Here."

She reached out to pull Jaide into her embrace — and both got a big surprise. Their minds merged as they had when looking for Jack, only this time it happened in an uncontrolled, wild rush. Jaide's thoughts collided with Grandma X's and became hopelessly entangled. For an instant it felt as though she actually *was* her grandma, with aching joints, a dodgy hip, and the weight of the world on her shoulders. Jaide sensed the battle that was taking place between Grandma X's incorporeal form and The Evil. The two were fighting for control over the storm. The Evil was trying to push back the wind and tide, to redirect the storm surge from its underground tunnels, and Grandma X was trying to keep the storm coming.

Jaide could also feel that The Evil was winning. There were thousands and thousands of minds under its control already, and though most were insects or animals, the collective force of them was like a great, overpowering mass slowly coming down.

But on three sides — north, south, and west — those minds were being held back, and not by Grandma X. It was as if there were physical barriers there, preventing The Evil from attacking from those directions. All that great weight of malignant thought was coming in only from the east.

But it was enough. Grandma X was being slowly overwhelmed.

"Grandma! I'll help!" cried Jaide. She looked up at the clouds scudding past above her, blinked as a raindrop fell straight into her eye, and concentrated her thoughts, trying to imitate what she felt Grandma X was doing.

"Jaide! No!"

Jaide had made a very bad mistake. She felt the storm swirl wildly at her command, as wily and slippery as ice. It didn't want to be controlled by anyone, much less her.

Grandma X reeled, struggling to contain the storm, The Evil, and Jaide's Gift all at once. Both of them staggered back across the widow's walk, lightning playing all around the house as the wind screamed even louder and thunderclaps rattled every window and shook the timbers.

Grandma X did something with her mind. Jaide felt a great outpouring of energy from the old woman, and instinctively pushed away and shut her eyes, just before a figure of searing white light burst out of the old lady and ran up into the clouds, the afterimage of its passage burning through Jaide's eyelids, accompanied by the loudest, most shattering thunderclap of all.

The next thing Jaide knew, she was lying facedown, stunned and deafened — but separate. Her mind was no longer mixed up with her grandmother's, although she could still feel strange echoes of it reverberating inside her skull, and she could not feel the terrible, inexorable pressure of The Evil aimed directly at her.

Slowly, Jaide pushed herself up and looked around. Rain was lashing down everywhere, but there was no more lightning, and the wind had dropped.

Grandma X was slumped against the railing. Her moonstone ring was dull, she wasn't moving, and it looked like she might very well be dead.

CHAPTER FIFTEEN

OUT OF THE
DRAINPIPE

The booming of surf pursued Jack as he ran through the subterranean tunnels. Occasional gleams of light came from drains and vents far above, but they were too small to crawl through or the grilles at their tops were too heavy to lift. He kept his spirits up by reminding himself that there simply had to be an exit. It was only a matter of finding it. He would worry about what happened next when he got there.

Hurrying under another high drain, he felt fresh, clean rain spattering on his head. He stopped and stood faceup underneath it for as long as he dared, trying in vain to get some water into his mouth. Not for the first time, he regretted leaving his pack behind, with his water bottle inside. He was parched. If Grandma X had appeared at that moment and offered him one of her hot chocolate potions, he would have drunk it without hesitation.

The next intersection was a T junction. He studied the options available to him. The left branch angled upward; the right way was flat. The air to the left smelled fresher, too, so that was the way he went.

When the tunnel suddenly dropped and opened onto a wide reservoir of rippling water, he was sure for a moment that he had chosen incorrectly. A waterfall roared out of a pipe above the center of the pool. There was another pipe in the water, through which the water was clearly designed to escape, but the flood was coming much faster than it was going. In the seconds he stopped to consider, the water level rose by nearly an inch.

He had almost turned back when he saw another tunnel on the far side, one accessible by a narrow ledge that skirted the reservoir. He could press himself flat and make his way around on the ledge, then pull himself up into the pipe. If he did that, he would be that much closer to ground level.

Everything said that he should take the higher pipe, but he instinctively felt he should go into the water, toward the submerged tunnel, even though he had no idea where it went. It could lead to a grille he couldn't swim past or to another reservoir that was full to the ceiling, where he would drown.

He looked at the water again, watching the winding current. If the water was flowing, it had to be flowing *somewhere*, and that somewhere might well be the sea, or the river.

But what if there was a grille or a full reservoir?

A slight wave came in and rippled across the water toward him, and as it did, it flickered ever so slightly with an image of Jaide's face, as though she was standing over the reservoir and being reflected in the water.

That was enough for Jack. He chose to go downward and jumped in. The chill of the water hit him like an all-over punch, even though he had already been sodden. It felt as though he was swimming at the South Pole. He gasped and splashed and tried hopelessly to get his breathing under control. How could he dive if he couldn't even hold his breath?

++Jackaran Kresimir Shield! We have found you!++

The voice spoke directly inside his head, but it was followed a second later by a stream of rats and cockroaches that poured out of the higher pipe and threw themselves into the water after him. If Jack had chosen that way, he would have walked right into that horrid mass.

++Wait!++ cried the voice as he gulped a double lungful of air and prepared to dive completely underwater. ++Do not go back to her! She means you ill. She sends storm and tide to flush you out — or drown you.++

"What?" Jack's held breath rushed out of him. "She wouldn't do that."

++If she cannot have you, she will kill you.++

The stab of ice in Jack's heart seemed colder than the water around him. He didn't believe it. His parents would never leave him and his sister in the hands of someone so monstrous. . . . But at the same time, he somehow felt that the voice was telling the truth. Grandma X had sent the tide in . . . but why?

Surely she didn't want him to drown, but there was also a ring of truth to the statement that if she couldn't have him, she'd kill him. . . .

But she's my grandmother, Jack thought weakly.

He was confused. He didn't know what to think. But either way, he was sure of one thing: Getting out of the tunnels was his first priority. If he didn't, he would drown, either way.

Rats splashed around him as he refilled his lungs and let himself fall into the water. With two quick kicks he was in the grip of the current. The pipe gulped him down whole, along with several wriggling rats, and sucked him violently through its depths. He tumbled and turned, bouncing heavily off several obstacles in the first dozen yards. He tried to guide himself with the odd kick or outthrust arm, but he was entirely at the mercy of the current. He could only protect his head and hope his breath lasted.

Light flared ahead of him, and suddenly he was flying through the air into muddy water, where he landed with a splash. He coughed and spluttered and went under twice before he was clear of the torrent pouring out of the storm water outlet. Only then did he manage to right himself and get a decent lungful of air.

When he had gotten his wind back, he wiped his eyes and looked around. He was outside! There was the river walk and, farther along, a squat building that looked like a groundskeeper's hut. The pipe had brought him out not far from where he had gone in.

Although the sky was gray and the rain growing heavier by the second, daylight and fresh air made him whoop for joy.

On the far bank, near River Road, an orange cat ran backward and forward, yowling and waving his tail in a question mark to attract the boy's attention. Jack looked at Ari wearily and considered his options. The police station was in the opposite direction. He could go that way and try to get help — but he suspected that the only way to get answers would be to talk to the cat, who had at least tried to warn him. And, as Ari himself had admitted, cats didn't take sides.

Jack wasn't a great swimmer, but he could make the short crossing. As he neared the shore, Ari ran up to him with his tail upright and quivering. The waterlogged rats that had accompanied Jack through the pipe went the opposite direction, squeaking piteously, their eyes returned to normal. There was not even a whisper of the voice.

"Come on. We have to hurry," said the cat.

"Wait a second," said Jack, hauling himself onto the shore. There was no chance of drying out, not with so much rain hammering down on him. "Hurry *where*?"

"The house, of course! Where it's safe! Come *on*, will you? This rain is going to get even heavier soon."

"Right. Cats don't like getting wet. But who says it's going to get worse?"

"Your grandmother," said Ari through his dripping whiskers. "She sent the storm in, after all —"

"What?! She really *did* try to kill me?"

"No! She sent it to flush you out . . . and to stop The Evil."

"The what?"

"The Evil! The thing inside those rats is coming to join us. Do you think we could get a move on now?"

Jack glanced behind him and saw the waters of the river darken as hundreds of rats and insects burst out of the pipe and began to swim toward him.

++Jackaran! Come back to us!++

Their glowing white eyes made Jack shudder. He understood instinctively that those eyes belonged to the voice, not to the creatures. It had taken them over and made them into one thing, the thing that Ari called The Evil.

Ari hadn't waited for an answer. Jack ran after him and, when he had caught up to the cat, grabbed him by the sodden scruff of his neck and turned his head around.

"What are you doing?" hissed Ari, wriggling.

"Just checking you're not possessed."

"Of course I'm not!" spat Ari, his eyes perfectly clear. "I'm a *cat*."

Jack let him go, reassured on that point, at least. Ari shook his shoulders to straighten himself out, and together they raced up the hill.

Kleo ran onto the widow's walk and came straight over to where Jaide crouched next to Grandma X. The rain didn't seem to bother her. She moved like a cat on a mission, straight to Grandma X's side, where she bent her head and spoke into the old lady's ear.

"Jack's safe," Kleo said in a distinct, cultured voice. "And he's on his way. Why are you lying down?"

Jaide jumped up from her squat with all the grace of a startled frog.

"What did you say?"

"I wasn't talking to — wait. You can hear me?"

"Uh, I guess so," said Jaide. "Unless I've gone crazy. More crazy, that is."

"More like you've woken up," said Kleo. She craned her

head over Grandma X's face and wrinkled her nose. "What happened to her? She's a lot deeper down than normal after a weather-working."

Jaide stared at the cat for almost a full minute. Was this another side effect of having shared powers with Grandma X? Or had she indeed gone crazy? Jaide didn't think so. And, besides, she figured she needed all the help she could get. A talking cat was really nothing compared to everything else that had happened.

"Um, Kleo . . . I tried to help her with the storm and everything, but it went wrong, and then I was in her head, and we got all mixed up, and now I can't wake her up, and suddenly you can talk to me and —"

The words came out in a wild rush that only stopped when Kleo put out a paw and touched her gently on the arm.

"Don't panic," said the cat. "You're a troubletwister. Things never happen in the proper order. Hearing a Warden Companion is a skill that Jack learned faster than you, that's all. A skill is a kind of knowledge, after all, and sometimes the seeds of knowledge can be passed along."

Kleo looked down at Grandma X. Her furred eyebrows bunched together in a close approximation of a human frown. "But we have a big problem now, if even her grand-daughter's touch cannot awaken the old madam."

Jaide's concern for Grandma X was broken into by the sudden recollection of what Kleo had said to her.

"Jack! You said Jack's safe!"

Kleo backed away from her, looking slightly nervous, as though Jaide was a bomb that might go off at any moment.

"Yes, Ari found him. I saw them coming — they're almost here."

Jaide ran down the stairs in one thunderous rush. By the time she reached the front door, she could hear its heavy handle turning. Without thinking, she swept it open, and Jack stumbled inside, practically falling on her. She hugged him tightly, not caring that he stank of mud and worse. She didn't care. He was alive. That was all that mattered.

"Jack! Thank heavens you're here. I need you to —"

"I need a shower," interrupted Jack wearily. "A really, really hot, long shower. And I'll even drink some of that hot chocolate."

"Jack, we were wrong about Grandma — and there's no time for a shower."

"What?" asked Jack. "You wouldn't believe what I've been through — I *have* to have a shower —"

"There really isn't a moment to waste," said Ari, just as Kleo appeared on the first floor landing and called out, "Jaide? The rain is easing, but your grandmother's not getting any drier."

"Yes, we're coming!" shouted Jaide. She took Jack by his muddy hand, both of them talking as they hurried up the stairs.

"You can hear the cats?" he asked.

"Yes," said Jaide. "I wish I could have before."

"How come you can now?"

Jaide opened her mouth, but no words came out. It just wasn't something she could easily explain. Having her mind mixed up with Grandma X must have helped her grow into her powers, but there was a lot of other stuff floating about in her mind now, too, most particularly the image of a handsome man about the same age as her father with floppy brown hair and a narrow black tie. He was bending over an open fob watch with a look of calm concentration on his face. Then, in the memory, he flipped it shut, looked up, and smiled directly at her. It was like a four-second film that kept playing over and over in her head, transplanted there from her grandmother's memories. It had to be the mysterious Grandpa X, or Grandpa Shield, or whatever she was supposed to call him. Her father's father.

"Uh, it just happened. Look, I need your help to get Grandma X inside," she told Jack. Very quickly as they ascended she explained what had happened on the widow's walk, including Grandma X's explanation about The Evil and Wardens and Gifts.

Jack listened carefully, but he was having difficulty taking it all in. Raising a flood to force him out of the sewers seemed a dangerous strategy. What if he hadn't found the exit in time? Why *not* just call in the police to find him? Did being a Warden, or whatever Grandma X was, mean doing things the hard way all the time?

"The phone's out," said Jaide. "Everything's out. Otherwise I would've called an ambulance for Grandma, too."

"Oh, yeah," said Jack. He hadn't noticed the lights were all off. He could see quite clearly, but now that he thought about it, he must be using his special vision. He supposed this was one of the Gifts that Jaide was talking about.

"I saw a lot of downed poles and wires on the way up from the river," Jack said. "It looked like a hurricane went across Dock Road."

"At least you're here now," said Jaide. "And . . . even though I shouldn't have tried to help Grandma X, the storm does seem to be getting quieter."

"Maybe it's done what it needed to," said Jack hopefully as he approached the hatch to the widow's walk. "Maybe it drowned The Evil. Got rid of all the rats and insects and everything."

"Don't be so foolish," said Kleo. She jumped up through the hatch and then leaned back to look down at him with narrowed eyes. "The Evil is getting stronger, if anything. Did you notice the weather vane as we came in?"

Jack nodded. "It was spinning like a top."

"That means The Evil is all around us here, but not *in* any particular hosts."

"So it's left the rats and the insects?"

"Yes. But it will only have done that if it's been able to move up to something . . . or someone . . . that suits its purpose better."

"That's bad, right?" Jack asked.

"Very bad," said Kleo.

"Let's not think about it," said Jaide. "We have to get Grandma X back down and into bed before we can do anything else."

"All right." Jack started to climb up through the hatch, out to the widow's walk.

"Wait," said Jaide, peering closely at him. Two red dots burned on his cheeks, as though he had a fever.

"Did The Evil try to get into *your* head?" she asked. "When you were down underground?"

"Yes." The way Jack spoke the one word suggested it was all he wanted to say about the subject for now, and perhaps ever.

CHAPTER SIXTEEN

NEVER ASK A CAT FOR HELP

It was a lot more difficult to get Grandma X off the slippery widow's walk and down to her bedroom than Jaide had expected. Jack was very tired and kept having to rest, and the top flight of stairs was a big problem. But somehow they managed to half drag and half carry Grandma X to her bedroom door without dropping her even once.

"Come on," whispered Jack as Jaide hesitated by the door. "Hurry up — I'm losing my grip."

Jaide turned the crystal handle, opened it, and peeked in, wary of some kind of magical surprise. It was a perfectly ordinary room, though smaller than she'd expected. There was a single bed, a narrow cupboard, a dressing table, and a bedside table. On the bedside table was a glass of water, a hairbrush, and two pictures in frames. The first was a black-and-white photo featuring the clock maker Jaide had seen in Grandma X's memories. The second photo was in faded color, of two young boys. Jaide wasn't sure, but she thought it looked like her father as a child with a twin brother. But since her father didn't have a twin, she figured it had to be some sort of trick shot with a mirror.

There wasn't time to worry about that. She returned to Grandma X and lifted her arms. Jack took hold of her legs. With a lot of grunting and numerous stop-starts, they managed to get her into the room and levered up onto the bed. Through all of it, Grandma X didn't wake even once. When she was settled, Jaide brushed the hair back from her face and hoped she was going to be all right.

Jack looked on, an extremely worried expression on his face.

"We should try the phone again," he said. "See if we can get an ambulance."

"Nothing like that will work," said Kleo with feline certainty.

"When I saw her all fallen over by the railing . . . I . . . I thought she was dead," Jaide said.

"Are you sure she's *not* dead?" Jack asked hesitantly.

"She's breathing," said Jaide. "I think. . . ."

Kleo leaped up onto the bed and gave Grandma X's face a testing lick with her little pink tongue.

"She lives. But she has delved deep into herself and exhausted her Gift trying to bring the storm under control after Jaide destabilized it," said the cat. "Troubletwisters are dangerous to be around. Your Gifts are unformed and unpredictable, and you haven't learned to control them."

"You shouldn't think of it as your fault, though," said Ari. "If The Evil hadn't managed to manifest here, somehow, all would have been well. In any case, you can't worry about that now. The Evil *is* here, and it wants you and your Gifts, so you need to work out what to do about it."

"We have to get help," said Jaide. "I know the phones and power are out, but maybe —"

"The whole town is cut off," said Kleo. "The Evil is strong enough now to make sure of that."

"So what can we do?" asked Jack.

"You need to look after your grandmother's body until her spirit returns."

"Where has it gone?"

"Very deep inside her innermost self."

"When will it come back?"

"Who knows? But the longer she stays there, the harder it will be for her to come back. Wardens have been lost that way before."

"What if The Evil attacks before she does? We can't stop it!"

"Alarms have been sounded. Help will come... eventually."

"Eventually!" Jaide protested. "That doesn't sound very good."

"All that can be done has been done," said Kleo.

"Well, that's not quite —" Ari began, but he stopped at a sharp glance from Kleo.

"What?" asked Jack. "Is there something *you* can do?"

"No," said Kleo. "We are constrained by an oath we took as kittens."

"There are some loopholes —" Ari stopped again as Kleo's tail slowly beat out three short thuds on Grandma X's bedspread. Ari looked imploringly at the twins, as though begging them to read his mind.

Jaide looked at Jack. They were both thinking the same thing.

Cats!

"Grandma X said we'd be safe in this house," said Jaide slowly. "But I guess without her, that's not true anymore."

Kleo didn't move one iota. Ari's whiskers twitched as if he was desperately trying to keep his mouth shut.

"Maybe not completely true?" said Jack eagerly, trying to interpret the weird vibe the cats had going. "Is there a way we can defend the house against The Evil? At least until Grandma X wakes up?"

Ari looked at Kleo and then down at the floor.

"Downstairs?" Jack guessed immediately.

Kleo's fixed stare turned withering.

"I didn't say a word!" Ari protested. "I didn't even mention the door."

"The blue door? That's it! We need to look in there!" Jaide exclaimed.

Kleo put her head to one side, looking pointedly away from Ari, and sniffed in disappointment.

"I didn't say 'blue' door," said Ari innocently. "It could have been a green door, or a pink door. . . ."

Jack was already heading downstairs, Jaide hot on his heels. With a loud tattoo of shoes they pounded down the stairs and to the front of the house.

They hesitated at the front door, thinking of the rain and The Evil still at large, until Ari caught up with them. Kleo came down more reluctantly behind them, still not looking at Ari, as though she wanted no part in the expedition.

"Is it safe to go out?" asked Jack, thinking of the white

eyes shining in the dark. "I mean, The Evil won't be right outside, will it?"

Ari sniffed around the base of the door and shook his head.

"Does that mean it won't be safe or that The Evil isn't right outside?" asked Jaide.

"The Evil is close, but it has not yet dared cross the boundaries," he told them.

Even with this assurance, the twins went out very cautiously, remembering the rats that had been in the yard the previous night. The rain had eased off a lot, but it was still sprinkling. The yard was a mess, with fallen leaves and branches, and out in the street a light pole leaned over at a drunken angle with a cable hanging off it, sparking occasionally.

There were no birds in the dark sky, and no sign of anything else, be it under the control of The Evil or not. It was quiet, the quiet after disaster, or the unnatural stillness found in the eye of a storm.

The twins hurried to the blue door, but the cats stayed behind, out of the rain. Jaide looked back at them and saw Kleo buffet Ari's ear with her paw, followed by a short, hissed "Fool of a cat!"

"How do we open it?" Jaide asked, thumping the door so hard it rattled on its hinges. It still didn't have a handle or doorknob. The cats didn't answer.

"Look!" Jack had stepped back and was looking up at the sign. "It's changed!"

The handwritten words now said: *The door is open. Lift the latch — but not on your side, that's the catch.*

Jaide read it through twice. It didn't make sense. "The door *isn't* open, otherwise we'd open it."

"Maybe it's not open on this side," said Jack, "but it is on the other."

"What's the use in that?" Jaide's frustration was mounting. "Why would Grandma X leave us such a stupid note?"

"It's a test," said Jack, suddenly remembering Grandma X's words, weirdly accompanied by the aftertaste of hot chocolate in his mouth. "She said, 'Some doors are not meant to be opened before their time.'"

"It's definitely time now. But how do we lift a latch on the other side?"

They stared at the door with identical expressions. This was a challenge, and they were determined to be up to it.

"It's a secret room for Wardens, right?" said Jack.

"I guess." Jaide could see the way he was thinking. "So you need a Gift to open it?"

"Grandma X probably does it with her spirit or whatever it was she sent to me in the tunnels. She just goes in there and lifts the latch."

"But we can't do that," Jaide pointed out. Even after joining with Grandma X, she wasn't sure exactly what her Gifts were. But she *was* clear on what they weren't — and sending out a spirit form was definitely not something she could do. "At least, *I* can't. Do you know what you can do now? Grandma X said your Gifts were of the night and darkness — but it won't be dark for hours and we don't *have* hours. Remember what Kleo said about Grandma X finding it harder to come back the longer she was away? We have to get help before we lose her forever."

Jack nodded and looked up at the sky. Though it was full of dark clouds and showers, there were also patches where the sun was breaking through.

"I can see in the dark," he said, remembering his experiences in the tunnels. "And hide in shadows."

He stopped and looked down at his own shadow, faint on the doorstep. Jaide followed his glance and then swiftly looked back at him.

"Yes," said Jack. He knew she had the same idea. "I can give it a try, anyway."

Jack closed his eyes and imagined his mind leaking out the soles of his feet and into his shadow by the door. Nothing happened at first, but then he felt a strange sensation, like cold water running down on the *inside* of his skin, from the top of his head to his toes.

He opened his eyes and saw Jaide above him, as if he was lying on the ground. Then he saw himself standing next to her, completely still — and he felt the shadow. All the shadows around him were connected, where they overlapped. Darkness bled and joined, allowing someone special like him to travel through it.

Shadow Jack slid under the door, into the shadows of the room. It was like being on a waterslide: easy to get started, but difficult to change direction or stop once you were going. It took him a few tries to get the hang of it before he was able to glide up the inside of the door, next to the latch.

It was a metal bar not much thicker than his thumb. Normally he could have lifted it without thinking. As a shadow, however, it was a completely different matter.

His shadow hand just slid over the metal and the bar didn't shift a millimeter. He couldn't interact with it at all.

Just as he was about to give in, a miniature whirlwind blew in from under the door and spun about on the floor. It went one way and then the other, before approaching the door. It hesitated there for a moment before turning on its side and starting to climb. But before it got close to the bolt, it fell apart, and the dust and tiny pieces of gravel it carried all fell to the ground.

"Dratnation!" said Jaide on the other side, utilizing one of the unique swear words their father invented when he didn't want the twins to hear what he usually said. Jack realized it had been his sister's whirlwind, and she had been trying to use her Gifts to open the door, just as he was.

Shadow Jack slithered down and under the door, then back into his own flesh-and-blood body. He was disoriented for a moment, particularly when he opened his eyes. The light blinded him for an instant, and his head spun from more than just the light. Jaide was squatting next to him, with the fingers of both her hands pressing against the bottom of the door. A thin whistling sound came from the far side, with the occasional tinkling crash.

"That's not going to work," Jack said, tapping her on the shoulder.

She didn't give up. "Give me a minute and I'll get it for sure."

"But you can't see, and that whirlwind is going all over the place. You need help from the inside."

She blinked and looked up at him. Understanding

dawned. "We need to do it together — me pushing and you telling me where to push!"

"Yep," said Jack. Then his face fell. "Uh, that's if I *can* talk as a shadow. . . ."

"Maybe we can talk inside our heads, mind to mind," said Jaide. "Grandma X could do it —"

"And so can The Evil." Jack shuddered. "I don't know if I can cope with mental voices after that."

"I know." Jaide remembered the feeling of The Evil trying to force its way into her mind. "But it'll feel different with us, I'm sure. Anyway, maybe your shadow-self *can* talk. Let's try!"

They turned back to the door. Shadow Jack went under and up again so he could see the latch. Jaide's miniature whirlwind followed a minute later.

Shadow Jack tried to talk, but nothing happened at first. He was moving his mouth, but no sound was coming out. Or at least that's what he thought, until he heard a voice on the other side of the door that wasn't Jaide's but did sound kind of familiar.

"Testing . . . testing . . . I can't make this work, Jaide . . . can you hear me?"

It took him a moment to realize it was his own voice, coming out of his body on the outside.

"Of course I can," snapped Jaide. It took a lot of effort for her to keep her miniature tornado going. "Which way and how far?"

Shadow Jack slid along the door a bit to get a better view.

"Move to the right about a foot . . . a bit less . . . a bit less . . . Perfect! Now go straight up . . . straight up . . . Stop! Go back down and left a bit . . . Left! Okay, start going up again, steady. . . ."

The latch shivered and rose up out of its cradle.

"Almost there! That's it!"

The tornado winked out, and Shadow Jack slipped down and under the door. A few seconds later, the twins leaned on the blue door with all their weight, and with a crash it finally opened.

The secret room was secret no longer.

CHAPTER SEVENTEEN

BEHIND THE BLUE DOOR

The twins slipped warily inside. Two crystal chandeliers fixed to the ceiling sparkled into life, revealing an unexpectedly large room, with one half flight of steps leading down to a lower level and another flight up to a mezzanine floor dominated by a huge mahogany writing desk covered by pots of pens, pencils, and feathery quills, plus stacks of receipts impaled on spikes. Shelves and display cases lined the walls, and they were filled with even more exotic items than the shelves inside Grandma X's house. There were clocks, crystals, telescopes, globes, goggles, and goldfish bowls — far too many things to take in at once.

The room itself was littered with objects too big to fit on shelves. Jack saw a tall rack heavily loaded with outrageous hats, a chair shaped like a dragon's mouth, and a bed board containing the repeated motif of a four-pointed star. Jaide's gaze lit on two cases full of gleaming jewelry, a gold suit of armor, and a fur coat that seemed to be made out of an entire bearskin, including its head. The air was thick with the stink of age and discovery.

"What *is* this place?" Jack asked.

"What the sign originally said, I guess." Jaide cast her mind back. "'Antiques and Articles' — something like that."

"So it is a shop?"

"It's a collection." Ari appeared from behind them. One ear was kinked over, but he seemed otherwise unharmed by Kleo's wrath. "Wardens are always looking for old things. The older the better. But not just any old things. They wouldn't like something that had been buried in the ground for a hundred years, for instance. They like their antiques to be worn in."

"Why?"

"Things that Wardens use take on power from their Gifts," said Kleo in a tight voice. She was sitting stiffly in one corner, beside a trio of large, faded umbrellas. "Particularly when it was made to do that in the first place."

"So are you okay to tell us things now?" asked Jaide pointedly.

"We are bound by our oaths to keep everything we know from all but full Wardens," said Kleo. "Until they are no longer secret. Like this room."

"You mean you can't tell us things until we practically already know them or can work them out anyway?" asked Jack. "Great."

Kleo didn't look at all repentant. "Sardines don't grow on trees," she said with a sniff.

"We're not looking for sardines," said Jaide. "We need to help Grandma before she's lost forever. Won't you even give us a clue?"

The cat met her gaze unflinchingly, and it was Jaide who turned away, feeling faintly ashamed. Promises were important. That was something her parents had hammered into her since she was old enough to talk. But surely when someone's life was at stake, that was the perfect time to break them?

"Troubletwisters are dangerous," the cat repeated. "You being in here is dangerous."

"More dangerous than The Evil?" Jack asked, picking up a skull that had once belonged to a small crocodile or alligator and looking in its crystal eye.

Before Kleo could answer, the crocodile's eye flashed and its jaws snapped open. Jack hastily put it back down, only just avoiding getting one of his fingers bitten off.

"One brass plate," chattered the reptile, "three inches by four, fixed by four two-eighth screws fashioned entirely from silver."

"What does that mean?" Jack asked.

The crocodile didn't answer.

"Be careful, for one thing," said Jaide. "Don't touch anything."

But she didn't follow her own advice, picking up a brightly colored tube with an eyehole at one end.

"Don't put it near your —" Jack started to say. But he was too late. Jaide was already looking into it. "— eye."

"Oh, yeah. Anyway, it's only a kind of kaleidoscope, but with letters." Jaide could see an endless stream of letters rather than random geometric patterns. "Just a whole lot of them, all mixed up . . . Hang on. . . ."

"What?" asked Jack. He was eyeing a short, very highly polished silver sword that was thrust into a block of very dark, gnarly timber.

"The letters spell something backward," said Jaide. "Write this down. Maybe it's another message."

"Write with what?"

Jaide pointed to the desk on the mezzanine without looking away from the tube. Jack reluctantly left the sword and ran up the steps. There were lots of different kinds of paper on the desk, but most of the pens were the really ancient kind with nibs, and some were just cut feathers. Only after a quick hunt did he find a modern ballpoint pen.

"Okay," he called out.

"Write this down," instructed Jaide. "Ready? P-o-t-s-s-r-e-t-s-i-w-t-e-l-b-u-o-r-t-a-m-m-o-c-s-d-r-a-w-e-h-t-o-t-k-o-o-l."

"Okay, that says 'look to the wards comma troubletwisters stop,'" said Jack, reading it backward. "Like an old telegraph. But what are the wards?"

"Grandma X talked about wards," said Jaide thoughtfully. "Whatever they are, I think they're meant to keep The Evil away. But she never said anything else about them."

"So what are these wards, Kleo?" asked Jack. But the cat had disappeared again. Jack opened his mouth to repeat the question to Ari, just in time to see the ginger tom's tail disappear under a leather chair.

Jack bent down to try to talk to the cat and accidentally knocked over a bronze cigarette lighter in the shape of an artillery shell that suddenly roared out a jet of fire four feet high. Jack dived out the way, and sheepishly emerged from under a table a second later, patting down his singed hair.

Jaide laughed, and backed into a globe of the world that spun around and discharged a ferocious spark of static electricity into her arm.

"Ow!"

"I told you. There are a lot of dangerous things in here," said Kleo's voice from somewhere hidden. "You need to be careful."

"It's not like we have any choice," said Jaide. "Grandma X could be dying up there! If you won't tell us exactly what we can find to help us, then we'll just have to keep looking."

"Kleo, I really think given the circumstances that the oath is flexible enough —" Ari started to say from his position under the lounge.

He didn't finish. Eight of the dozen or more clocks in the room suddenly started to chime frantically, the needles on three barometers swung to STORMY, two flags unfurled, a mechanical drumming bear beat out a staccato alarm, and the crocodile skull chattered its teeth.

"The Evil," warned Kleo, appearing from the inside of an ornate box with the lid on her head like a hat. Her back arched and she spat: "It's gotten strong enough to pass the garden walls and gate!"

Jaide looked around, her heart pounding. They'd left the door open, and coming straight at them was Luger, the pit bull terrier that had chased them the day before. Its eyes were shining white, its jaws were foaming, and its skin was encrusted with cockroaches, which were somehow now joined to the beast, their heads buried under its skin.

"Out of the way!" Jack yelled. Jaide dodged aside as in one swift motion Jack picked up the cigarette lighter and pointed it at the dog. A jet of blue flame shot out at Luger, who fell back, his cockroach coat all writhing legs and flapping wings. Jaide dashed forward and slammed the door as Jack sent another blast of fire through the closing gap.

Jaide slammed the latch down. The clocks stopped their frantic chiming, but the mechanical bear kept up a slow, disturbing beat on his drum, and the barometers stayed set on STORMY.

"Can The Evil get in here?" asked Jaide. She looked around for the cats. "Come on — you *really* have to help us."

Two cat heads appeared from under the lounge. They both looked at Jaide, then Ari looked very intently at Kleo.

"Oh, for goodness' sake," said Ari. "The oath says 'Wardens,' but these are very special circumstances, and these two are already more than your typical troubletwisters."

"I swore an oath, and I stand by it," Kleo said, then withdrew back under the lounge. Her muffled voice continued from somewhere behind it. "I know you do not, Aristotle."

"Can you please just answer the question!" snapped Jack.

"Seeing as I have no principles, I suppose I might as well," said Ari with a sharp look at Kleo. "Ultimately The Evil can get in here. But even withdrawn as she is, your grandmother's power still inhabits this house. The Evil will not easily breach the defenses."

"But if we're stuck in this room, we can't even check on Grandma!"

"It is fortunate, then, that we're not stuck here," said Ari. "Kleo, look out!"

Kleo poked her head out from under a rich tapestry depicting an elephant draped in robes and tassels, in the process revealing a hidden doorway.

"What? Oh, Ari!"

"Hey, thanks, Ari . . . and Kleo," said Jaide. The twins ran over to lift up the tapestry and looked at the steps behind it.

"Where does this go?" Jack asked. "We hunted all over the ground floor but we didn't find the other door."

"That's because the other end isn't on the ground floor," said Kleo. She lifted her nose and haughtily stalked up the steps.

Jaide followed her up. The steps ended in a wooden panel. As Kleo trod on the third step below it, the panel slid silently back to reveal the third-floor landing of the house above them.

"Uh, how can this come out on the third floor?" Jaide asked cautiously. "It's, like, thirty feet up, but there are only six normal steps."

"Architectural magic was one of your great-grand-father's gifts," said Ari, who was coming up behind, careful to keep Jaide's legs between himself and Kleo. "It was enormously troublesome when he was a troubletwister himself. He kept losing his bedroom, I believe."

Jaide stepped through the open panel, wondering what she'd feel as she did so. But it felt absolutely normal. She just emerged on the third floor next to Grandma X's bedroom. However she had managed to cross the intervening space, it was no different from stepping across an ordinary threshold.

"Wow," said Jack, jumping through and landing with a thud.

"I'll look in on Grandma," Jaide told him. "You check that the doors and windows on the ground floor are all closed and latched."

"I'll help," said Ari with a cautious glance at Kleo, who ignored him.

Jack thundered down the stairs with Ari at his heels and the artillery shell cigarette lighter clutched tightly in one hand. Jaide and Kleo went into Grandma X's room.

Kleo jumped up on the bed to sit at Grandma X's feet. The old woman was lying on her side with her hands cupped under her head and her mouth parted. She looked almost childlike. Her worry lines and wrinkles had smoothed away, as though she was completely oblivious to the troubletwisters' plight. Her eyes didn't so much as flicker when Jaide touched her forehead to see if she had a fever. Her skin was as cool as marble. There was no way to tell how much longer she had before she couldn't return. It might be hours, or minutes.

"Maybe we should try to carry her to a doctor," Jaide said. "Or one of us could go —"

"No mere human doctor can help her," Kleo said. "And if you leave the house now, The Evil will take you."

"So what can we do?" asked Jaide. "We have to do something! Maybe we could —"

She stopped talking as the moonstone ring on Grandma X's hand gave a tiny flash of light and the faint whistle of a breath came from between her lips.

"Quiet!" said Kleo urgently. The cat leaped to the bed board and leaned over Grandma X's face. "Listen."

Jaide leaned in, too, till her head was touching Kleo's ear.

"Ward damaged," Grandma X whispered. "Root of problem . . . must . . . fix ward. . . . Kleo . . . help them!"

Before Jaide could ask a question, the light in the moonstone ring faded. A soft breath came from Grandma X's mouth, but if it carried any words, they were lost as Jack thundered back, out of breath.

"There are hundreds of dogs outside! It's horrible — they're all white eyed and they've got insects all over them and they're completely quiet, just watching the windows and the doors. What are we going to *do*?!"

"Grandma just told us a ward is broken," said Jaide. "She said we had to fix it."

"What?!" Jack exploded. "We don't even know what they are! How can we fix that?"

"She also told Kleo to help us," said Jaide. She looked at Kleo very sternly. "You heard her, didn't you?"

"I'm not entirely sure that an oath made as a *kitten*, sworn in *blood* on a saucer, can be overturned by a mere instruction," Kleo said. She was about to go on when Ari suddenly stood up on his hind legs and gave a very nasty, hissing yowl. It gave Jaide and Jack a start, since Ari had always seemed so placid and under Kleo's paw.

"But then again," Kleo continued, both eyes warily on Ari, "I suppose that, taken with the circumstances, your heritage, her order . . . I have no choice but to obey."

Ari backed down and made a playful strike at his own tail, which was curling toward his mouth.

Jaide never thought she could feel such relief simply from a cat actually doing what it was told.

"So what are the wards?" she asked. "And how do we fix a broken one?"

CHAPTER EIGHTEEN

SOMETHING GROWING, SOMETHING READ

We'd best go back to the blue room," said Kleo. "Everything you need is there, and there's nothing more you can do here for your grandmother."

Jaide took a look out the window before they left. As Jack had said, the house was surrounded by white-eyed dogs, whose shaggy coats writhed and crawled with the insects that were becoming part of them. But even worse than that, Jaide thought, was the way they all turned their heads at the same time and looked up at her window. The dogs weren't just one breed — they were every breed. Hounds and poodles. Dobermans and dachshunds. German shepherds and pugs. It was as if every dog in town had been taken over by The Evil.

She couldn't see any people at all, or hear any of the usual traffic noises. It was strangely quiet, save for the occasional patter of rain as a remnant squall from the storm blew over.

Grandma X didn't move as Jaide brushed past the bed and headed for the door. She hated leaving her alone, but she felt a lot better knowing that her bedroom was little more than six steps away via the secret passage.

They went back down to the antiques store, where Kleo immediately started prowling around the room, diving over and under displays and peering into bookcases. "It's here somewhere. Ari, can you help me?"

"I would if you'd tell me what you're looking for."

"That piece she bought last month — in the roll, remember? She said it would be for the troubletwisters' room, when they were ready."

"Ah." The ginger head turned to consider the many alternatives. "Over here, I think." He disappeared into a half-open drawer and emerged a second later. "Yes. In here."

Jack pulled open the drawer and found several long, white fabric tubes, some as slender as wands, others as thick as a telescope. "Huh?"

"That one," said Ari, tapping one of the smaller ones with an outstretched paw. "Unroll it."

Jack did as he was told, revealing a square of embroidered tapestry that he held up to the light. Instead of HOME SWEET HOME, it read:

SOMETHING GROWING
SOMETHING READ
SOMETHING LIVING
SOMEONE DEAD

"What does that mean?" Jack asked.

"Every Warden knows this rhyme," said Kleo. "It's one of the first things they learn."

"But what does it *mean*?"

"The Evil comes from somewhere outside our world," explained Kleo. "But it can't come through just anywhere. It needs to find weak points, where it is easier for it to reach out and find suitable hosts. Portland is one of those weak points, and as in other such places all around the globe, Wardens have made wards to reinforce its natural defenses."

"Okay so far," said Jaide. "But what are these wards?"

"The wards are magical barriers that hold back The Evil and prevent it coming through into our world. There are always four wards, one for each cardinal point of the compass. They come in many different shapes and guises, but the tapestry you hold describes their general type. There will always be 'something growing, something read, something living, someone dead.'"

"Fine," said Jaide. "So what are the four wards of Portland?"

Each cat looked at the other, waiting for an answer.

"She never told me," said Ari. "What about you, Kleo?"

Kleo half lidded her eyes. "She never told me, either."

"You don't know?!" exclaimed Jack. "That's just great!"

"If you can't even tell us what the wards are," said Jaide, "how can we fix the broken one?"

"I'm sure you can work it out," said Ari in an encouraging tone. His words were somewhat undermined by Kleo's sniff. "That's one of the things Wardens do. Very clever at finding things out, they are."

"We're not Wardens . . . yet," said Jack. He didn't say aloud that the odds were against their ever becoming proper Wardens. It was far more likely they were going to get absorbed by The Evil and lost forever.

"But it's true we're good at working things out," said Jaide. "We got through the blue door, didn't we?"

"That is true," said Jack.

"Are there any places Grandma X used to visit a lot?" Jaide asked the cats. "I mean, more often than anywhere else? Any particular things she looked at?"

Kleo shook her head. "No."

"She usually inspected the wards in her spirit form," said Ari. "So no one could see where she went."

"You never followed her?" asked Jaide. "Can't you guys do that spirit traveling thing, too?"

"We could if we wanted to, I'm sure," said Kleo. "Not that we need spirit traveling to move about mysteriously."

"Your grandmother . . . ah . . . discouraged our *perfectly natural* curiosity," said Ari. "We had to eat dry food for a week the last . . . that is to say, we really, *really* don't know where she went. You'll have to find some other way to work out where the wards are."

Jaide looked toward the door. The Evil was out there, in all those hideous dog-insect creatures. It could be spreading into more living things; it could be doing anything; maybe it was going to attack at any moment, and they were stuck and clueless and she could feel a terrible panic in her stomach, rising up to choke her —

"She took us on a drive the day after we arrived, remember?" Jack suddenly said. "She seemed distracted, like she felt something was up but didn't know what it was. Maybe she was checking on the wards then, without us knowing."

"Yes!" exclaimed Jaide. "Good thinking, Jack!"

"We went to the cactus park," he said. "There was that really big, weird cactus there, the one she went right up to and looked at the top with her funny little binoculars."

"Yeah, I'd forgotten that," said Jaide thoughtfully. "I guess the cactus could be the 'something living'?"

"Or 'something growing.' She also took us to Mermaid Point."

"That's right. She said something about a giant —"

"That it was a her, not a him."

"So maybe the rocks are the giant!"

"Alive or dead?"

"Either way, it fits."

"'Something read,'" mused Jack, running a finger across the cable-stitched letters on the fabric before them. "What could that be?"

"A sign?"

"There are lots of those, even in Portland."

"A book?"

"We didn't go anywhere near the library."

"No, but Kleo's owner has the bookshop around the corner from here."

"If the ward was one of his books, and he sold it, what would that mean for Portland?"

"Okay, something else, then."

"It could be anywhere. We'll never find it!"

"Hang on! I wonder . . ."

Jaide was looking at a compass on the wall, an old brass compass with an internal card that had NORTH, EAST, SOUTH, and WEST written out in very large red letters, with all the lesser points in tiny black type.

"I've just remembered," said Jaide slowly. "When I tried to help Grandma X with the storm, I could *feel* The Evil pressing in on us — but only from one direction, from the east. It was like we had walls around us on the other sides, so that east was the only direction it could attack us from."

"So it must be the East Ward that needs fixing," said Jack. "But east of what?"

"This house," said Ari. "We know that much. The wards will be arranged around this central point."

"Where did she take us that's east?" asked Jaide.

"The graveyard," said Jack. "And the lighthouse."

As he said *lighthouse*, the crocodile skull started to chatter.

"One brass plate, three inches by four, fixed by four two-eighth screws fashioned entirely from silver, the plate etched in acid, the words made clear."

"What does that mean?" asked Jack.

"Who knows?" said Kleo. "That skull spouts off all the time."

"'The words made clear,'" mused Jaide. "Words to be read, like the rhyme says? One of the wards?"

The crocodile skull laughed maniacally, its jaw moving so much that its vibration shuddered it off the table. It fell into a woven wastepaper basket, which muffled its cackling until it fell silent a few seconds later.

"Words on a plate," said Jack. He bent down and very carefully retrieved the skull, making sure his fingers were not at risk. "Some of the stones in the cemetery had brass plates on them."

"There might be a brass plate in the lighthouse, too," said Jaide.

"There are lots of brass plates all over the place. How can we tell if one of them is the 'something read' ward?"

"The silver screws, maybe?"

"That's if the skull was talking about the ward and not some other plate," said Jack.

"There *are* instruments that indicate the presence of Warden magic," suggested Kleo. She pointed with her paw. "Ari, show them the flower."

Ari jumped across to one of the shelves and gently butted a tall silver cylinder with his head. Jack lifted it down, took off the lid, and he and Jaide looked at the glass flower inside.

"If you take it out, the flower will change color to indicate the presence of Warden magic," said Kleo. "Powerful magic makes it turn a very deep blue. I'm sure it would do that in the presence of a ward."

"So if we took this and held it near any brass plates we find in the cemetery or the lighthouse, it would tell us which one is the ward," said Jaide.

"How do we fix the ward, though?" Jack asked.

"Finding it is the first step." A plan was already starting to form in Jaide's mind. "Then we'll need to see what has to be done."

"But we're surrounded by The Evil," protested Jack with a shudder. "Those dogs . . ."

"I think I know how to find the brass plate and get back here without being caught by the dogs," said Jaide. She put the silver cylinder under her arm. "Let's go up on the roof again."

When Jack opened the hatch at the top of the last flight of stairs, he was surprised at how old the day was getting. Through a break in the clouds, the lazy afternoon sun was sinking slowly into the last quarter, sending long shadows across the yard below.

There were even more dogs in the yard now. Hundreds of them, made horribly shaggy and creepy by heavy encrustations of cockroaches and other bugs. Their eyes were white and they all raised their snouts together as they caught the scent of their human prey.

"At least they're only watching," said Jaide. "They'd come inside if they could."

"Somehow that doesn't make me feel any better," said Jack.

He looked farther afield. The yellow shoulder of a bulldozer was visible over the fence by the derelict house next door, but there were no people in sight. The storm had made everyone stay indoors. He swung Grandma X's opera glasses south, over houses along Cutting and Crescent streets, two curving streets south of Watchward Lane, then looked farther east. The roads had no moving cars on them, and there was a train stopped at the station just south of the Little Rock.

The old willows by the river were bent over in answer to the wind blowing along the river off the sea. Jack thought of the tunnels under those willows and the sewers that ran to the river and the sea. He fervently hoped he would never, ever see the inside of those sewers again.

Jaide also looked out. She saw nothing strange to the northwest, just endless fields of newer houses and land cleared for future development. The little church by the cactus garden showed no sign of interference. The hospital was brightly lit, the only big building to have lights on, but then it would have its own generators, Jaide guessed. She could also see several work crews on the far end of Main Street, raising power poles and doing something that sent sparks from their welders falling like magical sprays of jasmine.

But there were no workers doing anything to the fallen power poles near Grandma X's house, and there were no people on the streets nearby. It was as if the town had been selectively abandoned, and everyone had left the area within five hundred yards of the house.

Jaide turned her attention to the north. The coastal reserve was empty apart from two brave fishermen wading out on the sand flats. The dredger was safely docked. The rocks of Mermaid Point did look a lot like a sleeping giant, even from this angle, but she couldn't tell if there were rocks missing or any other obvious damage.

Waves dashed themselves white against the breakwater. Masts swayed and bobbed in the marina. Like the coastal reserve, the cemetery and church were empty. Mourning could wait for better weather, Jaide supposed. She tried to see any brass plates, but it was too far, and there wasn't enough sun for any bright reflections. Not that any of the brass plates they'd seen before were clean enough to shine.

The lighthouse was as lifeless as it always seemed to be. It was too early for the automatic light to be on.

That left only the Rock, and although Jaide scanned its steep flanks carefully, she found nothing to suggest that it was either home to the ward or under attack by The Evil.

"See anything?" Jack asked.

"Nope," she said. "You?"

Wind caught her around the body and tangled in her hair. She felt a sudden surge of weightlessness and quickly handed Jack the silver cylinder so she could hold on to the rail.

"Nothing useful, except it looks like it's going to rain again soon."

They both looked east. A vast storm front of dark clouds was building up on the horizon, its interior lit by intense flashes of lightning.

"It's going to be a vile night," said Ari from his position by Jaide's feet. "The first storm was your grandmother's work. The one coming stinks of The Evil."

"Much of the house's protection is built into its timbers, infused with your great-grandfather's Gift. He built this place as a wedding present for your grandmother," said Kleo. She was perched on the railing, ignoring the wind and the Evil-infested dogs below. "If a storm were to physically break a wall, that would weaken the magical defenses, perhaps enough for The Evil to come in."

"So we need to find the broken ward and fix it before the storm hits," said Jaide. "Almost certainly to the east."

"Yes," said Jack. He was still looking out to the lighthouse and the cemetery. "But how can we get past the dogs?"

"I'll glide there," said Jaide. She was almost airborne already, even though she was doing as her grandmother had suggested, thinking heavy thoughts and holding on to the rail.

Jack stared at her as though she'd gone mad. "You'll what?"

"Trust me," she said, with a glance up at the sky. There was a bright patch of sun above her, one that she thought would last for ten or fifteen minutes before it was obscured by the outrider clouds of the storm front. She could feel the sunshine pouring into her, fueling her Gift. Grandma X had said Jaide's powers were of the sun and wind, and she felt that to be true, as both were now powerfully present. "It'll be easy. I'll be there and back in a few minutes. I'll take the flower, and when we know exactly what and where the ward is, we'll work out how to fix it."

"Hang on a minute," said Jack. He looked around the sky. "I don't think it's a good idea."

At the same time Kleo said, "Jaide, wait! This is very dangerous. Your Gifts are raw and you have not been trained!"

"I know I can do this, for Grandma," said Jaide confidently. The sunshine was flowing through her, lifting her spirits, making her feel like she could tackle anything. "Give me the flower."

Reluctantly, Jack opened the silver cylinder and took out the flower. As he touched it, the glass changed from being completely colorless to a very light, cornflower blue. But as he gave it to Jaide, the color darkened to a richer, royal blue.

"See," said Jaide. "My Gift is strong right now. Help me up."

"Please be careful," said Jack quietly as he gave her a hand onto the top of the rail. She stood there for a moment, testing her balance. The wind scattered her hair across her face, and she felt a lightness in her stomach, a joy that came at least partly from the thought that she was special. In almost no time at all, it seemed, she had gone from being an ordinary kid to someone who could fly. No one else could do what she was about to attempt.

"Let go, Jack."

The pressure of his fingers around her ankles fell away. He looked up at her as she leaned forward into thin air and let the wind take her.

CHAPTER NINETEEN

THE RETURN OF SHADOW JACK

Jack bit his tongue in fear as his sister dived forward with the glass flower in her hand, then he gasped in wonder and relief as she was swept up by the wind. Banking to the left, she circled the house once and then, climbing steadily, took off toward the cemetery.

As her shadow crossed the yard, every dog guarding the house started barking. Jack looked down in surprise, because they'd been so silent before. He was even more surprised to see them all in a frenzy of distress, some writhing and biting at their insect-ridden backs, some rolling in the dirt, most of them barking madly but more than a few whimpering in abject fear instead.

They were behaving like normal dogs now. A Labrador looked up at him piteously, and he saw the whiteness ebbing from its sad brown eyes.

"The Evil has left them," said Kleo. "But where has it —?"

With a raucous chorus and a thunderous slap of wings, hundreds of birds burst out of the trees all around the house. White eyed and single-minded, they flew straight up to become a great winged host, a dark cloud of enemy birds that spread across the sky.

"Jaide!" screamed Jack to the small, retreating speck that was his airborne sister. "Watch out!"

Jaide heard Jack's cry but not the actual words. They were lost in the rushing of the wind. Air pressed close all around her, coiling and uncoiling like a restless, invisible snake. She felt safe in its insubstantial strength, and being so high above the ground didn't frighten her at all. She felt as though she could fly for hours, carried by the wind and warmed by the sun.

Then the first of the seagulls smashed into her back, squawking and pecking, and everything went horribly wrong. Surprise made her wobble and dip. She dropped the glass flower, and it tumbled away.

She started to fly down in a desperate attempt to catch it, but a magpie and another seagull swooped against her head, knocking her off course. More birds struck her back and legs, mobbing her from every side. Suddenly everything was feathers and claws, and she was falling, spearing toward the ground.

In despair she saw the flower hit ahead of her, turning to clear glass just before it shattered into a thousand pieces.

Fear stabbed through her, but it was overlaid by the furious determination that had fueled her ever since Grandma X had been injured. She wouldn't be knocked out of the sky by a bunch of birds — she *wouldn't*. She would blow *them* away!

Without even thinking about what she was doing, Jaide took in a very deep breath, filling her lungs and her cheeks to bursting. Then she blew it all out, turning her head so that the blast of air from her mouth hosed in all directions.

Far more than a human breath issued from between her lips. A great wind swept the birds away from her, but it also sent Jaide into a violent spin farther up into the sky, surrounded by a cloud of stunned and squawking birds.

Jack watched in horror, gripping the rail so tightly, he gave himself splinters without noticing. The birds had attacked Jaide all at once and she had gone into a dive; he'd seen the flower fall, but then the birds had been blown in all directions, and now Jaide was spinning wildly up into the sky.

He understood what was happening immediately. Jaide's Gift was out of control, exactly as Kleo had feared it might become. At least she wasn't falling anymore, but she was climbing way too high and way too fast.

"Jaide!" he called, waving. "Jaide! Come back!"

Jaide ran out of breath. For a moment she thought that this would stop the wild, ferocious wind that had blown the birds away and sent her into the sky. But it didn't. She was still surrounded by a jet stream that was driving her straight up like a rocket.

Far below her, she heard a faint cry.

"Jaide! Focus! Fly down here!"

Jaide didn't feel like she could focus. She felt like throwing up. The world was spinning, the wind was blowing madly, and she was suddenly freezing cold.

"Jaide!!"

But Jack's voice was like a lifeline. Somehow, she did manage to focus on it. She tried to imagine that his voice was a real lifeline, and visualized the remnant sunshine wrapping around his words, weaving a rope that would hold her down.

"Aim for the house, Jaide! Aim for the house!"

Jaide's rapid ascent slowed as she concentrated harder on being pulled back to the ground by her lifeline. The wind faltered and began to dart in different directions, as if it had lost heart. Jaide was jerked and shoved around, but she knew she was winning the battle for control.

"Down," she said firmly to the wind, and, amazingly, the wind ebbed. Jaide began to spin and flitter down like a leaf falling from a tree.

"Faster, Jaide! The birds are coming back!"

Jaide ignored the warning. The last thing she wanted to do was go faster. Her hold on the breeze was tenuous and she thought if she tried to change anything, she would plummet like a stone.

Immediately she wished she hadn't thought about falling, because then she couldn't think of anything else, and all of a sudden she *was* falling, the wind had dropped, and all her weight returned.

But she was almost at the roof of the house. Jaide hit the topmost turret hard, bounced off, and then, with a despairing cry and a wild grab, reached up and caught the moon-and-stars weather vane.

The birds swooped in but did not press their attack. Jaide clung to the weather vane and shut her eyes for several very long seconds.

"Can you move?" Jack was calling to her again. "Creep around to your right. There's a ledge there. If you climb down a bit, then across to the chimney to your right, I'll pull you in."

Jaide did as she was told with her eyes tightly shut. She didn't want to look down, and she never wanted to fly again. Not until she had her Gift completely under control, anyway.

Jack's hands caught her and pulled her over the rail.

"Well done," he said. "Though you do look like you're about to throw up."

Jaide gave him a furious look, rushed back to the rail, and vomited over the side. Jack patted her on the back as she said, "I would have been all right if you hadn't said anything."

"Sorry," said Jack.

Jaide was sick again, then she stood up straight and wiped her mouth.

"There goes that plan," she said. "What are we going to do now?"

"I had a thought," said Jack. He had remembered the odd little jump he had taken in the tunnels, from inside a mound of rats and bugs to safety inside a shadow. What if he could do more than just move his mind along a shadow — what if he could move the rest of him as well? It would have made getting into the blue room a lot easier than it had been, for a start. "The sun is going down. There are a lot of shadows. I can go and look for the brass plate instead of you."

"But I lost the flower," Jaide pointed out. She felt very down and defeated, an emotion made stronger because of its sharp contrast to how great she'd felt when she'd first flown off the house. "How will you know if you've found the ward?"

"Ari, Kleo, do you know of anything else I could use to find the ward?" asked Jack. "Something I can use as a shadow?"

Ari shut his left eye and stared out with his right, then shut his right eye and stared with the left. Then he opened both eyes and said, "No. I'm afraid not. Though a full Warden would just recognize the ward —"

"There *is* something," interrupted Kleo. "You remember the Warden Nickolanci, Ari? She came to see Grandma X last year and stayed for three days?"

"Yes," said Ari. "She brought rollmop herrings. You ate most of them."

"She is a Shadow Walker, like you, Jack," said Kleo. "She could manipulate and shape shadows, and she said something once, that she could use the *memory* of a shadow, if something had cast one long enough in the same place."

"What does that mean?" asked Jack. His mind was racing, thinking of the possibilities of manipulating and shaping shadows. He was very keen to give it a go.

"Nicki could use the shadow of an object when she herself was a shadow," said Kleo. "She could, for example, take the shadow of a sword and wield it. But I'm thinking that the flower was in that silver case for a long time, its shadow with it —"

"You mean I could take the memory of the shadow of the flower and use it to find the right brass plate!" interrupted Jack. "Though it wouldn't change color —"

"It would change tone or density," said Jaide, who was more into art classes than Jack. "I guess it would go black. But I'm not sure you should go out, even as a shadow. Who knows what The Evil can do to you? I mean, rats and birds might be nothing compared to what it can do with shadows."

"You tried your way," said Jack. "It's my turn now."

"It's not about turns," said Jaide.

"Can you think of anything else?" Jack pointed to the approaching storm. Below, the dogs had fallen silent again and were watching the house with creepy intensity. "We can't just wait until the storm blows the house down and The Evil walks in!"

Jaide looked at the clouds.

"I guess you're right," she said.

"All I need is a shadow to start with," said Jack.

They circled the widow's walk, looking for a point where the shadows intersected the house. There weren't many tall trees to the west, but there was a shapely elm behind one of the shops on Dock Road. Its shadow reached far across the front yard, just touching one of the drawing room windows.

"That'll do," Jack said, and he headed for the stairs. Jaide followed, glad to put the widow's walk behind them. She had gotten cold up in the high, thin air, the last of the sun was fading fast, and she no longer trusted the wind or her ability to use it.

Jack pulled back the drawing room curtains and looked out.

"The rats are back," he said. "A few of them at least. Over by the wall."

Jaide looked out, too. There weren't many of them, as Jack had said, but they had the milky eyes she had learned to fear. She saw a couple with normal eyes and was relieved for a moment, until she realized they were not really rats, but rat-shaped composites made up of cockroaches, earwigs, and other insects.

"Sentries," guessed Jack. "I wonder what the rest of The Evil is up to?"

"Be careful," said Jaide. "It'll be waiting for us to try something else."

"Hey, I'll be a shadow. What can go wrong?"

Jack regretted saying this the second it came out, but it was too late. Jaide looked as if she was going to go all Kleo-vs-Ari on him.

"I mean I'll be *very* careful," Jack said seriously.

"I wish Dad was here," said Jaide.

"Yeah," said Jack. "But he never is, is he?"

Ari opened his mouth as though to say something, but shut it again with a snap at a sharp look from Kleo.

Jaide didn't notice. She had gone back to looking at the watching rats as Jack settled himself on a chair. He opened the silver cylinder and put it on the floor, then placed his hand into the shadow of the elm where it fell through the window. He closed his eyes, even though he wasn't sure if that made a difference.

"Good luck," whispered Jaide.

Her voice grew faint as Jack's mind found the tree's shadow and slipped into it, like a fish into a stream. Following it was as easy as wishing. The world slid around him, gray and blurry, and when he looked up, he saw himself in the chair.

The silver cylinder was nearby, and it had something in it. The memory of the shadow. Shadow Jack reached in and pulled out a flower that had the color and consistency of a light, white mist. But as he touched it, it got darker and more defined, and he had no trouble holding it in his hand.

Shadow Jack slid along the shadow of the branch, out through the window to where the shadow of the trunk fell across the road. There was plenty of shadow to follow from there, and Jack slipped along to Dock Road, heading east. He lost his bearings for a moment, as light and shade crisscrossed everywhere, and it was hard to make out landmarks when he was pressed flat against the ground or vertically up a wall. Luckily, the lighthouse was visible from just about anywhere in the town, and even through his blurry shadow-vision he always found it again. All he had to do was choose shadows that led toward it and he would be fine.

That was the plan. But the farther he went, the harder he found it to move. It was as if an elastic band connected his mind and his body, and the more it stretched, the more difficult it was to go on. Every extra foot cost him more effort until it seemed like he was fighting harder and harder just to stay where he was. If he let go, he would snap back to himself in an instant.

Then, as Shadow Jack strained to move forward, he saw someone walking toward him along Dock Road —

a woman in overalls with a low cap on her head. Shadow Jack paid her no attention, beyond vaguely noting that it was the woman with the sad eyes who had been fixing the playground equipment, Rennie. He ignored her, all his energy focused on trying to move.

Come on, Jack, he said to himself, and he slid forward a few feet, not noticing that the woman had come up right behind him. *You can do it!*

Something grabbed him by the scruff of his neck and pulled him out of the shadow. All of a sudden, light flared and his strange vision changed back to normal. The shadow flower slipped straight through his fingers and fell back into the shadow, like water to the sea, mixed and lost forever.

Even worse than that, somehow Jack was back in his usual, physical body — but he was where his shadow had been. Standing on Dock Road, with someone — something — holding the back of his neck.

Desperately, Jack wriggled out of that grip, only to find himself taken by the arm and spun around to face Rennie. Her eyes were a fierce, glowing white, and though she spoke, her mouth didn't move at all.

++You can cease searching, Jackaran Kresimir Shield,++ said the woman. ++You have found us!++

"But — but you're a person!" he gasped, trying to pull away. The grip on his arm was immovable.

++All join us,++ said The Evil. Jack could feel the pressure of thousands of mostly animal and insect minds behind the words in his head. ++All desire to become one.++

"No . . ." said Jack. He tried to sound strong, but it came out weak. "I won't join you! I won't!"

++You will,++ said The Evil with a terrible, grim certainty. ++You brought us here, troubletwister. You and your sister broke the ward. Your inner nature wishes to join us — and if you do, you will become something far more powerful than any mere Warden.++

"No," whispered Jack. "That's not true. We didn't . . . I don't . . ."

But inside he was wondering if he and Jaide *had* somehow broken the ward. What if their uncontrolled Gifts had done it without them even knowing? Grandma X said troubletwisters were dangerous. Maybe they'd done it and she hadn't even known.

A treacherous part of Jack wondered what the point of being a Warden was if they couldn't stop a couple of *children* stuffing everything up. . . .

++It is destiny, Jackaran. Your destiny. You *will* join us, and we will keep you safe and sound forever.++

The Evil lifted Rennie's right hand and brought it down to cup the top of Jack's head.

Jack felt the force of The Evil magnify a hundredfold, and knew that if it managed to grip his skull, his strength would fail. He couldn't break free of the grip on his arm, so he didn't even try. Instead he let himself *flow* away, *all* of him away, dropping into the shadow at his feet with his entire being.

The Evil snatched as he fell, but it was too late.

But Jack couldn't move his physical self through shadow

very far. Despite his desperate attempts to get away, he popped out only a dozen yards off. The Evil in Rennie's body crossed the space in a blur of movement, far faster than anyone normal could run.

Jack jumped as it struck, and went into the shadow again. This time, he controlled where he came out, behind a tree. The Evil had to go around, and in those few vital seconds Jack managed to sprint some distance. Even so, Rennie was on him again in a second, and he only just managed to reach another shadow before her hand closed on his ankle.

He reappeared a handful of yards away, The Evil's host right behind. They proceeded halfway along Dock Road that way, Jack jumping in and out of shadows with The Evil hot on his heels. Then it occurred to him that he didn't have to follow the road at all. He could go anywhere the shadows took him, and as long as he reappeared in a new spot quickly enough to avoid being caught, he would escape.

He found the shadow of a long tree branch that took him over a shop, almost as far as Watchward Lane, and shadow-jumped there. But the constant switching into shadow with his real body was incredibly difficult. His head was spinning, he felt sick, and he couldn't focus his eyes.

Even worse than that, he'd been gone longer than he thought possible. The sun was nearly down. When it set, the shadows would go, too. What that meant, he didn't know. Would he be able to shadow-jump anywhere at all, or nowhere?

++Jackaran! Come back!++

The cry came from Rennie's throat, too, and the despair he heard in it was heartbreaking.

Jack dived again, forcing himself along a shadow that led to Grandma X's house. Too weak to go far, he popped out right in front of the gateway and fell facedown in the gravel.

He had just gotten up and was crawling along the drive toward the front door when he heard footsteps behind him, a measured, steady crunching on the gravel.

"Jaide!" he shouted, but his voice was affected by shadow, and came out as only a weak croak. "Ari! Help!"

++Why are you running, Jackaran?++ asked The Evil inside his head. **++This isn't a game.++**

Jack twisted around as white-eyed Rennie loomed above him. He tried to scramble back, but he was exhausted, all energy gone.

++Come here. Come to us.++

"No, no!" Jack shouted, steeling himself to resist the mental onslaught that he knew would overwhelm him in a few short seconds.

Rennie knelt down and lowered her hand. Jack jerked his head aside and, at that instant, saw something flash over his head. There was an incredibly loud *bong!* and Rennie flew backward and landed heavily on her backside.

"What the —?" she said in normal tones. But then her voice faltered. Her eyes, which had momentarily cleared, clouded again and she rose up like a puppet pulled by unseen strings, not moving her legs at all.

Before Rennie could get fully upright, Jaide stepped forward and hit her again with a large silver tray. As she went down for the second time, Jaide threw the tray on top of her chest, grabbed Jack under the arms, and dragged him to the front door.

As they half ran and half fell through the doorway, The Evil rose up inside Rennie. She was lifted high by its power and sent after them like a missile, her hands like claws, reaching out.

Jack and Jaide screamed as she flew straight at them, both of them tangled up on the hallway rug, for the moment completely defenseless.

Then Ari and Kleo slammed the door.

There was a violent, shuddering impact. The whole house shook, and The Evil vented its anger with a piercing scream that filled the twins' minds with images of raging fire and ice and destruction and unchanging death. It went on and on, then slowly faded, and finally they heard footsteps receding rapidly along the drive. They heard Rennie's ordinary voice calling their names, as though searching for them, until that, too, faded into silence.

"It's gone," said Ari from the window. "For now."

Jaide and Jack pulled themselves up and looked at each other.

"She almost got me," said Jack shakily.

He was shivering and wild eyed. Jaide had never seen him like this before, not even when he'd come back from the tunnels.

"It wasn't her," said Jaide. "It was The Evil. And besides, it didn't get you. You're safe now."

"I didn't make it to the cemetery . . . or the lighthouse," he said. "I'm sorry."

"Neither of us did," said Jaide. "We'll . . . we'll think of something else."

Outside, the wind picked up, and a light rain began to fall, both harbingers of the coming storm.

It was getting dark all over Portland, and would soon get darker still.

CHAPTER TWENTY

KNOWLEDGE IS HALF THE BATTLE?

By mutual, unspoken consent of children and cats, all four retreated to Grandma X's bedroom, pausing only to pick up candles and matches from the kitchen. Though no one said it, they all hoped that she would somehow be awake and could take charge, that she would rescue them from The Evil.

But Grandma X was still unconscious, and hadn't shifted from her curled up position on the bed.

Kleo and Ari jumped up next to her and both licked her face. Jaide knelt down and took her hand, holding it tightly. Jack went to the window and looked out the rain-swept pane.

"The lighthouse light hasn't come on," he said. "I'd have thought it would have a generator, like the hospital." He peered through the glass again and added, "Actually, it looks like they've got the power on everywhere else, except for our bit and the lighthouse."

"The Evil has grown strong enough to command anyone who might come close," said Kleo. Her eyes glittered in the candlelight.

"I'm sorry, Grandma," Jaide said quietly. "Sorry we didn't trust you, and sorry if . . . if we brought all this trouble on you . . . on everyone."

Jack turned back from the window and knelt down next to Jaide. He put his hand over Jaide's in what he hoped was a confident, comforting grip. He didn't voice the resentment he felt for being in their position. He had never asked to be a troubletwister, and he certainly didn't like the feeling that Grandma X had been keeping secrets from them. Perhaps his parents, too. Why hadn't they said something?

"We just want this to stop," he said. "Why won't you help us?"

Warmth blossomed under the twins' hands, and a soft light spread between Grandma X's closed fingers.

++Troubletwisters.++

Jack jumped. The voice came to him the same way The Evil's did, but it sounded like Grandma X, and it possessed none of the heavy pressure of that horrible presence.

"Grandma?"

++Troubletwisters?++

Jaide leaned close. Grandma X's mouth wasn't moving, but her voice was clear.

"We're right here, Grandma," Jaide said, holding more tightly to her hand. The cats pressed in close beside her. "Are you okay? What can we do to help you?"

A wisp of light danced on the old woman's forehead. There appeared a tiny version of Grandma X's glowing, ghostly form. Her eyes were closed and her expression was pained, but her voice was clear inside Jaide's and Jack's heads.

++**Lighthouse,**++ whispered the voice. ++**On the lighthouse.**++

"The lighthouse?" Jack asked urgently. "Is the broken ward on the lighthouse?"

++**Brass plate,**++ said Grandma X. Her voice was fading and the shining figure was beginning to flicker. ++**Brass plate.**++

"Wait, Grandma," said Jaide as Jack said, "Tell us more!"

++**Replacement. Blue room.**++

The ghostly image vanished, along with the light shining from between Grandma X's fingers. At the same time, there was a ripple of wind through the room, and all the candles guttered and went out.

Jaide fumbled for matches and cried out, "Jack! Check the window!"

"It's shut," said Jack, who could see perfectly well.

"Don't panic," said Kleo. "That wasn't the storm."

Jaide lit the candles and looked at Jack. He had an expression she had rarely seen before. It was one of determination underlaid by extreme fear.

"We need to replace a brass plate on the lighthouse," he said, relieved to be sure of something finally. "And there's a replacement in the blue room."

"Don't count your sardines before the tin opens," said Kleo. "We'll have to find it first, and that room is tricky."

"But at least we know where to look," said Jaide. "That's half the battle."

"It is?" asked Ari. "I would have thought it was more like ten percent at most."

"Come on," said Jack. He was looking at the window frame. It was shuddering with the impact of wind and rain, and the storm had barely gotten started.

Their arrival in the antiques store was met with a pronunciation from the crocodile skull.

"One brass plate, three inches by four, fixed by four two-eighth screws fashioned entirely from silver."

"We know *now*," said Jack, tapping it on the top of its cranium. "Thank you anyway."

"Where do we start looking?" asked Jaide.

"There's an old tool kit over here," said Ari, leaping in one direction.

"And I seem to recall a collection of brass signs in that box," said Kleo, pointing an elegant paw.

The twins followed the cats' directions, but while they did find a tool kit with various screwdrivers that would be useful for dealing with screws, silver or otherwise, the box of brass signs did not contain a brass plate.

Nor did the chest that held a complete bronze dinner set; or the small cupboard with the horse brasses; or the sack with the tarnished white metal and lapis lazuli coffee demitasse cups; or the inside of the grandfather clock that had lost its pendulum and was now full of stacks of what Kleo assured them were gold florins of a long-ago French king.

"There's too much stuff here," said Jaide after another thirty minutes of fruitless searching, with the sounds of the storm growing steadily all the while. The house was groaning, and there had been several thuds outside, probably from more power poles blowing over or big trees losing their limbs. "We'll never find it!"

"I don't suppose you can tell us," said Jack conversationally to the crocodile skull. "I might even let you bite my finger."

The skull's eyes lit up, which was considerably more eerie in the dim candlelight than under electrical illumination, and its jaws snickered *rat-a-tat-tat.*

"In the third drawer down on the left of the serpent-wound bureau of Indian teak," it said. Then it chattered a bit more, shivering itself along the table to orient its mouth directly at Jack.

Ari and Kleo were already at the bureau. Jaide followed them and opened the third drawer down on the left. She held her candle close and examined the contents.

"It's here, Jack," she said. Then she looked back. "I guess you'd better let it . . . try to . . . maybe just a nip . . ."

Jack nodded and very carefully extended the tip of his little finger toward the crocodile skull. It lunged forward, right off the table, and managed to tear off a tiny flap of skin and a bead of blood before crashing to the floor.

"Ouch!" exclaimed Jack, sucking his finger.

"Worth it," said Kleo. "Worth a whole finger, for that matter."

"Hey," protested Jack.

"You've got lots," said Ari, "and those famous opposable thumbs. Besides, it's only a scratch."

Jaide lifted out an open leather pouch that contained what she was sure must be the replacement ward. Everything was exactly as described by the skull. There was the brass plate, with its four silver screws, each in a little loop so they would not be lost. The screws had a strange spiral pattern instead of the usual straight groove or Phillips head.

The plate was the right size, and its deeply etched words said:

To all the Keepers of the Portland Light, past, present, and future, who serve to guard and ward against the darkness

"That has to be it," said Jack, who had come to look over Jaide's shoulder.

"Yes," said Jaide. "Now all we have to do is get this to the lighthouse."

Jack was about to speak when the drumming bear suddenly started smashing at his drum and every single clock in the room began to strike wildly. The face of a barometer shattered, sending glass raining onto a chess set below. The white knight jumped out of the way, the king retreated behind his castle, and the white pawns moved in a panicky rabble.

"The Evil!" hissed Ari.

The cat's voice was lost in a sudden noise that was even louder and more threatening than the storm. A very deep, angry, and mechanical bellow — the throbbing menace of some very big engine.

Jaide shut the leather wallet with the plate and screws and picked it and the tool kit up. Jack had paused to pick up the artillery shell cigarette lighter, but he was already ahead, lifting the tapestry that hid the secret passage while Ari zoomed through farther ahead.

A minute later, they were crouched out on the widow's walk once again, looking over the rails as the wind whipped at their clothes, the rain beat down on their heads, and water cascaded down their noses to join the rush from the gutters of the roof.

The throbbing engine noise was even louder than wind and rain.

"Where's it coming from, Ari?" shouted Jack. "Oh . . ."

Ari had not come out of the conning tower structure that shielded the steps, and there was no sign at all of Kleo.

"Down there," said Jaide, pointing into the yard of the abandoned house. "That's where it's coming from."

"But no one lives there," Jack said as he ran to see. "There are no cars."

Two headlights suddenly flicked into life next door. The engine roared even louder and the stench of exhaust came up to the twins. Then a noise was added to the mix. A grinding, clanking rattle that got louder as the lights moved forward, toward them.

"It's not a car. It's the bulldozer!" Jack cried.

"I guess The Evil isn't going to wait for the storm to knock the house down," shouted Jaide over the racket. "Is that Rennie again?"

Jack peered out into the night as gears crunched. He couldn't see the head of a driver in the cab. There was no one at the controls at all!

"That's impossible," said Jaide when he told her. "Although —"

"What?"

"Grandma did say that inanimate things become more lively when they're around Wardens. Maybe when The Evil is strong enough, it's the same!"

The bulldozer turned awkwardly on its tracks, shuffling backward like a bull backing up to make its charge. When it was lined up with Grandma X's house, Jack was sure it would crash through the fence and keep on coming.

Jack grimaced as he saw that there *was* something in the driver's seat. Hundreds of tiny shapes — crawling, linking limbs, straining to reach and pull at controls designed for humans —

Rats. Dozens of rats, forming the legs and arms of a human, without bothering to make a head.

"It's made a driver out of rats," said Jack.

Jaide shivered and with a trembling hand tried to shield her eyes against the glare of the dozer's lights. But she still couldn't see anything, and to her it looked like the bulldozer was moving of its own accord.

"We have to stop it," yelled Jack. He had to talk close to Jaide's ear so she could hear over the storm and the bulldozer. "If I can get behind it, I can climb on and into the cab. I'll flame the rats with the cigarette lighter . . . and switch it off, or wreck something important."

He swapped the artillery shell cigarette lighter to his left hand and scrabbled in the tool kit for a long screwdriver.

"I can't see anything," she said. "Those lights are too bright and everything else is too dark. There could be anything out there. Maybe you should stay inside — we could think of something else. . . ."

Jack was watching the bulldozer carefully. Though it was frighteningly loud, it was also slow and ungainly and it wasn't being driven very well. And if it took a lot of The Evil's power to control the creatures driving it, then there was less chance of any nasty surprises in the dark nearby.

"I can take care of it," said Jack firmly. He positioned his thumb ready to flip the top of the lighter and brandished the screwdriver like a sword in his other hand. "You get back to the blue room. Maybe there's some other magic thing that will help. Ask the cats, wherever they've gotten to."

"But, Jack, I really don't think —"

"Go!" said Jack. He ran to the front door, forcing himself to slow only minutely when his wet shoes slipped on the steps. Jaide hesitated, then ran back through the secret passage, into the relative safety of the blue room.

Jack hefted his two weapons and visualized himself cloaked in darkness. He imagined it wrapping around him, and after a moment, he felt a kind of soft, electric buzz along his exposed skin.

He opened the door and slid out into the night.

The roaring of the engine and the crunching of wood was horribly loud. The fence had resisted the bulldozer's initial push, requiring two attempts. On the second, the curved steel blade successfully managed to sweep all obstacles aside, and the heavy, articulated tracks behind it crushed the wooden splinters into the ground.

Snorting and rumbling, the slow but fearsome machine crept onto Grandma X's land and headed straight toward the house.

CHAPTER TWENTY-ONE

BULLDOZER!

Jaide could hear the bulldozer clearly, even inside the blue room. She winced as she heard the fence get smashed to pieces and the grinding crunch as the machine's metal tracks crushed the remnants flat.

"There must be something here we can use against a bulldozer!" she exclaimed. "Ari! Kleo! Think of something!"

"Like what?" asked Ari, peeking out from under the desk. "I don't think Grandma X has a rocket launcher."

"Don't grizzle, Aristotle," said Kleo. She was sitting in the middle of the room, slowly swiveling her head, bright blue eyes weighing up many possible things. "There are numerous defensive items here, but unfortunately we only know those devices Grandma X has employed in the past, and she hasn't needed to use many. It has been very quiet in Portland since we were born."

A smashing, tearing noise outside was a grim reminder that this was no longer the case.

"What about you, then?" Jaide asked the crocodile skull. "Is there something here that can stop that bulldozer?"

"Yes, yes, yes, yes, yes," chattered the crocodile skull. Its eyes flashed with excitement.

"Well, where — and what — is it?" demanded Jaide.

The crocodile skull clapped its jaws together.

"Num num num num num," it said in a rather horrible parody of someone eating something nice.

"Uh, okay, then," said Jaide. The skull had only taken a sliver of Jack's finger. She could bear the same kind of scratch, if it got them the information they so desperately needed.

She held out the little finger of her left hand cautiously and leaned toward the skull.

It lunged forward, using its chattering to move, and its sharp teeth shut on Jaide's finger halfway down the fingernail, nearly cutting off the entire tip of her finger.

Jaide stared down at the wound, too shocked to cry out or move or do anything. Blood started to drip down into her hand and onto the floor.

The crocodile skull crunched happily, burped, and said, "Music box made by Favre, for the discombobulation of The Evil. Tea chest with the mark of the blue oryx."

"Th-thanks," said Jaide weakly. She sat down in an armchair and pinched the end of her finger hard and raised her hand above her head to slow the bleeding. Susan had always made sure they had first-aid lessons.

"I'll get the first-aid kit," said Ari, and was off.

"I'll find the tea chest," said Kleo. "I think it's behind the walnut wardrobe."

Both cats leaped away. Jaide kept pressing on her bleeding finger, and flinched again as she heard the bulldozer outside change gear and bellow even louder than before, followed immediately by the screech of its blade sliding over stone or concrete.

Jack saw the rats straightaway. They stood on their hind legs like prairie dogs behind the bulldozer's controls, milky-white eyes focused firmly forward. Their heads didn't turn as he slowly moved along the front of the house. Either they couldn't see him or The Evil was completely absorbed in driving the bulldozer.

Jack kept his eye on them as he rounded the corner and started to make his way around the edge of the garden, circling wide to come back behind the bulldozer, concentrating hard on being part of the darkness. The vehicle lurched forward as he stalked it. It was almost at the house now, but had been held up by the roots of the giant fir tree and the remnants of the fallen garden wall.

In fact, Jack saw that the tree roots were actively working against the bulldozer. There were far more of them out of the ground than when he and Jaide had run past on their first day, and the roots were much larger, some of them as thick as his body. The roots were slowly twining up out of the ground in front of the dozer, and carrying with them huge squares of sandstone that must have once been the foundation of the garden wall.

But even so, the bulldozer was winning. Its long, sharp blade was cutting through the roots, and pushing the rocks aside. It would only be a matter of minutes before it cleared a proper path of attack and smashed into the side of the actual house.

Jack steeled himself for what had to be done. Tucking the lighter under one arm and the screwdriver through his belt, he ran straight at the back of the bulldozer, through the acrid cloud of its diesel exhaust, and jumped up on the engine right between the clanking tracks. There were cooling slats on the engine, giving him somewhere to grip, but they were hot. Jack involuntarily cried out even as he swarmed up and over, and crouched behind the back of the cab.

The hideous, headless body made of rats stopped pulling levers and swung around toward him, dozens of white rat eyes focused on him.

Jack pulled the lighter from under his arm, flicked the lid open and directed a great gout of flame into the cab. Rats squealed, the headless body disintegrating as its smoking, burning parts fled in all directions.

The gas in the lighter suddenly ran out. It burped a few last flames, then Jack threw it aside, and edged into the cab.

The bulldozer continued its inexorable forward progress.

Jack reached out to take the control levers, not knowing whether to push or pull but willing to try everything until he made it stop.

++Yessss, Jackaran,++ said the familiar, hateful voice into his mind. ++Drive forward. Kill the witch!++

"I'm not listening to you!" Jack cried. Under his hands, the bulldozer stopped, turned, turned again, and started in reverse, heading once more for the house, only backward. "I don't believe anything you tell me!"

++That is not true,++ said The Evil. ++We feel your doubt. We rejoice at your uncertainty. We know you will join us.++

There was power in The Evil's voice. Jack felt it sliding into his brain, growing stronger and more convincing. It would be easy to give in. Maybe it would even be the right thing to do —

"No!" he shouted. "Shut up! I'll never join you — never!"

The bulldozer turned again. Jack pushed and pulled on the levers, but no matter what he did, it wouldn't stop. If it kept going, it was bound to crash into the house, bring down a wall, and then The Evil would swarm in —

"Just stop, will you?" Jack let go of the levers and looked at the dashboard. There was a slot that looked like it would have held a key. If he could jam the screwdriver in there, perhaps, and turn it . . .

He reached down to draw the screwdriver from his belt, and was suddenly stopped in midmotion, as two strong arms wrapped themselves around him in an embrace so tight Jack couldn't breathe.

It had to be Rennie returning to do The Evil's will. Jack cursed himself for not keeping an eye out for the handywoman.

He kicked backward, but the grip didn't ease.

++We have you now, Jackaran Kresimir Shield.++ The voice was like an icicle in his mind. ++You were foolish to try to resist us. Your inner self wants to join us. Relax, and let us help you help yourself.++

Jack tried to say no, but suddenly his mouth wouldn't work. Spit drooled from his lips and his tongue felt numb.

He strained to fight, but barely managed to move a single finger before they all went dead.

++There. That's better, isn't it?++

Rennie eased her grip, and Jack slumped down, turning sideways as he did so.

Rennie smiled at him, an effect undermined by her white, staring eyes, the worms wreathed in her hair, and the rats coiled around her neck like a fat fur collar.

No, Jack wanted to say, *it's not better at all!*

++Be still,++ The Evil told him. ++There is no point in struggling.++

The only feeling Jack retained was in the little finger the crocodile skull had bitten. He wriggled it, but felt no triumph. What could he do with one little finger?

++We know the old Warden is dying,++ said The Evil. ++We feel it. She cannot help you. Surrender. You know you want to give in.++

Jack moved his little finger again, stretching it out. The long screwdriver was thrust through his belt. It was a Warden screwdriver, an antique, made *lively* by long contact with Grandma X. . . . If he could just touch it, maybe it would help him. . . .

++Surrender to us, and we will let your sister go,++ said the insidious voice. ++We are not greedy. One trouble-twister is enough.++

Jack didn't hear the words, but he knew The Evil was thinking *for now*. If he did give in, surely it would just use his Gifts against Jaide. But it was so hard to keep resisting.

He could feel The Evil forcing itself further and further into his mind, paralyzing more and more and more of his body. What was the point of fighting when he had lost the ability to fight at all?

++Perhaps this will help you decide,++ said The Evil.

Then it stopped his lungs.

The panic that Jack had just managed to keep under control burst free.

I can't breathe! I can't breathe! The terrified thoughts raced through his body, but none of his limbs could respond.

Only Jack's little finger moved. Fueled by his intense fear, it managed to stretch impossibly far and touch the cold steel of the screwdriver.

The Evil's control snapped the instant Jack made contact. The boy drew a great, shuddering breath that brought tears to his eyes. He drew the long screwdriver and dragged the point across Rennie's hand, scratching her from the knuckles to the wrist.

She shrieked and let go. Jack threw himself forward, thrust the screwdriver into the bulldozer's ignition, and twisted it as hard as he could.

There was a tremendously loud bang. Sparks flew everywhere. The engine coughed three times and died. The tracks clanked forward one more foot and locked in place.

The bulldozer was dead, but Rennie's hands came scrabbling back, gripping Jack's shoulders. He twisted desperately and slithered out the bottom of the cab, hitting the ground hard. But he was up again instantly, running for the house, the handle of the screwdriver hanging limply in his hand. The rest was gone, immolated doing its work against The Evil.

He'd just gotten to the front door when he heard the bulldozer's tracks start to clank again, followed by the screech of its blade across the ground. Neither sound was accompanied by any engine noise.

Jack whipped around in astonishment.

++**Come back, troubletwister,**++ called The Evil, straight into his head. ++**We will give you one last chance!**++

Jack didn't want another chance. No matter what he thought of Grandma X, he was sure The Evil's plans for him were too terrible to imagine. He ran inside, slammed the door after him, and immediately collided with Jaide, who was right behind it. She had a white bandage on one finger, a small screwdriver and the leather case with the replacement plate were sticking out of the pocket of her jeans, and she was holding a beautiful golden box the size of a small book in her hands. The cats were by her side, Kleo on the left, and Ari on the right.

"I killed the engine," said Jack. "But it's started again!"

"The Evil can make such things move of their own accord," said Kleo, "when it has sufficient lives to fuel it. It has grown strong."

"Very strong indeed," Ari agreed gloomily.

"So we've had it," said Jack. "It'll have the wall down in a few minutes, and the storm is getting worse!"

"Not if this works," said Jaide. "I was just about to take it outside and start it up, but I was worried about rats and stuff."

"The machine will be taking most of The Evil's power," said Kleo. "It will have little left to attack us."

"All right, then," said Jaide. "Come on!"

"Wait," said Jack. "What is that, anyway? And what happened to your finger?"

"Later," said Jaide. "Open the door."

"We're right behind you," said Ari, moving to put Jaide between himself and whatever lay outside. "After you, troubletwisters."

Jack opened the door. Kleo raced out ahead of him, hissing in warning. There were a dozen rats, with glowing white eyes, on the porch, but none of them reacted to the cat's presence. They crouched, frozen, staring fixedly at the approaching bulldozer.

Jaide opened the lid of the golden box, revealing a mass of rods and cogs. She set it down on the steps and took a butterfly key with enameled blue wings out of her pocket. She put that in the keyhole in the front of the box and slowly wound the spring.

On the other side of the house, the bulldozer cleared its way through the roots and stones and began to back up for its final, lethal run against the house. With its blade raised and the clank of its tracks barely audible above the roar of the storm, it was a strange and eerie threat.

Jaide let go of the key, and the music box started playing.

The notes were pure and crystalline, and they rang out through the night as clear as bells. Jaide recognized the tune; she felt as though she had been listening to it her entire life, but she didn't know what it was called.

As the music played, a series of tiny, jeweled figures sprang up from inside the box and began moving around the edges, telling the story of The Evil as it leaped from creature to creature in its bid to take over the world. Tiny insects were first, then small animals, then people. A miniature steam train with glowing red lanterns raced ahead of a storm with bloody lightning — machines and weather — followed by something Jaide couldn't interpret: a white circle with nothing but black inside. It rolled around the insides of the box like a soap bubble before sinking back into the innards, and the cycle began anew.

While the music box played, the world seemed to stop. Jack and Jaide didn't notice that the clank of tracks had ceased, or the frozen rats, or the cats stalking back toward them.

Jaide and Jack were lost in the music. The tune played over and over, drawing them deeper and deeper into its spell. The outside world had become irrelevant. Only the music mattered.

Something sharp dug into the back of Jaide's right hand, as something equally sharp stabbed Jack behind the knee. Both gasped and, looking down, saw the cats retracting claws into padded paws.

"Step away from the music box!" commanded Kleo. "Put your fingers in your ears and try not to listen."

Jaide felt as though she'd been wrenched out of a nice warm bath and dumped into icy snow.

"What did you do that for?" she asked petulantly.

"Put your fingers in your ears!" repeated Kleo sharply.

Jaide and Jack did as they were told. Though they could still hear and feel the music, its grip on them was lessened.

"Another minute and you might never have come back," said Kleo.

Jaide looked down at the music box and across to the immobile rats. Several frozen cockroaches and spiders had dropped to the ground nearby. The bulldozer was silent.

"This solves all our problems, doesn't it? We keep this playing and The Evil can't get in."

"Things like this can only be wound once," said Kleo. "And it won't play for long. It's old. Springs can break or cogs jam. It could end at any moment."

As if it heard Kleo's words, the music faltered for a second. The twins' hearts almost stopped in that moment of silence, as the rats and insects rustled forward, just a fraction of an inch. Then the music started again, and the figures continued to revolve.

"Go!" said Ari. "We'll guard here as best we can! Go!"

CHAPTER TWENTY-TWO

THE MUSIC WINDS DOWN

The twins hurried into the storm-addled night, the two of them alone against The Evil. Rain dashed down against them, and the wind blew it into their faces. It was cold, and even the exertion of their fast walk could not warm them. The moon and stars were completely hidden by the dense clouds, and it was very dark, as if a thick, heavy blanket had been thrown over the town.

Jack, who could see perfectly well, took Jaide's hand as she stumbled for the seventh time.

"Stay behind me," he said. "I'll guide you."

With Jack leading, they broke into more of a run. They knew time was short, even though they could still hear the gentle tune of the music box. Somehow it followed them, cutting cleanly through the sounds of rain and wind.

The tune had a familiar air, like "Greensleeves," but there was something modern about it, too. The rhythm was both jaunty and solemn, and its constant presence re-assured them that The Evil was contained behind them, at least for now.

This reassurance did not last long. As they skirted around the base of the Rock, the rain suddenly stopped.

For a moment this was a relief, until something flew into Jack's face. He brushed it away, feeling the hard carapace and wings of a beetle.

"Uh-oh," he said. Then he closed his mouth just in time, as many more beetles followed the first. It was like being hit by spiky hailstones. The twins struggled on against this assault until a beetle struck Jack's eye and he had to stop to wipe it away. So many more beetles smashed against them that the twins had to crouch down, facing each other, and shield their faces with their arms.

"Jaide! Blow them away!" Jack coughed. A beetle had crawled into his mouth as he spoke, its burred legs gripping his tongue.

Jaide reached out to the wind around them. She could feel it like it was part of herself, like an extra arm. She focused her mind on it, and then swung, making a mental swishing motion against herself.

She'd expected a sudden gust of wind, but got a miniature whirlwind instead. It lifted the twins off the ground and carried them forward a dozen yards, dropping them unceremoniously at the cemetery gate. But it kept going with the beetles, sweeping them far out to sea.

"Can you still hear the music?" Jack asked anxiously. The storm had lashed up the sea, and though the rain had stopped, the deep boom of the swell smashing into the rocks below the lighthouse was much louder now.

"Yes," said Jaide. "Only just, though. Come on!"

Hand in hand they raced to the lighthouse. Jaide smacked into Jack's back as he stopped before the door, sending them both stumbling against it.

"It's still locked," said Jack. The three big bolts were all padlocked. He tugged at the padlocks, but they didn't move.

"The music's stopped," said Jaide. She couldn't see a thing and was already imagining The Evil's creatures swarming toward her in the darkness. "Can you . . . can you see anything coming?"

Jack turned around. There was something moving between the headstones of the cemetery — a huge, dark mass that looked like a single, undulating thing, till he saw the dotted flecks of white that could only be thousands of tiny Evil-infested eyes.

"Mice," he croaked. "Uh, probably nothing to worry about, but maybe if you could use the wind to lift us up to the top of the lighthouse, that would be good."

"Mice?" Jaide didn't feel as confident as her brother after her airborne battle with the seagulls. "If it's only mice, what else is out there?"

At that moment, the mice all squeaked as one, with the voice of The Evil.

++Troubletwisters!++

The high-pitched squeal was like the amplified scream of an enraged crone.

"Hold both my hands!" shouted Jaide, reaching out to grab her brother.

Jack gripped her as if she was a life buoy and he was going under for the third and final time. Jaide felt the wind again, and visualized it as a cupping, gentle hand, coming up underneath them to carefully carry them just high enough to reach the walkway around the light, some one hundred and fifty feet above.

The wind answered, howling down. As the tide of mice poured around, between, and over the closest headstones, Jack and Jaide were lifted up and away.

But not toward the light. Instead, the wind swept them right off the headland and shot up above the sea, before dropping them with alarming suddenness toward the spray of the great, curling waves that were pounding the rocks below.

"No!" shrieked Jaide. "Up to the top of the lighthouse! Up!"

The wind dropped them another half dozen feet, into the crest of an enormous gray-green wave. Jack was almost torn from Jaide's grasp by the force of the water, even though he was only caught by the very tip of the wave.

"Up!" Jaide commanded desperately. She put all the force of her will into that one word.

The wind responded. The twins shot straight up into the sky, far higher than the dark lighthouse below.

"To the lighthouse walkway!" shouted Jaide furiously. She pointed down, initially in the wrong direction, until Jack hastily wrenched her hand around.

The wind spun them about and then left them entirely. The twins fell screaming, until the wind came back and snatched them up again, taking their breath away. A moment later, they flew wildly around the lighthouse below the rail, circling it several times as Jack desperately tried to reach out and grab hold.

Then, almost with a chuckle, the wind lifted them a fraction, just over the railing, and dumped them on the walkway, a twelve-sided mesh platform that entirely circled the tall, glass lamp enclosure.

Jack staggered to his feet and tried the door that led inside. For a second he thought it was locked, but the handle was just stuck. He forced it down, and the metal-framed glass door opened with the screech of long disuse.

"See if you can find a light," Jaide called out urgently. She was lying on the walkway, holding on to the railing. She hated not being able to see anything, particularly as her lack of sight made her more aware of the grasping wind. Even now it wanted her to join it again, to take off and fly far and free.

Jack was examining an electrical box on the low wall under the glass, which extended up another dozen feet. The box had several huge circuit breaker levers, all of which were down.

"Here goes nothing," he said, and pushed one up. Exactly nothing happened. He pushed the next one up, with the same effect. Then he pushed the last one, and this time there was a blinding flash. Jack reeled back into the main lantern apparatus in the center of the room. A second later he was thrown off as it started to revolve. Lying on the floor, he blinked rapidly, liquid black blotches dancing around in his vision.

"Thanks," Jaide said from the walkway. "I meant, like, the inside lights, not the *lighthouse* light."

Jack sat up. The huge reflector, twice his height and

four feet across, was rotating slowly, sending its dazzling light out over the sea, the beam slowly circling the bay.

"The mice are all around the base," Jaide said urgently. "They might already be inside."

Jack rushed to the rail and looked over. There was a surging mass of rodents completely encircling the base of the lighthouse. They were bound to find a way in, and would only take a few minutes to swarm to the top.

But that wasn't all. Jack spotted something else.

"There's something coming up out of the sea," he warned his sister. "Something really big."

Jaide looked out. She couldn't see anything at first, until the beam from the lighthouse swept across, briefly illuminating a huge, bestial shape that was pulling itself out of the raging sea and coming up the cliff. Hundred-foot-long tentacles preceded a vast oval-shaped body the size of a fishing trawler.

"It's made of seaweed and jellyfish," Jack said slowly. "Hundreds . . . thousands of them . . . Oh, it's falling back!"

A particularly big wave had smashed into the giant creature's back, loosening its hold on the rocks, and then the undertow had undermined its footing. But it was only a temporary reprieve. The creature sucked in more and more seaweed, jellyfish, and anything else that swam nearby, and grew even larger and stronger.

"We need to find the plate!" Jaide shouted. She ran inside and started searching around the low wall under the windows. She saw no brass plaques, but she did see numerous examples of graffiti etched into the stone. Light keepers and visitors to the lighthouse had been memorializing it for decades, it seemed, including the occasional dating couple. At the base of a narrow iron ladder leading up to the very peak of the lighthouse, where a tall lightning rod invited the heavens to do their worst, she saw *SAH ♥ HJS*, and realized with a jolt that they were her parents' initials, before they were married. She couldn't imagine them ever being so young, or so delinquent as to graffiti a public monument!

Jack didn't notice the initials. His eye had caught something even farther up the lighthouse, something that had flashed brightly as the beam of light passed underneath.

It was a small brass plate above the twelve-foot glass window of the lantern room, next to the narrow iron ladder.

"It's here!" he shouted, pointing. The ladder was wet, and the rungs were thin and slippery, but he was up it in an instant. The brass plate was screwed into a wooden beam that was part of the window frame, but it was two feet from the ladder. Jack had to hang on with one hand and reach across.

Once, the old plaque might have been identical to the one Jaide had below. It had the same words, but they were faded, and the brass itself was riddled with tiny black cracks, like veins.

Jack leaned out and touched it, and the plate flaked away beneath his fingers, leaving only remnant corners around the silver screws.

"Quick!" he shouted. "Give me the replacement and a screwdriver!"

Jaide came up halfway, gripping the ladder with all her strength. When she had to pass the plate and the screwdriver with her right hand, she looped her whole left arm through a rung and locked her elbow. Even so, her feet were lifted off, and the wind almost had her before she could get a grip with her other hand again.

Heavy, thought Jaide. *I'm heavy, heavy, heavy.*

She managed to get back down to the walkway and hold on there, the wind howling around her, encouraging her to let go. But even over the wind, she could hear a frenzied scrabbling and squeaking at the hatch in the lantern room as the mouse horde tried to get through.

On the headland, the giant creature finally managed to get out of the sea. It half crawled, half flowed toward the lighthouse, and as it did so, it began to elongate. Its existing tentacles split into several thinner, longer ones. Jellyfish, seaweed, crabs, squid, and hundreds of different types of fish dripped from the creature's composite form as it oozed forward, and it left a glistening, flopping trail fifty feet wide.

It took Jaide only a few seconds to recognize that its leading tentacles had reached the base of the lighthouse and were feeling their way upward.

She was so intent on the squid-monster that the appearance of a woman's face at the edge of the walkway came as an incredibly awful surprise. She was milky eyed, and her face was bruised and battered, with dried blood caked under her nose and mouth. Rat heads now grew out of her shoulders, bursting through a cloak of cockroaches shielding her from the rain. But far, far worse than that were the spiders that supported her, hundreds of fat, hairy spiders that had encased her in a coat of webs, the webs they had used to carry her up the side of the lighthouse.

++We have been looking for you,++ said Rennie. ++And now we have found you.++

The woman grasped the rail, and the spiders peeled off her, swarming up the railing, trailing their webs behind them. The wind blew some away, but there were many, many more spiders to take their place. They quickly wove a rope that Rennie used to swing herself up and over the rail.

++Now we have found you.++

Rennie was shouting aloud, her impassioned cry echoed by rats and cockroaches and the towering sea creature, but the sound was a mere whisper compared to the mental scream of The Evil inside Jaide's and Jack's minds.

++We will never let you go!++

Jaide *did* let go, and let the wind take her — driving her body straight at Rennie like a missile, her clenched hands thrust out ahead of her.

She struck Rennie in the chest and felt The Evil reach out from Rennie, but the contact was too fleeting. Rennie flipped backward over the railing in a shower of dislodged cockroaches and was gone.

Jaide spun over, too, but she did a somersault in the air, a violent fishtail, and then a kind of strange thrashing butterfly swimming stroke that somehow delivered her back to the walkway, where she landed on spiders and did a screeching dance across to, and up, the ladder.

"Rennie . . . she . . . uh . . . *it* is still there," said Jack, who was looking down through the diamond-shaped mesh of the steel walkway. Jack had instantly recognized her, even though she was now a hideous recombination of human, rat, and insect. "Hanging on a web, twenty feet under. The spiders are going to help her, that squid thing is getting closer, and I can't get the last stupid screw out!"

Jack could see the huge tentacles reaching out toward them, and the main body of the creature pulling itself along behind. He could smell it, too, an incredibly powerful, rancid fish smell stronger than anything any fish market had ever managed, even on a hot day.

"Let me try," said Jaide, tugging on his leg.

Jack climbed down the ladder and Jaide shimmied up past him.

"Hang on to my legs," she told him as she leaned over again and put all the strength of her shoulder, arm, and hand into the screwdriver. It *was* very stiff, and for a long, horrible moment, she thought she, too, might not be strong enough. She gritted her teeth and strained until her fingers burned.

Slowly, the last of the old silver screws began to turn.

"Yes!" Jaide shouted in triumph.

But as the last screw teetered out and fell, the fading powers of the East Ward of Portland finally died.

Now there was nothing in the east to stand between The Evil and the town.

Jack and Jaide felt the ward go, and the sudden surge in The Evil's power that came with it. Both of them almost fell off the ladder from the mental shock as they were struck with a thousand superfast, flickering images of The Evil's triumph. They saw that horrible milky-white glow spread across the eyes of everyone they'd met in town, from Rodeo Dave to the schoolteacher, Mr. Carver. They saw the doors of Grandma X's house bursting under the weight of rats and other vermin, and Ari and Kleo being ripped apart. They saw the mice pouring into the lantern room of the lighthouse. They saw themselves holding out welcoming arms to the tentacle of the giant squid-thing —

"No!" screamed the twins together.

The vision disappeared, blown away by their scream.

The Evil had not triumphed — not yet.

"Give me the plate!" shouted Jaide. "Keep holding my legs!"

Jack handed her the leather case that held the plate and screws, then wrapped his arms around his sister's legs and the ladder, his hands in a monkey grip on the far side. Every time the bright light of the lamp swept over him, he felt his strength waver. Only in the dark did he feel strong.

Help me, he thought to the night. But it was as if there was a barrier now between him and his Gift. A thick, threatening barrier, which had to be a manifestation of The Evil's growing power. *Help me!*

++There is no help for you here,++ said The Evil's voice out of the storm. ++Except from us.++

"Why would you help us?" said Jack.

++We will help you because only we do not want you to die. Where is the witch when you need her? Where are the Wardens? They do not care as we care. They are not your true family.++

Jack shook his head. He didn't want to believe the voice, but his determination was flagging. Everything it said was true. Grandma X hadn't helped him when he was in the tunnels — all she had done was send a storm, which might have drowned him had he not gotten himself out. She hadn't helped Jaide when the birds had attacked her. And she wasn't helping now, when all of Portland was in danger. Even the cats were at best reluctant allies. They didn't take sides, Ari said, which meant they weren't on Jack and Jaide's. No one was.

Furthermore, Jack thought, everything he knew about The Evil came through Jaide, the cats, or Grandma X. No one had given it the chance to speak for itself.

"What are you, really?" Jack asked The Evil. "And what do you really want?"

++Open your mind to us, Jackaran Kresimir Shield. Open your mind and find out!++

"Can't you just tell me?"

++No words can contain us.++

"What?" said Jaide from the top of the ladder. She could hear Jack talking but couldn't make out the words over the storm. She was leaning out into space, held only by her brother's strength. She had the replacement plate in one hand, the screwdriver and the first screw in the other, and the bag in her teeth.

Jack didn't answer her. Jaide brushed salty spray out of her eyes and pressed the plate into place against the beam. The brass shone in defiance of the storm and The Evil. Jaide slotted the first screw into the hole made by its predecessor. It turned straightly and smoothly, as though it wanted to go in. She fitted the screwdriver on, and quickly tightened the screw.

++Tell her to stop,++ the voice told Jack.

"Why?" he asked it. "What difference does it make if she does?"

++All the difference in your world. Accept our embrace and know an end to fear and grief.++

"And happiness and love as well!"

++All emotions are one. When you join us, you will understand.++

"I don't know," said Jack. The Evil *looked* horrible, but so did Brussels sprouts, and they were supposed to be good for you. Could Grandma X and the Wardens really have it the wrong way around?

++The Wardens keep your father from you. Tell your sister to stop, or you will never be allowed to see him again.++

Jack stared out into the night, knowing that The Evil must have a tiny foothold on his brain to be able to read that small, creeping doubt. Why *hadn't* his father come with them to Portland? Why had he abandoned them the day their house exploded?

"Got it!" cried Jaide, sliding her finger into the leather case and pulling out another screw. She put that in place, turned it once with her finger, and —

A tentacle smashed down ten feet away, wrapped itself around the railing, and pulled. Steel shrieked in protest, and the tentacle tore a whole section of the walkway off the side of the lighthouse.

At the same time, the bloodied, white-eyed Rennie struggled up the other side, webs dangling from her in all directions like parachute shrouds.

++Tell her to stop!++ The mouths of the rats on her shoulders moved in unison with her words. ++Tell her to stop, Jackaran Kresimir Shield, or we will stop her for you!++

Jack stared, frozen, as the tentacle struck again. This time it did not tear away the walkway, but came questing forward. Another tentacle followed, reaching about like a blind snake seeking its prey.

Jaide started on the third screw, frantically pushing it into place with cold-chilled fingers and leaning far out in her efforts to do so. Were she to drop the screw, it would almost certainly be lost. There was no walkway underneath them now, and nothing but The Evil to catch anything — or anyone — that fell.

"Hold me properly!" she called to Jack. His grip shifted as though he was growing tired. She wasn't worried about falling, but being blown away by the gale would be bad enough. There was no time left now for mistakes.

Jack stared back at Rennie as she tried to climb over the rail. The webs that had helped her before were a hindrance now, all tangled and confused. Cockroaches squished under her fingers, making her grip treacherous. Jack thought she might be trapped there, but that hope was dashed as a tentacle came toward her, wound itself around her chest, lifted her out of the tangle, and deposited her on the desperately leaned-over walkway near the ladder and the twins. With staring white eyes, Rennie looked up at Jaide as she screwed in the third screw, oblivious to Jack's struggle below.

"Leave her alone," Jack said. "It's me you want, not her."

++Tell her to stop.++

"But she doesn't understand —"

++Tell her to stop.++

"Wait —"

++We have waited long enough. She must stop!++

Rennie started to climb toward the twins, her slimy fingers groping through the diamond mesh, her white eyes fixed on Jaide as the girl pushed in the fourth and final screw.

A sigh of relief had just begun to form in Jack's throat when a tentacle suddenly whipped up over his head.

It hung in the air for a second, then the very tip curled around and flicked Jaide away from the plate, just like someone whisking away a fly. She fell on Jack, and both of them ended in a tangle, hanging off the rung of the ladder with only a six-foot length of bent and slanting walkway between them and the long fall to certain death.

A length of walkway that had Rennie on the other end.

Jaide looked at Jack in despair. The screwdriver was gone, dropped as she scrambled for a hold on the ladder.

Both twins looked up and saw the fourth, final screw teetering where Jaide had put it in and done a half turn with her fingers.

The tentacle came back again, brushing over them as it smashed blindly at the lighthouse. The whole structure shook as the tentacle hit, and Jaide saw the last screw fall, like a single silver teardrop, to be lost forever. They had no way now of finishing what they had started.

The East Ward could not be replaced.

"No," sobbed Jaide. "No . . ."

++Yessss!++ cried The Evil, entirely in their minds. Rennie's voice was silenced by cloying webs. **++It is pointless to resist. And now you will join us, both of you.++**

"No!" shouted Jack. He let go with one hand and held out his palm toward Rennie. "It's me you want. Spare her."

"Jack?!"

"I'll go with you." Jack was almost babbling, reaching out desperately to Rennie, who continued her slow climb toward them. "I'll go with you — just let Jaide go!"

The Evil laughed. They had never heard it laugh before, and the sound was more horrible than anything they had ever imagined. It came from the throat of every animal and insect surrounding the lighthouse. It came from Rennie. It came from the storm itself, thundering and rumbling.

++It is too late, Jackaran Kresimir Shield, *much* too late, to bargain with us!++

The twins felt all the power of The Evil gather around them and flow into Rennie. She would be the agent of their assimilation. The Evil would flow into them through her hands.

"So good, so good to have my children back," mumbled Rennie in her normal voice, though the white never left her eyes. Somehow that was even more horrible than hearing The Evil speak through her.

Still mumbling, Rennie dragged herself another foot up the broken walkway, her powerful fingers gripping the mesh as hand over hand she edged closer and closer. The rats growing from her shoulders squeaked in happy anticipation and the cockroaches rustled in applause.

Jaide averted her eyes. She couldn't look at Rennie as she approached. The lighthouse beam swept over them, and she saw her parents' graffiti just inches away from where they clung to the bottom of the ladder.

SAH ♥ *HJS*

Inspiration nearly blinded her, just for a moment. She knew what they had to do — if there were only time left to do it!

"Jack," she said, "give me your hand!"

He didn't hear her. His whole attention was on Rennie's slow but inexorable climb toward them. He was transfixed by the horror of what was going to happen. He could still hear The Evil laughing. It seemed to fill up his whole world.

"Jack! Your hand!"

He snapped out of his daze. "What?"

" 'Something read,' the rhyme goes," Jaide was saying. "Something *read*. Maybe it doesn't have to be that plaque. Maybe it doesn't even have to be words. Just letters might do if we make it happen — look!"

He looked where she was pointing and saw the graffiti. "But we don't know how to make it into a ward."

"How do we know we can't? We're troubletwisters! A week ago we didn't know we could fly or shadow-walk. Who knows what we can do?"

Jack grinned suddenly, and it was like the clouds parting.

++Join us!++ screamed The Evil as one of Rennie's clawing hands reached for Jack's leg. Behind her, all around the lighthouse, thousands of white eyes stared out of the dark. **++Join us at last!++**

In reply, Jack and Jaide entwined their hands together and pressed hard against their parents' graffiti.

As their palms touched the stone, a terrible scream exploded in their minds, to be repeated a split second later by every throat for miles.

++Wait!++ shrieked The Evil. **++Do not — ++**

"'Susan Anne Hungerford loves Hector Jamieson Shield,'" whispered the twins together. "Be the East Ward."

Silver light streamed through the carved initials, like molten metal following a mold. They felt their Gifts drawn to the light. Jack's sense of shadow and darkness drained away from him, and his vision dimmed, so that he could only see by the lighthouse's sweeping beam. Jaide felt the iciness of the wind, but nothing more, and no longer needed heavy thoughts to stay on the ladder.

But they didn't mind this ebbing of their Gifts. They knew instinctively that it was only temporary, part of the creation of a new ward and the containment of The Evil.

They could feel The Evil going, retreating back whence it came. The huge squid-thing was breaking apart, leaving tons of flopping marine creatures piled high from lighthouse to sea. Masses of mice were fleeing in all directions, their running columns crisscrossing with those of spiders and cockroaches, fierce battles happening at every collision.

"What have you done?" said Rennie sadly in something approaching her ordinary voice, although a hint of The Evil's power remained. "Why won't you join *me*?"

Her clawlike hands reached out for them. The rats and bugs in her flesh writhed in anger and pain, and her mouth was twisted in some deeper agony.

Jack acted instinctively, drawing back his feet. The woman's fingers grasped for his toes, but missed. She fell back down the walkway, rats screeching and her hands scrabbling for a grip. But she failed, sliding over the edge without a cry, her staring, all-white eyes fixed upon Jack and Jaide as she fell into darkness.

Jaide hugged her brother with her one free arm. He shifted his position to be more secure, then hugged her back.

Around them, the storm was fading. The wind had changed direction, and there were patches of clear sky opening up to show starlight and the promise of light from a still-hidden moon.

But the storm had left its mark. Water surged up the river and spilled onto Main Street on both sides. The lights in the town were off again, save for the distant hospital and the sweep of the lighthouse.

A moth flew up against Jack's face and he flinched. But it was just a normal insect, drawn by the light.

Jaide's plan had worked. The Evil had left Portland.

"We did it," she said, staring at the graffiti they had turned into the East Ward. The silver light was fading from it now, and soon it would look no different from any other graffiti, but they knew it was special, and that it would last.

"We sure did," said Jack, grinning like a loon.

The twins butted their foreheads together in their ancient and time-honored ritual of triumph.

"Ow," complained Jaide. The only problem with the ritual was that someone's head always hurt more than the other's.

"Brr," said Jack, feeling the cold more than the pain in his skull.

"We need to get back and check on Grandma and the cats," said Jaide.

She looked over at the door to the lamp room. The walkway was now a good three feet under it, slanting down to a gaping hole, and was slippery and wet.

"Do you think we should try to reach the door?"

"We have to," said Jack. "We can't hang on here all night."

"I can't do anything with the wind now," said Jaide. "If we fall . . . we fall."

Jack examined the walkway very carefully the next time the light came around.

"It'll be okay," he said. "We can hold on to the bottom of the window frames. They stick out."

"I guess," said Jaide.

"You're the climber," Jack pointed out.

"All right."

Gingerly, they both left the ladder and, holding on to the window frames, managed to clamber to the door and get inside.

Jaide shut the door behind them. It clicked, and the slight sound was immediately followed by an incredibly loud explosion that rattled all the windows, while a simultaneous flash of lightning blinded the twins. An almost horizontal stroke of electricity struck through to the lamp itself.

That's not right, thought Jack. *There's a lightning rod up top, and lightning doesn't go sideways, and . . . oh no!*

He grabbed Jaide and pulled her down.

"The Evil!" he shouted, even as his vision cleared.

Thunder answered him, rolling out across the bay.

"No . . . no . . . it can't be," said Jaide.

"It would be wrong," said a voice, "to think you've ever seen the last of The Evil. But in this case, it might be gone for a while."

Both twins looked up. There was a man crouched on the top of the lamp, smoke rising from his clothes. More amazingly still, they recognized his voice.

It was Jack who put the impossible into words.

"Dad?"

CHAPTER TWENTY-THREE

LIGHTNING AND TIGERS

Hector Shield swung himself down from the top of the lantern and landed with a light thud on the platform next to the twins. His hair was even wilder than it normally was, and his flapping coat was singed. He looked as though he had come down a chimney. There was a wild light in his eyes as he embraced the twins, drawing them into a very tight and smoky hug.

"I came as fast as I could, my dear troubletwisters," he said. "When a ward fails, there is an alarm. The signal reached me just after I arrived in Venice, where the weather was annoyingly fine. Luckily things were stormy at this end or I might have been even longer. Am I the first here?" He looked around and, without giving them the chance to say anything, said, "Good. Are you all right? Where's your grandmother?"

The twins didn't realize for a second that it was their turn to talk, and their reply was a rather jumbled account of everything that had happened in the previous days.

"Hmmm," he said. "Mother is even tougher than she looks, and it is not unusual for a Warden to fall into the kind of sleep you've described when they have overtaxed their Gifts. Speaking of Gifts, it looks like yours have really been going to town. All perfectly normal, but perfectly worrying, too."

"Dad," said Jaide, slightly muffled by his shoulder, "why didn't you tell us about being a Warden? And us being troubletwisters and all?"

"Didn't your grandmother explain that to you — that it's dangerous to know too much too soon?"

"Yes," said Jaide. She felt angry now, almost as much as she was relieved to see him. "But *you* should have told us!"

"Would you have believed me?"

Their father smiled in his lopsided way. His nose was just a little too large, which made his face seem slightly unbalanced.

"Yes," said the twins. "Of course."

"Um," said their father, looking contrite. "Well, the truth is that Warden parents are usually the worst — ah!"

He stopped and suddenly went to the window. The twins joined him and followed his gaze downward. A long, muscular shape was loping across the parking lot. The lighthouse flash gleamed off sharp, curving teeth. Jack gasped. It was a saber-toothed tiger!

It disappeared from sight, but a second later there were three loud cracks from below, followed by a booming thud.

"Padlocks," said their father. "And the door. Not subtle, not subtle at all."

The metal staircase below them rang like a crazy xylophone as the tiger ascended.

The twins looked at their father. They had no fear left in them now, just a kind of incredibly weary anxiety.

Hector chuckled with something that sounded very much like relief.

"I should've known Custer would be next. Don't be frightened. Tiger-shape is just how he gets around — and it's a deal more comfortable than lightning, I bet."

Heavy footsteps reached the lamp room, but what emerged out onto the hatch wasn't a tiger of any kind, but a high-cheeked man with long, flowing blond hair. His eyes were close-set and intense. He was dressed entirely in brown suede and leather, with a fur collar. He was, against all odds, perfectly dry.

"I received the signal," he said. "But the ward is up?" Taking in the contents of the lamp room, he performed a double take on seeing Hector. "What are you doing here?"

"Never fear, Custer," said the twins' father. "It's all under control. These two just got themselves in a bit of a tangle."

"Not surprising, if you were lurking about."

"No, I swear. All I did was answer the alarm."

Custer's stiff disapproval eased slightly.

"Well, lucky you came in time to bring everything under control, Heck."

"What?" said Jack. "*He* didn't do anything."

"It was us," said Jaide, her indignation a match for his. "We replaced the East Ward!"

"Replaced? I hardly think so." Custer chuckled, patting her heavily on the head. "All's well that ends well, I guess."

"Yes," said Hector. "The ward's fine," he announced, almost as if he'd fixed it himself. "That's what matters."

Jack and Jaide swelled up in outrage.

Before they could say anything further, however, there was a bright flash outside, and a twisting, golden tendril of light grew out of the new ward, shot past the open door and Custer, split into two, and plunged into the hearts of the twins.

Jaide felt her Gift return in a rush and reached out to the wind around the lighthouse, welcoming it back. Jack felt energy pouring into him, fierce and uncontrollable, and had an overwhelming desire for the calming surrounds of darkness. The lighthouse's lamp suddenly dimmed, and even the stars above seemed fainter.

"Whoa," said Hector, reeling them back into his tight embrace. They felt his Gift warring with theirs, trying to bring them under control. For a moment it looked as though he might lose, even with a father's strength and determination, until Custer put his hand on Hector's shoulder.

The men strained against the wild, fierce power of the twins. Custer's hand grew thicker, stronger. A tiger's paw dug into Hector's shoulder, prompting a wince of pain. Blood trickled down the inside of Hector's shirt.

Slowly, the adult Wardens prevailed. The wild wind around the lighthouse calmed, and the darkness receded. Jack and Jaide felt their Gifts settle back into place, raw and ready to rise up at the slightest provocation, but contained. For the moment.

"That ward's amplifying things rather too much. Let's damp that down a little, shall we?" said Custer. "Now, where *has* she put that pesky thing?"

He went outside and leaned across to tap the shining graffiti with one neatly trimmed fingernail. The light flickered and faded away. "There's been quite enough excitement around here for one night, by the look of things."

"Indeed," said Hector, adding significantly but without explanation: "Twins, eh?"

"Aye." Custer nodded. A look of intense sadness flickered across his face, and then vanished.

"Well, I'd better get the kids home, where they belong, and just make sure my mother is all right," said Hector. "Will you watch here, for the moment? Tidy up whatever you can?"

"All right."

"Thanks for coming so quickly."

"Anytime, my friend."

"And if anyone should ask, you didn't see me, okay?"

Custer tapped the side of his nose with old-fashioned solemnity.

Hector ushered the twins down the stairs ahead of him. It was difficult to talk over the ringing echoes of their footfalls. Manic moths, confused spiders and cockroaches, and a few bewildered mice made their descent even more unpleasant. By the time they reached the bottom, the twins were too exhausted to think of much beyond their longed-for beds.

But they still had questions.

"Where did you come from again?" asked Jack.

"I told you. Venice."

"*The* Venice? In Italy?"

"Is there any other?"

"There are lots of Portlands," said Jaide.

"Ah, but none like *this* Portland."

With a hand on the small of their backs, he guided them across the parking lot and through the headstones. The rain had started again, but it was only a drizzle, and the icy chill of it had eased.

Though he'd said he wasn't worried about his mother, Hector kept up a cracking pace, and the closer they got to the house, the quicker he walked, the twins having to really stretch out to keep up.

"It's good to see you both," Hector said as they half jogged, half walked through the drizzle. "Even under such circumstances. I've missed you."

"So why did you go away?" asked Jack.

"And why can't anyone know you're here?" asked Jaide.

"It's the curse of being a Warden," he said, "and the parent of troubletwisters. Your Gifts can give you amazing powers, but they are not safe and easy, and rarely can be used without consequences, particularly with other Wardens around. You have to be careful. More troubletwisters have died or fallen as a result of mishandling their own Gifts than have been simply taken by The Evil, and parents are often, inadvertently of course, the cause of that. Until your Gifts are under control, you could harm yourselves, each other, or those you love."

The twins nodded thoughtfully. They were beginning to understand that — and to have a clearer idea of exactly what had happened the day their house had exploded.

Their Gifts had awakened, drawing The Evil to them, and when Hector had intervened those very same uncontrolled Gifts had nearly killed them all.

"But why didn't you tell us before?" asked Jaide again. "Why didn't we come to Portland until now?"

He sighed. "That was your mother's choice, and my mistake. When we met, she didn't know what I was, and I didn't tell her. It wasn't until you two were on the way that I knew I had to fess up. Your mother wasn't happy, and she was afraid for you. She wanted a normal life. She wanted nothing to do with my world . . . with all this."

He waved a hand, encompassing the night, the dissipating storm, and the house ahead.

"I tried," he said. "I really tried, but nature can't be repressed, and a Warden's work is never done. It was bad luck that I returned from a Warden quest when your powers were full to bursting — but something would have happened eventually."

"And The Evil would have come," said Jack, remembering the staring white eyes in his parents' bedroom.

"Yes. It always comes, whenever it can find a chink between its world and ours," said Hector. "We must always fight it off, for our sakes, and for the sake of your mother and the billions like her. Almost there!"

Behind them, the beam of light from the lighthouse suddenly flashed on and swung over the town. Hector and the twins glanced back, and Hector smiled.

"You know, I broke my leg in that old lighthouse when I was your age. I've still got the scar."

"But you always told us you were flying a kite," said

Jaide indignantly, who had heard the story a thousand times and knew a sudden change of subject when she heard it. "You never mentioned the lighthouse!"

"I was flying a kite, more or less," he said. "But I never told you before about the electrical storm we . . . I summoned. I was lucky I only broke my leg. I could have been electrocuted — or caught by The Evil. My lightning weakened the ward, and it . . . The Evil had been waiting for that opportunity."

Jaide thought about this and felt a stab of guilt. Had she and Jack done something to weaken the ward in the first place? For Jack this was already a familiar anxiety, having had it suggested to him by The Evil. He was thinking back to his father's arrival. It wasn't the first time Hector's reappearance was associated with a thunderstorm.

"But you learned to use the lightning?" he asked his father, full of wonder. Moving in shadows was pretty good, but it was nowhere near as excellent as traveling by lightning, all the way from the other side of the world.

"Yes. It's not easy and it has its risks. Don't even think about trying it," Hector cautioned as they ran up the front steps and into the house. "In fact, I want you to promise me something. It's not terribly fair of me to ask you this, since I was never very good at it myself, but it's important, and I hope you'll do it for me."

"What is it?" asked Jack and Jaide together.

"Let me just check on Mother and then —"

"I'm fine, Hector, thank you," said Grandma X. Her sudden appearance at the top of the stairs made Jack and Jaide jump nervously. She started to come down, a cat on either side of her. Ari's tail stood up like an aerial apart from a one-inch kink at the end, and Kleo's back fur was frizzed as though with static electricity. The wildness of Grandma X's hair was a match for the look in her eyes.

"I'm not sure it is wise of you to visit," continued Grandma X. "Given the troubletwisting that has already gone on —"

She stopped and cocked her head to one side and the cats' ears flicked up.

A moment later they all heard the squeal of tires as a car turned in to the wet, cobbled road.

"Ah, I expect that will be Susan," said Grandma X.

Hector looked at the door, indecision obvious on his face.

"She can't know what happened," said Hector. Grandma X nodded, and he hurried Jack and Jaide through the back door and into the yard. He stood with them for a moment under the trees and put a hand on each of their shoulders.

"Now, that promise . . . I want you to do everything your grandma says, no matter how weird it sounds. Do you understand? I ask you both as your father and as a Warden. Your lives — and the life of our family — depend on it."

"So she'll teach us about becoming Wardens?" asked Jaide.

"Yes, and you'll teach her a thing or two, I bet."

He smiled, but Jack wasn't willing to laugh just yet.

"I wish *you* could teach us."

"So do I, but having me around would only throw you off. And the lessons are hard to learn, and often the teacher has to be very strict. I'm not sure I have the stomach for it, to be honest. I'd want to protect you . . . both of you . . . and that's not the way it works."

He might have said more, but Susan's car was already skidding to a sudden halt on the gravel drive.

"Promise me!" said Hector urgently.

"All right," said Jack.

"Jaide, what do you say? Quickly!"

She had never seen her father so agitated. "Yes, I promise, but —"

"I love you both." He kissed the twins on their foreheads and backed away. "Remember that, and stay where you are. You might want to cover your eyes, too."

Neither twin so much as blinked as their father pulled a pitted metal rod with a sharp end from his coat pocket. They both recognized it as the one they had found in his suitcase that fateful day when their Gifts had woken. Holding it in his right hand, Hector made several quick passes across his body, each of which left a pale blue line hanging in the air. The lines formed a complex sigil that, once completed, began to shimmer like heat haze. The purple glow returned. Hector Shield raised the rod above his head with both hands and braced himself.

"Who in an orchestra is most likely to be struck by lightning?" he called to his children. "The conductor. Get i —?"

He vanished into a flash of bright blue energy, and once again deep thunder rocked the town.

On the other side of the house, a car door slammed. The sound acted like a starter's pistol for the twins. They sprinted back inside and up past Grandma X, the cats jumping aside to make room. They ran to the bathroom on their floor and stripped off their wet clothes, toweled their hair dry, and leaped into pajamas.

"Is that you, Susan?" Grandma X's voice floated up to them. "What's going on?"

The cats came into the bedroom as Jack and Jaide hurled themselves into their beds and mussed up the covers.

"She woke up when the ward was restored," said Kleo to the twins. "I didn't have time to tell her everything."

"Are congratulations in order?" asked Ari, his penetrating gaze darting from one twin to the other. "Or was it your father's work?"

"We did it, but there's no time to tell you about it now," said Jack. He was more worried about his mother and what she might say to Grandma X.

Right on cue, Susan came in. She was wearing her emergency services uniform, and a radio squawked at her belt, but she ignored it. Grandma X followed her. Her feet were bare under her dressing gown, and for the first time Jaide noticed she had silver rings on her toes.

"Are you all right?" Susan asked. "Was it . . . was it something to do with . . . did you make it happen?"

"Make what happen, Susan?" asked Grandma X. "I don't know what you mean."

"You know very well!" The words tumbled out of her in a rush. "They've declared a natural disaster in the town.

Some kind of localized hurricane, they said, but I knew better."

"We're fine," said Jaide. Jack nodded and gave a very unconvincing yawn.

Susan ran to sweep them up in a tight embrace, dragging both of them out of bed and onto the floor in the middle of the room.

"I'm so glad you're all right. I've been so worried. You don't have to be afraid now. You're safe."

They returned the hug, feeling in its tightness the panic their mother had suffered. They wanted to tell her the truth, but knew she would never understand.

"It's okay, Mom," said Jaide reassuringly. "Just a big storm. We slept through most of it."

"Really, we did," said Jack, catching Grandma X's eye over his mother's shoulder. "It wasn't scary at all."

"Really?"

Susan pulled back slightly and looked each child directly in the eye. They knew that procedure: She was looking for any sign of fibbing. It was only then that both twins realized that they *were* fibbing — to protect her from worrying, but also to stop her from taking them away from Portland and their grandmother, where they needed to be if they were ever to get their Gifts under control.

"Honest, Mom," said Jack.

Jaide added, for the appearance of it, "You're such a worrywart."

"I had no idea this morning, Susan," Grandma X said calmly, "that the weather would turn like this. Otherwise I would never have let the kids out of my sight."

"Of course not," Susan said, letting the twins go at last. "I heard they closed the school. They might as well have stayed at home anyway."

"Not to worry. I was happy to pick them up when Mr. Carver called. Come on to the kitchen, Susan," Grandma X said. "You look frozen through. I'll make you something hot."

"Well, all right, but I can't stay long. I've volunteered to help out the local squad. The flood has ripped up trees and washed cars away, and a couple of roofs have come off. . . ."

The twins followed their mother, the cats, and Grandma X to the kitchen. Grandma X turned on the radio, then bent to light the stove. The twins and their mother listened to a very excited voice reporting that an enormous pile of sea life had been deposited near the lighthouse by a freak waterspout.

"I hope life isn't always this . . . interesting . . . in Portland," said Susan with a weak smile.

"The twins will be safe with me," Grandma X promised.

The voice on the radio carried on about the town's sole missing person, who had just been found near the lighthouse and who, though apparently injured, had refused treatment before hurrying away. Jaide hardly registered the woman's name, Renita Daniels, before Susan turned the volume down and gave her children another hug.

"Back to bed for you, I think," she said to them. "I'm so glad you're safe."

"I'll fix you some hot chocolate, Susan," said

Grandma X, with a knowing glance at the twins. "Good night."

The twins kissed their mother and dutifully headed upstairs to the room they guessed they should now think of as their own. A dose of Grandma X's memory-erasing potion might not ease their mother's anxieties about Wardens and Hector and their house blowing up, but it would at least make her forget about that morning.

The less she knew about their new life in Portland, the better.

A COMPENDIUM
OF THE EVIL

The cats followed the twins back to the bedroom and jumped up onto the beds, Ari at Jaide's feet and Kleo at Jack's.

"Don't think you can go to sleep without telling us exactly what happened," said Kleo bossily.

"We really would like to know," said Ari, in more conciliatory tones.

"All right," said Jaide.

They were still talking when Grandma X tapped quietly on the door and then poked her head around.

"Well done, troubletwisters," she said.

"How are you feeling?" Jaide asked.

"Considerably better than I did earlier, thank you, Jaidith."

Grandma X came in and picked up their dirty clothes, wrinkling her nose as she lifted Jack's shirt.

"That singed smell is so distinctive. . . . It is such a pity Hector couldn't stay. But that's the way it must be." She pulled a regretful face, and the twins knew that she missed her son just as much as they missed their father. "Now, I see you have been in my antiques store."

"We only went in to —" Jack began, but Grandma X held up her hand.

"You did what was necessary, in the grand tradition of Wardens, and you did so in a very messy way, in the less grand tradition of troubletwisters."

"What happened to the music box?" asked Jaide. The cats had already told her that when it had stopped, The Evil had attacked the house, but the rats and insects hadn't gotten in before the ward was replaced.

"It is now merely a very fine early-eighteenth-century music box, and nothing more," said Grandma X. "So I will sell it on eBay."

"That crocodile skull took off the end of my finger," said Jaide, brandishing her bandage. She'd forgotten about it in the events of the night, but now it was starting to really hurt again.

"The Oracular Crocodile is something of a trickster," said Grandma X. "You only need to give it a drop of blood, dripped from a spoon or the like. Never let it actually bite you. We'd best have that seen to in the morning, in case it festers. You might need a stitch or two."

Jaide pulled a face. She was generally brave when it came to doctors, except where needles were concerned.

From the pocket of her dressing gown, Grandma X pulled the brass compass the troubletwisters had played with in the drawing room the day she had tested them to see where their Gifts might lie.

"I can also tell from this that there has been a change in the wards. Didn't you get my message about the plaque?"

"We did," said Jaide, "and we tried to fix it."

"But The Evil stopped us," said Jack, "and so we had to make a new ward instead."

Grandma X raised her eyebrows. "Just like that?"

"Well, we don't really know how we did it. . . ."

"Only that we did," said Jaide. "Custer checked it and everything was fine. Did we do something wrong?"

"Not at all, not at all. You simply did something very difficult, something that normally takes years of practice and an astonishingly well-matched pair of Wardens to achieve. It always takes two, you see, to ensure the new ward is completely secure."

"We're twins," said Jack brightly. "That must be why it worked for us."

"Indeed. But in that regard you are not unique. All troubletwisters are twins, but not all twins are trouble-twisters."

Before Jaide could untangle that sentence, Grandma X produced something else from under her apparently inexhaustible nightgown.

"Now, I have brought something else to show you, something that is normally kept safe in the blue room, where it cannot be interfered with by anyone."

It was a huge blue folder the size of a very fat encyclopedia. They flipped it open to reveal a great mass of different-size pages loosely held together by a spiral binding. The pages at the front were modern computer printouts, but as Grandma X flipped the pages to the back, the paper got thicker and older, with some of it typewritten and some of it in beautiful, flowing handwriting. The pages right at the bottom were not paper at all, but vellum or parchment, and the writing was particularly ornate, with gilded capitals and little illustrations. There were also many other full-page drawings, maps, and diagrams throughout the folder, the earlier ones hand drawn and the later ones obviously done on a computer.

"Next time something like this happens, this is where you come first." Grandma X closed the folder and showed the children the spine, where a card had been stuck in the plastic sleeve. The whole loose-leaf collection was called *A Compendium of The Evil*.

"Wardens have fought against The Evil for millennia, with varying degrees of success. This *Compendium* contains as much of our collected experience as has survived the perils of both The Evil and history in general. Every Warden in this current era has one. Use it as needed, and you will be wiser for it. But be aware that it will not always answer you, and you may not be able to find things you have just now glimpsed, for this is not as simple a pile of old papers as it seems, and there are things that troubletwisters should not know, or should be spared the knowledge of. But if ever you cannot ask me something for any reason, you may ask the *Compendium*. Think of what you want to know, browse through the pages, and if it is something you can be told, you will find the right paper."

The twins nodded, sensing that with this small piece of advice their tutelage had properly begun. Where it would lead them they didn't know, and what perils lay ahead they couldn't imagine, but they were on the path now. At least they *had* a path.

"I'm glad you understand," said Grandma X, "because

tomorrow you're going to write down everything that happened to you and put it into the *Compendium* yourselves. If necessary, it will illustrate your work —"

"*It* will illustrate it?" asked Jaide.

"Well, it would be more accurate to say that it will find the Warden best able to illustrate whatever is required," replied Grandma X. "Perhaps one of you may have that Gift, of drawing the thoughts and writings of others. But apart from other Wardens, you mustn't ever tell anybody else what you write about —"

"Except for Warden Companions," said Kleo. "Like us."

"*Some* things may be told to Warden Companions," continued Grandma X with a quelling glance. "But secrecy is a matter greater even than life and death for us. We are part of an unending struggle against a terrible opponent. We risk our lives and fight great battles, but the rest of the world must not know of the existence of The Evil."

"Why not?" asked Jack.

"Because it is a sad fact of human nature that there are people who fall easily under The Evil's sway," said Grandma X bleakly. "There are even those who would volunteer to join it, or work for it, or who would sell themselves or others for things The Evil can give."

"Oh," said Jack thoughtfully.

She studied him a second longer than was comfortable, then added, "Not even Wardens are immune."

He looked away, hoping she was only guessing how The Evil had tried to turn him against her, and swearing that she would never know.

"Did we really damage the East Ward?" he asked.

"Perhaps," she said. "It was old and damaged by your father once, and your presence here might have weakened it to the point of failure. But it wasn't something you did deliberately, and you did put things right in the end, didn't you? I wouldn't spare it another thought — except to listen to me when I tell you to be careful, in the future."

"Yes, Grandma." Jack couldn't tell if she was telling the whole truth or being kind, but either way he did feel a bit better.

"Will you tell us about the other wards tomorrow?" Jaide asked. "And will you show us where they are?"

"All in good time," their grandma said. "We have to get your Gifts under control first. You would not normally have learned of the wards so early in your development as troubletwisters."

Jaide nodded. She was already firmly convinced of the need to get their Gifts under control.

"What about school?" asked Jack. "Do we really have to go back when it opens again?"

"I'm afraid so. The rest of the world won't stop while you learn what it means to be a troubletwister." She smiled fondly at them. "Now, I think it is time for sleep. Cats, you may retire, too."

"Good night," said Kleo to the twins. "You have done well."

She jumped up and licked Jaide's face, then leaped over to lick Jack, who was less keen. Ari followed suit, but he did not lick Jack, merely butting his head against him.

"It is an honor to work with you, troubletwisters," said Ari gravely.

Grandma X watched the cats walk out, then came and kissed the twins herself.

"You have done extraordinarily well," she said. "And I am proud of you, *grandchildren*."

Grandma X turned out the light. A moment later they heard her soft tread on the stairs, so different from the sharp beat of her daytime boots.

"I guess this isn't turning out as bad as we thought," said Jack. "Apart from no television."

"I guess so." Jaide yawned. "But what was it she said about twins and troubletwisters?"

"Hmmm?" answered Jack. His thoughts were elsewhere. "You know, it would be *so cool* to travel by lightning. . . ."

Jaide didn't answer. She was already asleep, and within moments, so was Jack.